WELSH FARGO

To Paddy Marks, to whom I owe the title; to Jennifer, who can read my writing; and to Myra, who can read me.

WELSH FARGO

Harry Secombe

All the characters in this book are fictitious, as is Panteg, which is not to be confused with any other Panteg. However, there is a Swansea, which will be confused.

H.S.

FIRST PUBLISHED IN GREAT BRITAIN IN 1981 BY ROBSON BOOKS LTD., BOLSOVER HOUSE, 5-6 CLIPSTONE STREET, LONDON W1P 7EB.

British Library Cataloguing in Publication Data

Secombe, Harry
Welsh Fargo
I. Title
823'914(F)   PR6069.E2/
ISBN 0-903895-87-0

Printed in Great Britain by Biddles Ltd., Guildford.

one

The crow cawed dismally as it flapped through the rain which slanted like steel stair-rods through its feathers. It landed awkwardly on top of a telegraph pole, shook itself in a flurry of droplets and, hunching its back against the elements, looked down with a jaundiced eye upon the scene below.

A ribbon of road stretched for nearly a mile across a gorse-clad common before disappearing in a series of S bends down the slope of the mountain. Twenty feet from where the crow sat, a bus was pulled up at the roadside. Under it lay a man, his legs sticking out stiffly from beneath the front wheels. Other people stood around in various attitudes of impatience.

Curious now, the bird shifted from one leg to the other as the voices drifted upwards.

"Come on, Dai, get the damn thing going. We'll miss the match." A mufflered, tweed-overcoated male figure detached itself from the group around the bus and kicked none too gently at one of the protruding feet.

A large lady with a shopping basket over her arm bent as far as her bulk would permit and plucked at one of the trousered legs. "I was supposed to meet our Emrys at the Middle Market Gate at one o'clock. It's that now."

She was joined by another lady, shorter and thinner and shriller, who jabbed the point of an umbrella at the hidden half of the man under the bus. "Dai Fargo, if this contraption doesn't start within the next five minutes I'll have the council after you."

The man she was addressing winced as the points rammed home — the ferrule and the civic threat. He lay, spanner in hand, looking up in bewilderment at the track rod, suspension and the gear box, trying to stem the flow of oil which dripped gently but relentlessly upon his round, puzzled face. "I'm doing my best, Miss Thomas."

The sister of Alderman George Thomas, headmistress of Panteg School and self-appointed scourge of the Valley, thrust accurately with the umbrella into an area of Dai's anatomy of which, as a spinster lady, she should have had little knowledge. "Your best is not good enough," she said, delivering an end-of-term report.

Dai gave a little cry of pain as his body jerked upwards, bringing his head into contact with the front axle.

The crow did a little dance of excitement on top of his telegraph pole. A small flock of sparrows, intrigued by the action, settled neatly on the four wires of a nearby electric pylon. Dai Fargo lifted his head from the road and, groaning, turned it sideways. He caught sight of the way the sparrows had positioned themselves on the wires and wondered what was familiar about the pattern. Then he realised that they formed the opening bars of Handel's *Hallelujah Chorus*. He banged his spanner in rhythm on the underside of the bus as he sang the notes. Suddenly the oil stopped dripping and he was able to locate the trouble. He did what was necessary and, smiling broadly, emerged from under his vehicle. "Hallelujah — it's a miracle, folks," he cried, waving his spanner at the sparrows who flew away in alarm.

The crow cawed noisily and, with the air of one not wishing to appear in too much of a hurry, took off into the lessening rain. It circled the bus once, and then as Dai Fargo cried "All aboard!" it swooped down and left a calling card on Miss Thomas's hat.

"That's supposed to be lucky," said Dai, not without malice.

As the grumbling passengers settled themselves back in the bus, a short, bandy-legged man appeared from amongst the gorse bushes wearing a chocolate brown uniform too large for him. Over one shoulder hung a bell-punch on a leather strap and on the other was suspended a metal ticket container which banged against his hip. From a distance he looked like a Mexican bandit who had lost his hat and his horse.

Dai Fargo waited by the chugging bonnet until his conductor came up to him. "Where the hell have you been for the past twenty minutes? I've had to handle the passengers and the bloody engine." His voice rose into a soprano register.

The conductor fiddled with his fly buttons and flicked his tongue over his projecting teeth before answering. "Had to take a leak, mun, you know I have this weak bladder." His beetling brows registered a hairy alarm.

"Weak, be buggered." Fargo seized him by the lapels of his uniform and dragged the conductor to the side of the bus. "It's strong enough when you're guzzling pints in The Bricklayers' Arms. Like a camel then you are."

An umbrella appeared from the window above them and came to rest sharply on Dai's curly head. "Camels can go for days *without* liquid. Now put poor Mr. Williams down and get us to Swansea before the shops close." Miss Thomas rapped once more on Fargo's round skull, producing a musical note.

"F," said Dai automatically, releasing his hold on Bryn Williams's uniform jacket.

"Eff yourself," said the conductor, scuttling back into the bus.

Fargo started after him, changed his mind, and, after picking up his oily cap from the road in front of the bus, squeezed his burly frame into the driver's seat. Behind him a chorus of angry passengers directed a barrage of abuse at his broad back.

"Be too late for the game," moaned Leonard and Stanley Roberts, two rabid Swansea Town Football Club fans.

"Hear, hear," said Muriel and Gwen, two ladies of easy virtue.

"Emrys will think something's happened to me," complained stout Mrs. Megan Walters to her companion, the umbrella-wielding Miss Thomas.

"Time we had a *real* bus service into town," shouted the

disguised voice of Bryn Williams as he rang the bell for the bus to start.

Dai slammed the ancient Leyland into first gear and slowly crept into second. As he gathered speed on the slope leading to the series of S bends he began singing *Nearer My God To Thee* in a vibrant tenor. The rest of the bus's occupants gradually took up the hymn in three-part harmony and, as the worst of the dangerous curves was being negotiated, the intensity of the singing increased, all animosity forgotten. And so the dilapidated brown and white vehicle with FARGO emblazoned on either dented side rattled into the outskirts of Swansea, exuding all the fervour of a revivalist meeting on wheels.

One hundred years ago Panteg had consisted solely of a valley farm of that name through which ran a pleasant little stream. The valley, formed by a tributary of the main Tawe River, had remained isolated throughout its history by virtue of its position. To get to it the ancient traveller had to climb out of the Swansea Valley and down a precipitous track into the bowl surrounded by wooded hills which was Panteg.

Then along came the Industrial Revolution and in the frantic search for coal in the South Wales valleys, man gouged out the heart of the farmland and tore down the trees and sank a deep shaft into the rich seam which lay beneath. The mine owners built rows of terraced houses for the workers, a chapel and a church to take care of their spiritual needs, and the public houses were set up to induce forgetfulness of the awful conditions in which the miners worked.

The one road into and out of Panteg remained precipitous because it was cheaper to build a railway tunnel to take the coal away down to Swansea Docks, whence it was shipped across to the continent or routed via the main lines to the greedy factories.

Now, in the year of our Lord nineteen hundred and thirty-three, there was a surplus of coal and the Depression bit as deeply into the lives of the people of Panteg as the drills which had carved up their valley. Old young men stricken with coal dust in their lungs walked slowly up the shabby streets, stopping for breath every few yards, whilst others lay coughing their lives away in front parlours on beds brought down from upstairs to save them the impossible climb. Mothers prepared meals they were ashamed to serve, pretending to their families that they had already eaten.

And yet there was love in abundance; a clinging together in adversity, and always humour — the sly Welsh humour — and, of course, there was the singing. In Ebenezer Chapel the walls shook with the sheer volume of sound produced by choir and congregation, and there was power in the plainsong at St. Peter's.

As Dai's bus was disgorging its disgruntled passengers in Swansea that Saturday afternoon, in Panteg a large ex-heavyweight boxer called Tommy Rees was attempting to hold up the Co-op in Fabian Street. Not wishing to be recognised, he wore a cloth cap down over his eyes and in each cheek he had placed a ping-pong ball. He joined the queue of shoppers waiting to pay for their purchases at the cashier's desk, shuffling along with his head down. When it came his turn, he put his hand in his jacket pocket and pointed his forefinger at Lily, the cashier.

"What do you want, Tommy?" she asked.

Taken by surprise at being recognised, the ex-boxer breathed in sharply, causing one ping-pong ball to be sucked into his throat. Fighting desperately for air he fell on his back to the ground, a position in which he had been photographed so many times in his short career that his manager had seriously thought of renting the soles of his boots to an advertising agency. An ambulance was called and he was taken away on a stretcher.

A shadowy figure lurking behind a pillar clucked his tongue in annoyance. "Sod it!" he said loudly.

James Henry Fargo lay tucked up in bed at 33 Gwydyr Terrace, Panteg. It was the end house of the row and because of this afforded a view up the valley, away from the colliery workings which provided what work there was for the area in these bitter years of the Depression. The birds under the eaves chattered incessantly in the early spring evening.

A book lay on the counterpane before him but his eyes were focused on a large bumble bee which buzzed fatly against the window, the top half of which was lowered by eighteen inches. He closed his eyes and willed the bee to have enough sense to climb up over the top pane and away to freedom. When he opened them again he saw that the frantic insect was still hurling itself at the same corner of the window frame. His twelve-year-old mind was torn between the desire to set the bee free and the fear of being stung in the process. And anyway, Nana Fargo had told him to "stay under the clothes, there's a good boy, otherwise you'll be off from school for another week".

He looked around his room for something he could persuade the bee to crawl on to so that he could then shake it out of the window. Through the brass bedstead at his feet he was able to see the red and blue flower-patterned jug and wash hand basin on the table near the door, standing out in relief against the stark white of the opposite wall. Behind his head was a framed picture of Holman Hunt's *Light of the World*, and, apart from a high-backed chair in the corner by his bed, there was nothing to assist him in an effort to help the berserk bumble bee to escape. Then he thought of the copy of *True Confessions* he had secreted behind his pillow after having sneaked it out of his grandmother's bedroom. Perhaps he could persuade the insect to climb on to that. He considered the risk involved. If she caught him with it there'd be trouble. It was an American publication "for adults only" with pictures of ladies holding torn blouses with one hand and fending off amorous, fully-clad gentlemen with the other. There were stories which hinted at things he had vaguely heard about, and letters to the agony column from girls who signed themselves "Distressed, Detroit" or "Worried, Washington". James Henry had a few questions to ask the magazine himself, and toyed with the idea of signing himself "Panting, Panteg".

The buzzing increased in intensity and he started to reach

reluctantly beneath his pillow. The door opened with a bang and his grandmother bustled in bearing a tray of tea and toast. "Here's your supper, James Henry."

The boy leaned back quickly against the pillow, suddenly pale with the thought of discovery.

"There's white you're looking." The old lady pulled back the top of the counterpane so that tea would not be spilled on it and put the tray on the boy's lap. "That's right, sit up tidy, there's a good boy. Nana must get you up and about for the carnival next Saturday." She plumped up the pillows behind his head and stood back from the bed with her arms folded across her cross-over pinafore, her head to one side as she smilingly surveyed her patient.

James Henry took a slurp from the thick cup marked "Property of Ebenezer Chapel".

"Your Uncle David will be back from Swansea soon, then you'll be right for a good old laugh."

The boy grinned at the prospect of having his uncle sit with him, joking about the day's events. In the background the bee buzzed with renewed effort.

"That old bee bothering you, boy bach?" His grandmother took off a carpet slipper and splashed the struggling insect against the window pane. She wiped the mess away with a handkerchief taken from the pocket of her pinafore. "There you are. That nasty old thing won't trouble our James Henry any more."

The boy pushed the tray away from him. "I don't think I want anything to eat, thank you, Nana."

"Aah! Never mind, love. I'll leave it on the chair by your bed in case your appetite comes back." She fussed over him, straightening the sheets and putting the counterpane back into position. "There you are. Have a little read," she said, handing him the *Palgrave's Golden Treasury* which had occupied his lap before the advent of the tray. Then, planting a smacking kiss on his forehead, she went out and closed the door behind her.

James Henry looked at the faint mark on the window where the bumble bee had met its doom, and shuddered. "Poor thing," he thought. "If only I had been able to get the magazine under its feet I could have saved its life."

His hand groped under his head and produced *True Confessions*. He listened carefully for his Gran's descending footsteps down the stairs, and turned to page 38. *"'No, please!' I cried as he began to unbutton the top of my dress, 'You can't (continued on page 113)."* He leafed through the pages of advertisements for developing the bust and creams for removing body hair until he reached the continuation of the downfall of Miss Ethel X in the back seat of a Stutz Convertible in Peoria, Illinois. *"'. . . do that!' My pleas were smothered by the ardour of his kisses . . ."* The boy grabbed a piece of toast from the nearby tray and stuffed it into his mouth, chewing with an abandonment which matched that of Miss Ethel X. Why worry about the birds and the bees — this was the real thing.

Downstairs in her kitchen his grandmother unwillingly poured tea for her next-door neighbour, Mrs. Ceinwen Rees, who had just dropped in to borrow some sugar.

"Money's a bit tight this week, and now with Tommy taken ill today . . ." she finished the sentence with a shrug of her bony shoulders.

Mrs. Fargo helped herself to milk and sugar and stirred her tea reflectively before replying. "You *must* be hard up if your Tommy's taken to eating ping-pong balls."

Mrs. Rees paused in mid-sip, her little finger held delicately outwards. Her eyes like jet beads looked into Mrs. Fargo's and slid away almost immediately towards the loudly ticking clock on the mantelpiece. "Your Dai is late again, I see." She laid a slight emphasis on the word "again", and finished the upward motion towards her thin lips; the curve of her nose was buried briefly within the circumference of the cup.

"What do you mean by that, Ceinwen?" The old lady sat ramrod straight in her chair.

"Well, it's just that everybody in Panteg is saying that we need a new bus service." Mrs. Rees replaced the cup in the saucer and pointed to the timetable headed "FARGO'S BUS SERVICE — EFFICIENCY OUR WATCHWORD" which hung on the wall near the dresser. "That's the laughing stock of the village, that by there. Efficiency? You're better off walking. Morris the Coal's horse and cart passed your son twice on the way into Swansea last Wednesday, and they were both going uphill at the time."

Before Mrs. Fargo could spit out a reply, her son's one and only bus wheezed into the yard at the side of the house where the garage and workshop stood. She got up without a word and went into the pantry, returning seconds later to thump a sugar bowl on the table. "There, take it — and don't forget to bring the bowl back."

Ceinwen Rees seized the bowl and with a tight nod turned and went out through the back door just as Dai Fargo barged his way through the front door and slammed it noisily. He came in from the hall and kissed his mother on the cheek. "Hello, Mam." The smell of engine oil and leather was strong in the little kitchen.

"Take your cap off, David." She never called him Dai. "Sit down, your supper's getting dry."

Her son removed his cap and jacket, hanging them on a hook on the back of the door through which Mrs. Rees had just exited, and sat down at the table. "Who was that in here just now?"

His mother went to the oven at the side of the fireplace and took out a plate of fish and chips. "From Hughes the Hake," she said, laying it before him. Then, in answer to his question, "That sneaky old bitch, Ceinwen Rees."

"What did she want, then? I heard that her Tommy's been had up for trying to hold up the Co-op. There's excitement for you. Not after money for bail, is she?" Dai laughed into his plate.

"No, just a loan of some sugar."

"Not again! She's always bloody borrowing. Didn't give it to her, did you?"

"Don't swear, David. No, as a matter of fact I didn't."

"Good."

"I gave her a bowl of salt instead."

Her son banged the table with his hand, clattering the crockery and upsetting the vinegar. "That'll shake her." He swung his great head from side to side with delight. "Oh Mam, Mam."

His mother cut him three great slices of bread from a cottage loaf and buttered them for him. "You're half an hour late again tonight, David. People are complaining about it. That old cat next door was rubbing it in just now."

"I know, Mam. It's worrying hell out of me. I could do with a new bus. Let's face it, the only thing worth keeping from this one is the starting handle. But where are we going to get the money from?"

"You could always try robbing the Co-op."

"Aye," Dai chuckled. "I'm sorry for poor old Tommy — he's never been the same since he got that hammering in Treherbert. He was finished as a boxer after that."

"Yes," said Mrs. Fargo, standing up and starting to clear the table. "Nasty business. Mind you, that Gwyneth Pugh was a big girl. If the policeman hadn't dragged her off Tommy in time she'd have killed him, by all accounts. Hell hath no fury like a woman scorned."

"Indeed, indeed." Dai licked his lips nervously. "Talking about that, Mam, Elspeth is getting a bit fed up with waiting. After all, we've been engaged for twelve years now and neither of us is getting any younger. I mean — I'll be forty-seven next birthday." He took a deep breath. "It's time we got married, Mam."

Mrs. Fargo clutched her heart and sank heavily into the armchair by the fire. "Get me my tablets from the top drawer in the dresser, quick."

Her son moved quickly, though with a certain amount of resignation, to do her bidding. He filled a glass of water from the tap in the kitchen sink and handed it to his mother along with two pink tablets. "Here you are, Mam."

"Thank you, David." She threw her head back, put the tablets on her tongue and took a long drink from the glass. When she had finished she let her head rest against the back of the chair for a while, eyes closed, her hand still held against her billowing bosom. Dai took the glass from her limp fingers and regarded her with more than a hint of suspicion. His mother opened one eye slowly, saw his steady gaze and closed it immediately. "Don't worry about your old Mam and your little nephew James Henry. We'll manage somehow. I'll just have to sell my shares in the company and we'll go and live with Bryn and Bronwen."

"If you mention that useless idiot again I *will* leave home. He hung about doing nothing when we broke down this afternoon on the Common while I had to fix the engine *and* sing *Bless This House* four times to keep the passengers happy."

"He's your sister's husband and you know your father promised faithfully on his deathbed that Bryn would always have a job as conductor as long as there was a Fargo bus on the road." His mother's voice had strengthened in the thirty seconds since she had taken her tablets.

"There won't be a Fargo bus on the road much longer if things go on as they are. There's no money about for one thing, and I can't afford to go on employing that fool as a conductor. Bryn Williams had to get Dad drunk on a flagon of Hancocks ale before he got that promise out of him. Anyway, the same night Dad also made a solemn vow to come back and haunt Albert Matthias for refusing to serve him after stop tap, but I haven't noticed Albert's hair going white overnight, and that was ten years ago."

"He's getting a bit grey at the sides, though. God moves in a mysterious way, boy bach." Mrs. Fargo folded her arms and nodded wisely.

"I'm off upstairs to see young James Henry. How is he today, by the way?"

"He seemed a little stronger this morning, but when I took his tea and toast up not so long ago he looked a bit pale, poor little dab. It was his chest that took his father away." Tears came into her eyes and she felt for a handkerchief in her pinafore pocket. Shaking out the remains of the bumble bee, she blew her nose heartily.

"Aye, but it was a little Cockney from Peckham who took his mother away." Dai remembered the day five years ago that his sister-in-law had left the note on the kitchen table telling them that she was running off with the English grocer from Pantycellan Street. And him with a wife and four children of his own! Since then James Henry had been more like a son to him than a nephew, and Elspeth, his long-suffering fiancée, loved them both dearly. "Come on, Mam, the boy's only got a touch of 'flu. You're being over-protective, mun." Dai patted his mother gently on the cheek and went out of the kitchen and up the narrow stairs to James Henry's bedroom. He took the stairs surprisingly lightly for a man of his size, not wanting to wake the boy if he was sleeping. He opened the brown varnished door, turning the white china knob quietly.

James Henry, oblivious to all outside interference, was well into Ethel X's astounding revelations, his sensitive young features flushed with her exertions.

Dai stood at the foot of the brass bedstead looking at him indulgently. "Your Nana said you were looking a bit pale. I'd say you were running a fever myself." He moved forward and took the magazine from the boy's frozen grasp. "Duw, there's rich reading for an underfed mind. Liable to bring you out in heat bumps."

Dai looked at the fear in James Henry's face at being discovered with the forbidden publication, and laughed. "It's all right, boyo, I won't tell your Nana." He reached into his trouser pocket and drew out a paper bag. "Here you are, suck one of these hard-boiled sweets. Sugar's supposed to be good for shock."

The boy caught the bag as his uncle threw it, spilling some of the sweets on the bed. "Thanks, Uncle Dai. Ooh! There's lovely." He picked up one of the sweets and examined it. "Hey! My favourites."

Dai grinned as the lad popped into his mouth an orange-coloured sweet the size and shape of a small goldfish dusted with sugar. "Careful you don't swallow the thing."

James Henry shook his head, unable to speak, the sweet filling his cheeks with its contours.

"I'd better take this back to your Nana's bedroom before she misses it." Dai tucked the *True Confessions* into the front of his striped flannel shirt. He put his hand in his back pocket and brandished a comic he had bought for the boy. "Try this for a change. It'll keep your temperature down."

"*The Magnet*, is it? Thanks, Uncle Dai." His nephew picked up the comic from the counterpane and started thumbing eagerly through the adventures of the boys of The Remove, who were as far removed from him and his limited experience of life as the man in the moon.

Dai left him to become acquainted with Bob Cherry, Harry Wharton, Billy Bunter and Company, and went back downstairs. He passed through the kitchen and opened the back door. "Just going down the 'dub'," he called to his mother as he headed for the outside toilet at the bottom of the garden.

Once inside he bolted the door, parked himself on the bum-polished seat, and taking the *True Confessions* from inside his shirt, began to read where James Henry had left off. As he got more absorbed in the story he wondered vaguely what the fare was to Peoria, Illinois.

two

Bryn Williams sat nursing a cup of coffee opposite a shadowy figure in the dimly-lit back room of Panteg's Italian café. Nearly every small town or large village in South Wales possessed such a place — either a Bertorelli's or a Cascarini's or a Bracchi's — and Panteg was no exception. There is an affinity between the Welsh and the Italians — a love of singing, a similarity in shortness of stature and breadth of character, and a common dislike of being owed money. This last characteristic was manifest as the owner of the café slammed down a steaming capuccino before Bryn's partner.

"Thatsa da last you getta for notting. You costa me hundreds and pounds worth of free coffee. Whatta you think I run here, bach? I already shutta da shop."

A head, its hair seemingly made of patent leather, thrust itself into the light thrown by the shaded lamp over the table. The face had the texture of white dough, and was rescued from anonymity by a large, scimitar-like nose and a thin pencil-line moustache which started from within the recesses of both nostrils and finished abruptly at each end of a full, sensuous mouth, from which a cigarette drooped. The hooded eyes looked up menacingly at the Italian, transfixing him as a ferret would a rabbit. A fat, beringed hand reached up and clutched the lapel of the other man's white linen jacket.

"Look, buddy." Smoke wreathed upwards from the hardly moving lips. "I don't like that kinda talk, see." More puffs of smoke punctuated this Welsh-accented parody of American gangster talk, causing the speaker to snort. He hung on to the lapel as he went into a spasm of coughing, his other hand plucking the cigarette from his lip. He gave a little cry of pain as the Woodbine tore away a strip of skin in the process.

The Italian removed himself easily from the other's grasp and backed out of range.

Bryn hastily picked up the cup of fresh coffee and handed it to his friend. "Drink a drop of this, it'll stop you coughing."

It was gratefully accepted, the recipient gulping down half the contents before feeling the scalding effect. "Aaaargh!" he choked, tears streaming down his cheeks.

"Sorry, Sid." Bryn wrung his hands nervously. "I mean, Mr. Jewell — er, I mean, Boss."

"Serves-a him right." The little café proprietor watched in satisfaction and left the room. He walked into his bright little parlour where his wife and daughter sat on a settee before the fire. His mother-in-law, clad from head to foot in black, sat motionless in a high-backed chair slightly to their left.

"That man makes-a me sick, mun. He rentsa my back room and don' pay da money. He drinksa my coffee and always say 'Put it in da bill.' Why he pick on my place to have dese meetings?"

His wife looked up from her knitting, her olive-skinned face serene. "Alberto Capone, you too soft-hearted."

"Our Mam's right. You let everybody walk over you." His daughter's voice held none of her parents' Italian candences but was, on the contrary, pure Swansea Valley.

Alberto stroked his daughter's dark curls and smiled. "Teresa, carina mia. You Daddy can look after hisaself."

"Look after *him*self," corrected his twelve-year-old offspring. "*My*self, *your*self, *him*self, *her*self, *our*selves, *them*selves."

"Thatsa lotta people to look after." Alberto laughed at his own joke. "Hey, Mamma, thatsa lotta people to look after!"

His mother-in-law stared back at him expressionlessly. The

smile died on his face. She had never forgiven him for uprooting her and her daughter from her native village in Sicily and bringing them to this heathen land. From the day she had first set foot in Wales she had never spoken to him. She gave him the age-old sign which has roughly the same meaning all over the world. Teresa giggled and Alberto gave her a sharp look. She dropped her eyes and, blushing, pretended to read her magazine. Her mother, Maria, missing the by-play, calmly carried on with her knitting. Alberto turned his back on his daughter and replied to his mother-in-law's gesture with a coarser one, only to receive an even cruder sign in response. He shrugged his shoulders in defeat and sat heavily on the settee.

In the back room Bryn Williams had poured coffee from the cup into a saucer and was blowing hard on it.

"Never mind blowing that bloody coffee. You've blown my cover — you said my name in front of that wop." Sid Jewell forced the words out through his burning mouth. "I've gone to a lot of trouble hiring this room and coming only at night-time on that bloody bike all the way from Morriston, and you've just told him my name." Sid's phoney gangster accent had disappeared now and his speech was as Welsh as Bryn's.

He waved his hand in front of his open mouth in a vain attempt to cool it. Bryn watched him anxiously. It was difficult to know how to handle Sid — not that he had known him for long.

They had met in a pub behind Swansea Market one Saturday three weeks ago when Bryn, who was technically on duty, had caught him with his hand in the money satchel he wore across his shoulder. When challenged, Jewell had smiled at him and gone on rummaging amongst the silver and coppers.

"Just looking for change of half a dollar, buddy," he drawled calmly in his best American. "Have a drink on me, pal." Sid palmed two shillings from the satchel and put it on the counter.

"Thanks. Australian, are you?" said Bryn, who was, to say the least, gullible.

Over the pints of Hancocks best bitter, Sid — keeping his attention on the buxom barmaid — had listened with one ear to the conductor's tale of injustice: how Dai Fargo treated him badly, and him being his brother-in-law as well. He went on to describe his job, saying how tough it was, just the one bus operating between Panteg and Swansea, not being paid for overtime, and not even getting danger money when they took the wages from the Glanmor Colliery Head Office to the Colliery at Panteg every Friday.

Sid had perked up suddenly at this piece of information. As he pumped Bryn for more details, a great plan slowly began to take shape in his mind. All his life he had been a petty crook, starting at the age of six when he had caught his mother in bed with the milkman. He had demanded sixpence to keep quiet as well as a ride on the milkman's cart. It was not a completely successful initiation into crime because the milkman had slapped his horse so that Sid was thrown off the back of the wagon. This was the way most of his schemes went. What he gained on the swings he invariably lost on the roundabouts.

He had been everything from a bookie's runner in Newport, where he was born, to a cinema projectionist in Splott. That was where he had picked up his fake American accent. He revelled in Chicago gangster films and watched avidly each time he ran them. Cagney, Edward G. Robinson, Paul Muni — he knew them all, along with their dialogue. When a reel he particularly enjoyed came up he was not averse to playing it over again, in spite of the stamping and shouting from the infuriated audience. This had eventually got him the sack. He had called the manager a "dirty rat" and got punched on the nose. That night he had returned to the cinema projection room and set fire to it. He watched the blaze from across the street, the light from the fire glinting in his eyes. On the other side of the city, the cinema owner rubbed his hands with delight on being telephoned with the news, and ran to the desk where he kept his insurance policies. He checked the small print. "Ruth," he cried to his wife in the bedroom. "Somebody's done us a favour. We can buy that bungalow in Porthcawl after all."

Since then Sid had kept pretty low. He had heard that the police were after him to establish his whereabouts at the time of the fire, and he had drifted down west to Swansea, where he had arrived just two days before his meeting with Bryn.

Faced with the disgruntled conductor's information he began to plot his next move. The great plan, the big "heist" he had always dreamed of, could become a reality. He needed a team around him, that was the snag. Bryn, after two more meetings, was easily talked into betraying his brother-in-law, having already done so many times with his ticket returns, but he was hardly the strong-arm man Sid needed to pull off the job of hijacking the Colliery wages from the bus.

To acquaint himself with the scene of the projected crime, Sid wandered around Panteg one Sunday afternoon. However, his snap-brimmed black trilby, tight-fitting dark striped suit and two-toned shoes contrasted strangely with the cloth caps and crossed-over white mufflers of the locals. He retreated quickly into the nearest café and ordered a cup of coffee. While he was waiting for the coffee to arrive he looked up at the window and saw the legend ENOPAC LA. It took him some time to work out the lettering the right way around, but when he did his heart gave a leap. This must be fate, he thought. Al Capone, his idol, the greatest of them all. This feller must be a relation. When the coffee came, he stood up and seized the little Italian by the hand. "Great to meet you, Al, goddamit." He looked over his shoulder and then back to Alberto's puzzled face. "Let's go in back and have a gabfest."

He was led into the little store-room at the back of the shop by the bewildered café proprietor who soon disillusioned him about his antecedents. "I come-a from respectable famiglia."

"O.K., O.K." Sid was disappointed, but decided that there must be a good reason for him to have been led to this place, and talked the Italian into letting him hire the back room.

As he was leaving, Tommy Rees came in through the door of the café carrying three large cartons of coffee. "Where d'you want these, Al?"

"Over bya dere." The Italian pointed to the room which he and Sid had just vacated.

"Right ho." Tommy barged through the door, his right

shoulder taking away part of the lintel.

"Mama mia!" Al smacked his hand hard against his forehead.

"Sorry, Al." Tommy's battered face was creased with anxiety.

"Thass aright." The Italian shrugged his shoulders resignedly.

Sid eyed Tommy's big frame with mounting excitement. Here, he thought, is the man I'm looking for, the muscle, the third member of the team. "Hey, kid."

Tommy turned, dropped his burden, and looked around, finally fixing on Sid as the man who had spoken to him. He smiled suddenly as a child might. "That was what they used to call me in my fighting days. Kid Rees." His left arm came up level with his shoulder and he dropped into a boxer's stance. He flicked out his fist at the electric light fitting which was on a level with his head. It swung away from him violently, and on its erratic return caught him squarely on the forehead. "Bit out of practice." Tommy shook his head dejectedly.

Sid had momentary qualms about his choice, threw them off, and put his arm around the boxer's huge shoulders. He began to talk quietly to him.

Thus was born the Taffia — a name which Sid conjured up for the three of them. He drew up rules for the gang which included always being addressed as Boss: his real name was never to be mentioned, hence his fury now.

"I take the bloody trouble to come in by the back door every time we have these meetings, covering up all my tracks, and then you go and blurt out my name." Sid touched his mouth carefully, feeling for blisters, the fake rings dull in the light.

"Sorry, Boss." Bryn was all contrition, his fingers, green from handling small change every day, twisting nervously. He was getting apprehensive about the impending robbery and would have been far happier with a pint in front of him at The Bricklayers' Arms than with the cup of coffee he had just drunk.

"Then there's that Tommy Rees. I set him a simple exercise today — fixed him up with a foolproof disguise — and he buggers it up by swallowing one of the ping-pong balls. I went through it with him time and time again. It was an easy snatch.

He could have grabbed the money and got away before anybody stopped him. The bike was there at the kerb waiting for him — I even lent him my own clips — put 'em on for him before he went in the shop. Risked my cover as well to watch him do the job, and he cocks it up." He sighed. This hadn't been his day.

It hadn't been Tommy Rees's day either. At the hospital two large male nurses in the casualty department had pounded him heartily between the shoulder blades, making him disgorge the ping-pong ball along with his lunch.

He was now being interviewed in Panteg police station by P.C. Burns, a tall, thin Scotsman with a lugubrious countenance whose dogged method of questioning suspects had earned him the sobriquet of "Third Degree". But even he was near to admitting defeat with this one.

"For the fiftieth time, ye canna pretend this was your ain idea, Rees. Whae put ye up tae it?"

Tommy frowned hard in concentration. Burns waited, his patience fraying. The minutes ticked away on the large round clock on the whitewashed wall where peeling "Wanted" posters and a calendar from Jones the Butcher clustered together for comfort.

Five long minutes went by and then the boxer raised his head. "I can't understand a word you're saying, mun." He sounded genuine, as indeed he was. Burns's accent was almost incomprehensible to ordinary Welsh ears, and even more so to Tommy's cauliflower variety.

The constable turned abruptly on his heel and walked out, seething with frustration. He knocked on the door of his superior across the passage. "Sergeant Powell, are ye busy?"

"I won't be long, boyo." The sergeant's voice was calm and unhurried. He was at the moment questioning "Flasher" Roberts, who stood before him.

Powell was leaning back in his chair, his feet perched comfortably on his desk, and his hands clasped over his burgeoning paunch. "Been a naughty boy again then, have we? Showing off in front of the ladies, eh?"

Roberts, bearded and shifty-eyed, shuffled uncomfortably in his too large raincoat. "No, I never done nothing. Them women was telling tales." His voice was a high-pitched whine.

The sergeant studied him for a while then, slowly taking his feet from the desk, leaned forward confidentially. "Come on now, Flasher. We all know what you've been doing. Mind you, you must have got something there to be proud of." He winked knowingly at the other, toying with a big ebony ruler as he talked. "From what I've heard you must have got the biggest and best in Panteg, perhaps even in the whole of South Wales."

Flasher Roberts managed an uncertain, snaggle-toothed grin and shook his head.

"Oh, go on. You must have." The sergeant looked around the room conspiratorially and returned his gaze to the man before him. "Let's have a look at this thing you're so proud of. It's frightened the life out of half the women and children in Panteg. Come on, there's only us two here." His voice had dropped to a whisper.

Flasher reddened and then giggled.

"Just man to man, boy bach. To satisfy my curiosity, that's all," Powell wheedled.

"All right, then." Roberts opened his raincoat and revealed himself. He was naked from his waist to his knees, to which he had tied the cut-off remnants of his trouser legs.

"Well, well," said the sergeant. "What a whopper. Put it on the desk by here and I'll measure it for posterity."

Flasher, proud now of his manhood, flopped it on the blotter which the sergeant pushed towards him.

"Hold still, now." Powell picked up the heavy ebony ruler and brought it crashing down on Roberts's pride and joy.

The resultant scream brought Burns running into the room.

"It's all right, lad. Flasher here has just caught himself on the edge of the desk. Nasty."

Roberts hopped around, clutching himself.

"Go on now, bugger off," said Powell. "And if I ever catch you at it again you'll go inside for a couple of years."

Flasher pushed past Burns in a crouched rush for the door.

"Sort of primitive justice, I suppose you young coppers would call it, but I guarantee we won't see Flasher back here again. It won't look so attractive in a truss." Powell heaved himself to his feet and turned to his constable. "Before you do anything else, change that blotting paper." He twirled the ends of his trim military moustache. "Having trouble with Tommy Rees, are you? When you've finished tidying my desk you go on home. I'll talk to him."

The boxer, having heard the scream, looked apprehensive when the sergeant came in.

"It's all right, Tommy bach. Just straightening out old Flasher Roberts's problem for him. Well, not exactly straightening it — flattening it more likely." He smiled reassuringly at Tommy.

Unlike most people in Panteg, he had a soft spot for the ex-boxer. He had brought momentary fame to the village when he had won his first few fights, beating opponents carefully selected for him by a manager who had high hopes for a title, there being a shortage of heavyweights at the time. Then along came Tommy Farr and Jack Petersen, and Tommy went tumbling down with a monotonous regularity. But of all the fights he had had in the ring, none was as momentous as the one he fought in Gelli Street, Treherbert with Gwyneth Pugh.

Sergeant Powell was the policeman who had dragged her off him, being severely mauled in the process himself. That was before his promotion to sergeant and his subsequent move to Panteg.

The battering by Gwyneth — a monolithic woman who claimed Tommy was the father of her child, though there were two rugby teams and several tradesmen who might have claimed the dubious honour — had finished the boxer's already declining career. He became a figure of fun, and because of his inability to concentrate on anything for long, he now relied on people like Alberto Capone to give him odd jobs.

"What's all this about trying to hold up the Co-op, then? That's not your form, Tommy. Pinching oranges off a stall, or doing a bit of running for a bookie, aye, but not holding up the bloody Co-op in broad daylight. Whose idea was it?"

Tommy looked down at his feet and considered his reply. He had promised the Boss — whose real name he didn't know — that he would keep the Taffia oath, and besides Bryn had warned him that they would set Gwyneth Pugh on him if he gave anything away. He suddenly stiffened as he surveyed his feet. "Hey, I've got odd socks on, look." He pointed down to where his trouser bottoms finished three inches above his ankles, revealing a brown sock on his left foot and a black one on the other.

"I know, and when you get home you'll find another pair like it." Powell was weary and felt unable to cope with Rees's tangential thinking. He made a snap decision. "Listen now, Tommy. I'm going to let you go home. There's not much of a case against you — you had no weapon on you and the evidence is confused to say the least. Report back here Monday and I'll see whether the Co-op manager will change his mind about preferring charges. Right?"

Tommy laughed delightedly and started shadow boxing around the room to show his pleasure. He cuffed the hanging light shade over the table, receiving it on the bridge of his nose on its return.

"Out of practice you are, boyo," said Powell kindly.

"Treacherous things, them lampshades," Tommy growled, rubbing his face.

"All right then, off you go — and don't forget to report back here at eleven on Monday."

The sergeant opened the door for him and watched the boxer skipping away up the street. There remained a nagging doubt in his mind that something was not quite right about the escapade in the Co-op. It wasn't like Tommy at all. He wondered if there was somebody else at the back of it. His reverie was interrupted by a call from his wife to come and get his supper. "Coming, beauty," he cried, hastening to obey.

Tommy's mother welcomed him with a lack of warmth. "Stupid idiot! All the village is talking about you. What's got into you? If your father was alive he'd turn in his grave." She looked towards the wall where the silver-framed photograph of her husband hung. He was standing stiffly to attention in the uniform of a South Wales Borderer, alongside a chair in Chapman's Photographic Studios, Swansea. "Died whilst on active service for his King and country" read a small commemoration plaque built into the frame. Bert Rees had actually been killed by a tram as he reeled back blind drunk to his barracks in Cairo, but Ceinwen had always kept this fact from her only son.

"Sorry, Dad." Tommy turned towards the picture of his father and bowed his head.

"I should think so, too," said his mother, shovelling three laden teaspoons into his cup of tea from the bowl she had borrowed from Mrs. Fargo.

Tommy picked up his cup and wandered over to the fire. Above it on the mantelpiece stood a row of cups and trophies he had amassed in his amateur boxing days, along with one from his professional fights. He fingered them lovingly as he drank his tea.

"Another cup, Tommy?" His mother was calmer now.

"No thanks, Mam. I'll have a glass of water instead. This tea's made me thirsty."

three

James Henry Fargo, lying in his bedroom on Sunday morning, could hear the hymn-singing from Ebenezer Chapel through the open window, and even though the Chapel was two streets away he could make out his Uncle Dai's driving tenor voice leading the congregation along the Glory Road. He smiled to himself. Today he was allowed to get up, and if he dressed up warm his Nana was going to let him go on the outing to Parkmill down on the Gower Coast. He started to dress himself, anxious to show her that he was well enough to go out. She came in as he was pulling on his grey flannel shorts.

"There's a lovely boy, then. Getting up, are we?" She beamed at the tousle-haired little lad. "Oh, you are looking better today. Let me help you on with your little socks, then."

His grandmother knelt down and, making him sit on the bed, fussed him into his grey woollen stockings, turning the tops down just below the knee so that the red bands showed in a nice even line. She buckled his red and white belt with the silver snake clasp around his waist and tied the laces of his brown canvas gym shoes. Taking a hairbrush and comb from the little table by the door, she made him face the mirror while she brushed his hair. She carefully examined the roots for nits and, finding none, parted his hair at the side, making a dead straight white line. When she had finished she looked over the top of his head into the mirror. "Oh boy bach, you are the image of your poor Dad." Taking him to her she rocked him against her bosom, letting the tears for her dead son flow freely.

James Henry, who had no memory of his father, allowed himself to be patted, waiting patiently for his grandmother's tears to subside. He was aware of her corset digging into his chin and he wondered whether the ladies in *True Confessions* wore them. If they were anything like the heavily laced-up one that his Nana was wearing, most of the tales of woe in the magazine would have had little chance of happening.

"There's a silly old Nana you've got. Oh dear, I've spoiled your hair." His grandmother wiped her eyes and blew her nose and started to look again for his parting. "Got to look nice for the trip to the Gower."

"I'm glad Auntie Elspeth is coming." James Henry felt a warm glow come over him when he thought of his Uncle Dai's fiancée, and even though she was also his school-teacher, he worshipped her. He was sure she didn't wear a corset, because she was all soft when she cuddled him.

Watching his face carefully in the mirror, his grandmother brushed his hair with increased vigour. "Keep still, boy," she said sharply.

"Be thou still my strength and shield," sang Dai Fargo, holding on valiantly to "shield" as the basses and baritones came in underneath like a mighty organ with "strength and shield", then all together with a thunderous repeat, "Be thou sti-ill my-y strength and shield."

Dai wiped his perspiring face with his handkerchief and sat down with a sense of achievement as the Reverend Iorwerth Jenkins, B.A. made purposefully for the pulpit.

At the other end of the village, Elspeth Owens and her father knelt on hassocks, heads bowed as the Vicar of St. Peter's prayed for the "health of King George the Fifth, Queen Mary, Edward, Prince of Wales and all the Royal Family."

Elspeth sneaked a look at her watch. She was meeting Dai at half past two and she had to get her father home for dinner first. The Reverend Courtenay Dowler, M.A. (Cantab) was noted for the length of his sermons, but she fervently hoped he might relent on this bright Sunday morning and let his congregation off lightly.

The Reverend Iorwerth Jenkins had no such intention. He stood stock still in the pulpit, his shock of white hair framing his head like a hirsute halo, surveying his flock in a grim, brooding silence. Suddenly he lifted his right arm and swinging his bony forefinger in an arthritic arc around the chapel he cried, "Sinners!"

The sibilance of his "s"s fell in a harsh rain on the first three pews. Their occupants leaned forward to receive it, as if seeking a second, more personal baptism.

"'Ye shall keep the sabbath therefore; for it is holy unto you: every one that defileth it shall surely be put to death: for whosoever doeth any work therein, that soul shall be cut off from among his people. Six days may work be done; but in the seventh is the sabbath of rest, holy to the Lord: whosoever doeth any work in the sabbath day, he shall surely be put to death.' Exodus, Chapter 31, verses 14 and 15. Cut off from among his people, friends." The Minister paused to let the echo of his thunder die away into the musty recesses of the Chapel. He leaned forward in a confidential manner, arms folded on the front of the pulpit, his voice muted now. "And yet it has come to my attention that one of the senior members of our Chapel intends this afternoon — this *very* afternoon — to gallivant off down to the seaside." He let the last word rise to the top of his register, pinging around the building and coming to rest squarely on the conscience of his target in the gallery.

Dai Fargo sat transfixed in his seat.

"An outing has been arranged for those stupid enough to be taken in by the Godlessness of this man. Today they will be paddling in the sea instead of praying on their knees. But what a price they will have to pay."

"A bob there and back," whispered Jammy Wicks to his mother.

"When they get on that bus today they will be taking the first step on the rocky road to perdition." The Minister thumped the pulpit with his fist.

"Just a moment, Reverend." Dai Fargo was on his feet. "I would like to have a word." His tenor rang clear in the silence broken only by the creaking of necks turning in his direction.

This was an unheard-of event in the history of the Chapel. No one had ever contradicted "The Thunderer" on his own ground. Those singled out for personal attacks always took their public scourging in silence. This was almost a Biblical confrontation — a Dai and Goliath. Those members of the congregation who liked and respected Dai hoped that he had not left his slingshot at home. Those who were on the side of the Minister, a faction led by Miss Thomas the headmistress, hoped to see him reduced to a pulp for his temerity.

"You would dare to stand up in the House of God and defy his appointed representative?" Iorwerth Jenkins's tone was milder than his wide-eyed expression of outrage seemed to merit.

Dai was surprised to find himself standing. He had acted purely on impulse. He felt the same as he had done sixteen years before when he had faced a German machine gun post. Then, he had hurled a hand grenade; today he clutched a Moody and Sankey hymn book. "It's not defiance, indeed. You just called me Godless in front of all the people by here."

The Minister spread his arms wide and looked around at his congregation in astonishment. "Did I mention Mr. David Fargo by name?"

His faithful followers shook their heads in silent denial.

Dai's face went redder. "There's only one bus service in this village . . ."

"More's the pity," said Miss Thomas loudly.

". . . And there's only one outing arranged for today. So therefore you are talking about me, and if you are talking about me, then you've just called me Godless."

The Minister allowed himself a smile. "I bow to your superior logic, Mr. Fargo." He bowed deeply, a theatrical gesture. "If the cap fits, wear it."

"Hear, hear," Miss Thomas remarked, nodding her cloche-hatted head.

"She'd look better in a cloth cap," said Jammy Wicks out of the side of his mouth. His fat mother suppressed a titter in her handkerchief.

"I don't see anything Godless about taking a few sick miners to get a breath of fresh air at the seaside. I don't think God would object to that, somehow — especially when I'm only charging half price."

"Hear, hear," said Jammy Wicks loudly.

Dai sat down, quivering with a combination of anger and embarrassment.

"I appear to have offended our bus operator friend, who apparently knows more of the working of God's mind than I do." Iorwerth Jenkins put a hand to his ear and listened. "Do you hear a hum in the air, brethren?" His voice was almost a whisper.

The congregation looked at each other in bewilderment and adopted various attitudes of strained listening.

The Minister allowed himself twenty seconds of silence and then pulled out all the stops in his vocal organ. "That noise, brothers and sisters, is the sound of our founder, the great Charles Wesley, spinning in his grave."

Dai Fargo stood up again, but this time he walked out of the gallery and down the steps towards the Chapel door. When he reached it he turned to face the Minister. " 'And He said unto them, "What Man shall there be among you that shall have one sheep and if it fall into a pit on the sabbath day will he not lay hold on it and lift it out? How much then is a man better than a sheep? Wherefore it is lawful to do well on the sabbath days." ' Matthew, Chapter 12, verses 11 and 12. Thank you." Dai bowed as theatrically as the Minister had done and went out of the door.

The Reverend Courtenay Dowler stood in the porch shaking hands with his parishioners. A tall, stooping figure, his head bobbed up and down on his long thin neck like an ostrich doing a mating dance, as he acknowledged the faint praise which damned his sermon for being too long. "Thank you, thank you," he said in his high Anglican voice, smiling absently into each face. His manner changed abruptly as Elspeth and her father came out into the sunshine. He seized her hand with his two bony ones and caressed it. "Ah, Miss Elspeth. You look charming as always. You light up the church with your presence."

Elspeth blushed to the roots of her auburn hair and tried to retrieve her hand from his skeletal clasp. The Vicar held on valiantly. "Are you coming to the Vicarage after church this evening? I'd like to talk to you about forming a Girl Guide troop. My housekeeper is making some Welsh cakes and . . ."

"She's going on an outing to the Gower," said her father, thumping his walking stick on the ground to emphasise his displeasure.

"Oh!" The Vicar temporarily loosened his hold on Elspeth's hand and she took the opportunity to remove it. "On *Sunday*?" There was gentle reproach in his watery eyes.

"It's the only chance Dai has got to take some of the sick miners for a breath of sea air. And he's doing it at a special price so that they can afford it. Some of the village children are coming too. It won't do them any harm either." Elspeth was vigorous in Dai's defence.

"Yes, yes." Dowler nodded his head twice, letting it bob gently for a while as he considered what she had said. "An errand of mercy, eh? I believe there's something in St. Matthew's Gospel where our Lord defends such an action on the sabbath."

"Matthew, Chapter Twelve, verses eleven and twelve," said Elspeth. "I looked it up for Dai so that his conscience wouldn't be too troubled. He liked it so much he learned it by heart."

"Very good, yes." The Vicar was all smiles again, though the repeated mention of Dai Fargo's name had taken the warmth from them.

"I think it's disgraceful, myself." Evan, Elspeth's father, did not approve of her engagement to the bus operator either.

"Come on, Dad, off to go. I've got to get your dinner for you before I meet Dai, and the joint's been in the oven long enough." She glanced at the Vicar to make sure that her hint at the length of his sermon had taken effect, but he had already turned away and was bobbing his head over the hand of P.C. Burns.

"Verra guid service, Reverend, but what evidence have ye *really* got that there were only two loaves and two fishes among five thousand people? Now, it seems tae me that . . ."

The policeman's Sunday morning theological argument dwindled into the distance as Elspeth hurried her father up the street.

"Why don't you marry the Vicar instead? He fancies you, gel. You're thirty-eight, remember."

"I remember, all right." She shuddered. The thought of being Mrs. Courtenay Dowler was too awful to contemplate, yet at the same time she felt a chill come over her at the prospect of still being a spinster at the age of forty. It was about time Dai sorted his mother out.

At that moment Dai's mother was sorting him out. "You told the Reverend Jenkins *that* — in Chapel?" Mrs. Fargo leaned against the dresser for support. "I'll never be able to hold my head up in the Sisterhood again. Get my tablets for me, quick."

"Oh, come on, Mam. I'm not going to sit like a dummy in Chapel while that old fogey has a go at me." He gave his mother her tablets and poured her a glass of home-made pop from a large brown glass flagon. "He's never liked me from the very first day he came here."

"It was your fault for dropping his luggage off the roof of the bus when you brought him up from Swansea Station." Mrs. Fargo sat down at the kitchen table and patted her bosom. "What's going to happen to the Panteg Male Voice Choir now?

You can't go back to Ebenezer after this."

"Well, I can rehearse them in the garage." Dai, who had formed the choir mostly from members of the Chapel, was still too angry to realise the possible consequences of his action. "Get them all in there — a bit of a squeeze, perhaps. Good for sound in the garage, too. Nearly as good as the Chapel."

"Don't be so daft, David. If it rains on that corrugated iron roof you'll never hear yourselves sing." His mother had risen and was laying the table for dinner. The word lunch was never used for a midday meal except by the Vicar, a fact that constantly puzzled his housekeeper. "Go and call our James Henry in from the backyard. Dinner's nearly ready."

James Henry, who was sitting on a broken kitchen chair in the cluttered backyard reading *The Magnet* in the sunshine, readily abandoned his comic. His gastric juices had already anticipated the call. The smell of roast lamb, roast potatoes and cauliflower had drifted deliciously over him for the past half-hour.

"Put something in front of his nice clean shirt. He mustn't have gravy all over him before he goes on the outing. There's enough trouble already, indeed."

Dai ruffled James Henry's hair affectionately and tied one of his mother's aprons around the lad's neck. "Eat up, boyo. You'll soon be big and strong like your fat old Uncle Dai." He patted his belly and grinned.

"Yes, eat while you can, boy bach. The way your Uncle David's going on there'll be nothing on the table at all soon except the knives and forks."

"Oh, Mam, don't upset the boy." Dai winked at James Henry and tucked into his full plate as if he didn't have a care in the world.

Elspeth removed her apron and turned to her father, who sat reading a paper in his armchair by the fire which he insisted be lit even in the summer. As an ex-foreman at the Colliery retired on compensation through an accident to his leg while working underground, he was entitled to free coal, and being the man he was he would rather use it than give it away. "Are you sure you'll be all right now, Dad?"

"Go on out, gel. I can manage on my own." He looked at his daughter over the top of his glasses. "Don't bother to clear away. I'll do it." He picked up *The Empire News* again.

Elspeth was a little puzzled about her father's behaviour over the past few weeks. Before that he had always grumbled when she went out and behaved like a latter-day Barrett of Wimpole Street. Since his wife had died ten years ago he had leaned heavily on his daughter for everything. Now, even though he had not altered his dislike for Dai Fargo — thinking him not good enough for his only daughter — he was almost pushing her out of the house. She went upstairs to change for the outing, shaking her head in disbelief as she did so.

In his one room digs in Morriston, Sid Jewell sat in a torn Paisley dressing-gown, toasting stale bread in front of a broken gas fire. On the table behind him lay a map of Panteg and District, a pair of second-hand Army surplus binoculars, and a time-table for the Fargo bus company, augmented with details — furnished by Bryn — of the special Sunday trip. Saturday's *South Wales Evening Post* was strewn across the unmade bed which took up the rest of the room.

Sid stared thoughtfully at the cracked ceiling as he worked on his plan to ambush Dai's bus. The details were uncertain at present because of Tommy Rees's apprehension by the police. He would have to do the job soon or he'd starve. He drummed his fingers on the arm of the chair, glumly contemplating his future.

The toast burst into flames on the end of his fork, singeing his fingers.

"Sod the bloody thing!" He stamped on the burning bread in anger, forgetting his feet were bare.

Downstairs his landlady and her husband were having their Sunday meal. Mr. Donovan looked up at the ceiling. "Thought you said that new lodger was an actor."

"That's what he told me, anyway." The landlady pushed cabbage on to her fork and conveyed it to her mouth.

"Sounds more like a dancer to me. Fancy practising on a Sunday." He listened again. "Doesn't seem to have much sense of rhythm."

His wife looked at him disdainfully. "What do you expect for seven and six a week — bloody Nijinsky?"

Evan Owens sat up eagerly as the latch of the back door clicked open.

"Come on in, love. She's gone off on the outing."

Mrs. Wicks giggled in the doorway. "Are you sure it's safe?" She moved towards the chair.

"Come by here, my little plump beauty." Evan reached for her with outstretched arms.

The widow sat carefully in his lap. "Watch your bad leg, then."

"Will Jammy come looking for you?" Evan's breath was hot on her neck.

"Not likely." She giggled again. "He's upstairs trying on my frocks."

four

James Henry stared out of the window on his side of the bus, his eyeballs large in their sockets. His euphoria had reached a degree he had never before experienced. As they drove into the outskirts of Swansea the advertisements on the hoardings burned into his brain like the window in his bedroom did when he looked hard at it and then quickly shut his eyes and waited for the squares to appear behind his lids. On one poster a pig pulled a cart containing sausages — "Drawing his own conclusion" read the inscription. The Bisto Kids sniffed appreciatively at visible tendrils of gravy aroma which hooked into their nostrils from a joint of roast beef. A man in striped pyjamas sat astride a giant bottle of Bovril on a stormy sea. "Elsie and Doris Waters" proclaimed Swansea Empire posters in large letters, and James Henry felt vaguely proud that these famous ladies had deigned to come so far from Broadcasting House and actually appear in a town which itself was not very far from where he, James Henry Fargo, lived — namely Panteg, Near Swansea, Glamorgan, South Wales, Great Britain, Europe, The World.

Beside him, Elspeth sat watching the back of Dai Fargo's neck as he negotiated the winding roads into Swansea. She had heard about the scene in the Chapel from her headmistress, Miss Thomas, whom she had met in Balaclava Street on her way to Dai's house.

"Disgraceful behaviour indeed from a deacon of the Chapel,

defying the Reverend Jenkins on our Lord's sacred ground." The elder woman's eyes had narrowed. "You are off on this ungodly outing, too, aren't you?"

"Yes, and it's no business of yours what I do when I'm out of school." Elspeth had tossed her head with a rare show of rebellion and hurried on down the street.

"Damned, you will be!" Miss Thomas had cried to her retreating back.

"Oh! Bum to Miss Thomas," said Elspeth aloud.

"That's what I say." Teresa Capone leaned forward from the seat behind her and tapped her school mistress approvingly on the shoulder. Her grandmother, sitting beside her, looked out of the window with the same intensity as James Henry, oblivious to everything but the parade passing before her eyes.

"I don't know what you're talking about." Elspeth blushed through an angle of 360 degrees and shook her pupil's hand from her shoulder.

From the other sixteen worn leather seats came the beginnings of a Welsh hymn as the six sick miners and their wives scented fresh air and freedom. *Calon Lan* they sang, and Dai, conducting with one hand and driving the bus with the other, led the harmony.

Sid Jewell, cloth-capped and mackintoshed, lay on his stomach on Cwmgorse Common. He put his binoculars to his eyes and waited amid the gorse for the Fargo bus to come into view. With his battered pocket watch on the ground before him, he intended to determine the time the bus took to cross the Common on its way into Swansea. He had already decided vaguely that this was the point on the bus's return journey from Swansea to Panteg on Friday at which he would attempt his hijacking of the Colliery wages. It was open countryside and the chances of success were higher than they would be anywhere else on the bus route.

In the distance he heard the unmistakable clanking of Dai Fargo's Leyland and he swung his binoculars towards the bend in the road around which the bus would appear. A figure blocked his view.

"Trouserless" Tom Daniels, a professional house painter and amateur Casanova of 3 Howell Crescent, Port Talbot, arose from his prone paramour, a barmaid from The Mason's Arms, and smashed the binoculars from Sid's grasp.

"Bloody peeping Tom," he cried, emphasising each word with a heavy blow.

The unfortunate Jewell clawed himself desperately to his feet, and leaving behind an even more battered pocket watch, fled the field.

Trouserless Tom was content to let him go, honour having been satisfied, and conscious of the fact that his lady friend had not.

"Now where was I?" he said, regaining his previous position.

"Ooh, there's awful you are."

Dai applied the brakes gently three hundred yards before the "Shepherd's Teas" sign came up on the bend in Parkmill, judging to a nicety the end of the chorus of *Aberystwyth* and the amount of pressure the thin tread of his tyres would take.

"All out, folks."

Dai's passengers needed no second bidding.

"Duw, I'm dying for a pee," said one old miner, struggling to his feet. Elspeth helped him to stand up. "Sorry, Miss," he said, "but when you've got to go . . ."

"You've got to go," Elspeth finished the sentence for him.

"Perhaps you can help him to find it," called a bronchial voice from the back.

"Take no notice," whispered the old miner to Elspeth, who had gone red with embarrassment. "Some people haven't got no respect for ladies." He descended the steps of the bus carefully, holding up the rest of the passengers. He stopped on the bottom step. "Mind you, if you've got a pin on you . . ."

"Oh, go on with you," Elspeth laughed as she handed the old chap over to Dai, who took him from her and set him on the way to the corrugated iron toilet marked "Gents".

"Come on then, butties." The bus slowly emptied. The last to leave were Teresa and her grandmother, who clutched her grand-daughter's hand tightly and looked around her with a mixture of caution and belligerence.

James Henry had already jumped down from the bus and stood alongside Elspeth and Dai as they watched Teresa and her Gran hesitate before taking the final step.

"Upsadaisy," said Dai, reaching out with both hands to lift the old lady off the step. As soon as she felt him grasp her waist, she burst into a gabble of what sounded like Italian oaths and pummelled Dai's head with her horny old fists. "Bloody hell," said Dai, setting her fairly gently on her feet.

Teresa still stood on the last step. "Well, aren't you going to help me down?" She addressed her question to James Henry, who had been engrossed in his Uncle Dai's efforts to help the old lady to the ground. James Henry offered her a hesitant hand which Teresa took firmly in hers and helped herself down on to the grass verge outside the café. As she did so he felt a tingle run through his hand from the contact and his whole body lit up as though he had been struck by a bolt of lightning from the inside. Teresa thanked him with a tiny inclination of her head and disengaged her hand immediately. James Henry remained rooted to the spot, his head thrust forward and his blood singing an age-old melody to which his red corpuscles had yet to find the words.

Elspeth nudged Dai, who was still smarting from Teresa's grandmother's assault on his person. "Hey up, Dai. Our James Henry's been smitten. Look at his little face."

Dai looked towards his nephew, who was still transfixed as he stared almost uncomprehendingly at the retreating back of the girl who had suddenly changed his life. "Like St. Paul on the road to Damascus," said Dai, grinning. "Or Petrified, Peoria in my Mam's magazine."

"What magazine?"

"Never you mind. It's too naughty for you to read. Come on, James Henry — tea should be ready. It'll take your mind off other things."

"Oh hush, Dai." Elspeth clucked reprovingly at her fiancé and, putting her arm around James Henry's shoulders, she led him gently towards the café.

Inside, the miners and their wives were already sorting themselves out as to who should sit where at the trestle tables which were set out in two long lines. Tea urns were steaming away alongside piles of sandwiches and cakes, and slices of boiled ham lay on plates beside gleaming knives and forks.

"Haven't seen such a lovely do since they buried Mr. Preece Top Farm," exclaimed one goitrous matron as she sat down after first assisting her breathless husband to a place beside her.

There were cries of "Hear, hear!" and other remarks of appreciation, and the company set to with a will. All except James Henry. He had been placed next to Teresa and was too distracted by her nearness to take an interest in the food in front of him.

Dai, who sat on his other side, tapped him on the arm. "Come on, boy bach, eat up. I thought the fresh air would give you an appetite."

"I'm not very hungry, thanks, Uncle Dai."

Teresa, who had nearly finished her ham, turned towards him. "Can I have your ham, then?" she asked, anticipating James Henry's reply by spearing the meat with her fork.

"Help yourself." James Henry's voice squeaked an octave higher than normal.

"Ta." Teresa salted her spoils and, turning again, gave him a crumby smile of thanks. He reddened and a fine trembling began at the pit of his stomach and permeated his whole being. Had he been a tuning fork he could have pitched an A for the whole of the Swansea Valley.

After tea the waitresses cleared the tables and Dai announced that the afternoon was now free for everybody to do what they liked as long as they were back at the bus by six o'clock. The party broke up into groups of those who wanted to see the sea, which meant an impossible climb for most of the miners, and those who wanted just to sit by the roadside or go for a gentle ramble up the Valley. Thus, Dai, Elspeth, James Henry and Teresa and her grandmother began to head for Three Cliffs Bay and the others took the softer option.

The view from the top of the cliffs was magnificent.

"Duw, there's lovely," said Elspeth, clutching Dai's hand tightly.

"Aye. That's Devon over by there." Dai pointed across the sparkling water to a faint profile of hills on the horizon.

They stood in a group near a wooden bench half hidden in the ferns. Teresa's grandmother sat on it heavily and arranged herself for an afternoon nap, grumbling in Italian beneath her breath at the climb she had made. Her granddaughter had chatted incessantly to James Henry on the way up to the cliffs, even taking his hand at one point. His own contribution to the conversation had been monosyllabic; he was still too overcome by Teresa's presence to say much. He didn't know what had come over him. After all, he knew Teresa from the playground in school and had even played games with her. But then she had been merely a little girl from a junior class. Now she had become a princess in a fairy tale.

"Why don't you two go and play for a bit?" Dai's hand clutching Elspeth's had tightened considerably and he felt a familiar yielding in her palm. He knew of a shady depression away off to the side of the path where the ferns grew high and would comfortably hide a courting couple.

"Do you think they'll be all right on their own?" Elspeth was as anxious as Dai to find a hiding place, but her instinct as a teacher made her feel responsible towards the children.

"Of course we will, Miss Owens," Teresa said with utter confidence. "Won't we, James Henry?"

He nodded dumbly, thrilled with the sound of his name on her lips.

Elspeth hesitated as Dai tugged urgently at her hand. "Are you sure, now?"

"Grandma's here, anyway," Teresa nodded towards her grandmother, who opened one eye and glared balefully at Elspeth.

"All right, then. But keep away from the cliffs now, won't you?" The last sentence was delivered over her shoulder as Dai hurried her away.

Teresa sat down on the grass and patted the ground next to her. "Come on, silly, sit down by here."

James Henry sat gingerly, feeling the grass. "It's not damp, is it? My Gran says if you sit on damp grass you can get piles."

"I know that, too." Teresa tossed her head impatiently. "I bet you don't know what piles are though, do you?"

"Yes I do." James Henry had no idea, but as a boy he had to pretend a kind of superior knowledge.

"What are they, then?" She looked directly into his eyes, taunting him. "If you can't tell me the proper answer you'll have to pay a forfeit, and do anything that I tell you to do."

The boy began to sweat. This strange girl was upsetting his whole nervous system. He looked away from her. "I *do* know but I haven't been very well and I've forgotten, that's all." He was now near tears.

"You don't know, you don't know!" the girl whispered into the boy's face, her triumph, though muted, still complete.

"All right, then, *you* tell me what they are." James Henry's retort had no real defiance in it.

"They're lumps on your bum and they bleed when you go to the lav to do number two. So there." Teresa sat back on her heels, picked a piece of grass from beside her and tickled James Henry's face with it. "Didn't know that, did you? Well, my Mam's got them, see, after she had me."

All these revelations were too much for James Henry. He got up and ran towards the cliff top. Teresa ran after him, laughing.

"Come on, you're my slave now. You've got to do everything I say."

The boy threw a stone towards the sea. "Bet you can't throw that far."

The girl picked up a pebble and hurled it so far that it splashed into the water. "There," she said, setting her hands firmly on her hips, facing him. Her eyes were alive with mischief. "See that beach down there? I'll bet I can get down there quicker than you can. And you've got to do as I say because you owe me a forfeit and you're my slave, so there."

The boy's heart shifted rapidly from his boots to his mouth at the thought of tackling the cliff. "There's a path over by there, but it's not very safe. And Auntie Elspeth said we weren't to go near the cliffs."

"Cowardy custard! You're a rotten little coward and I thought you were brave."

"I've had a cold and I've been in bed for days with it and I've got to wear my scarf when I go out because I've got to keep warm." James Henry was abjectly apologetic.

Teresa turned her back on him and made for the path down the cliff. "Cowardy custard!"

James Henry wavered, torn between the new-found feeling he had for this girl and his natural timidity. "All right, then, I'm coming." He ran after her, his heart pounding.

"Don't, Dai. Dai, stop it! Somebody'll see us." Elspeth struggled warmly in the ferns.

"Why do you have to wear these old passion killers? They can't do your circulation any good, and they certainly aren't any good for mine." Dai's face was suffused with the effort of the fight to breach Elspeth's elastic defences. "Come on, mun, take the things off. We *are* engaged."

"You'll have to wait until we get married. I've told you that thousands of times." Elspeth was breathless — a physical condition which was perfectly obvious to Dai as her breasts, freed from her slip, heaved under his nose.

Dai groaned and fell away from her, panting. "There's no justice. It's not as if you're a virgin. Good God Almighty, you couldn't have enough of it that night when your father went to London for the Final."

"Yes, and I've never forgiven myself." Elspeth sat up and crossed her arms over her breasts. "You took advantage of me with those two Green Goddess cocktails you gave me." She shot Dai a sidelong look. "I didn't know what I was doing."

Dai rolled over onto his back and chuckled. He stuck a blade of grass between his teeth and chewed on it for a while. "Instinct, then, was it? There's a wedding night we'll have when you're fully conscious."

Elspeth laughed in spite of herself and cradled Dai's head in her arms. "Oh, I do love you, Dai, but be patient, there's a good boy."

Dai reached out and gently stroked her breast. "Patience is a virtue. I've had enough of bloody virtue."

Elspeth moaned softly. "Oh God, here we go again," she said.

James Henry clung like grim death to the root of the tree which had broken his fall. Away to his right Teresa hugged the cliff face with outstretched arms. She stood on a narrow ledge with a sheer drop of two hundred feet below her.

"Mam, oh Mam." The lad cried for a mother he could hardly remember. "Uncle Dai! Nana!" He had followed Teresa down the steep cliff path until his nerve gave out when she had decided to take a short cut diagonally across the face of the cliff. "Coward," shouted the girl as he hesitated. "I'm not, I'm not!" Tears came readily now. He had been stimulated, challenged and humiliated all in one brief afternoon. Enough was enough. He wasn't going to follow this crazy girl any further. He had begun to run, stumbling, back up the path. His action caused loose earth to crumble beneath his feet and he lost his balance and fell. The next thing he knew was that he was hanging from a stunted tree and Teresa was marooned on a ledge because the rest of the track she was following had disappeared in the small avalanche he had started.

"Save me, James Henry," screamed Teresa, her dress billowing around her legs.

The boy forgot his own fear for a moment and concentrated. If he could swing his body to the left there was an outcrop of grey stone below him which could offer him a chance of getting back up the cliff. "I will. I'll save you. Hang on." He shut his eyes and heaved himself sideways along the cliff face. His feet touched the outcrop tantalisingly, sending more loose earth tumbling down into the sea, and he swung back again. He tried once more, and this time it worked. Holding on to the tree root with his right hand, he shifted his weight on to the projection now beneath his feet. With his left hand he felt the rock gingerly, looking for a crack into which he could thrust his fingers. He found one, carefully transferred his grip to it, and balanced himself on the rock. He was calmer now, and by turning his head he could see Teresa silently watching his movements from her own precarious position. There was another crack further up the cliff. If he could get his hands into it he could reach a clump of small bushes which he remembered was near the path where he had slipped and fallen. Don't look down, he told himself. Don't look down. The process was diabolically slow and it seemed an eternity before he reached the bushes. He sobbed with relief, then, remembering his priorities, wiped his face on his sleeve and pausing only to wave reassuringly in the direction of Teresa, he scrambled back towards the top of the cliff.

"Uncle Dai, Uncle Dai . . ." The shouts probed Dai's reluctant consciousness. He was about to reach the heights he had achieved during the time of Evan Owens' absence at the Cup Final. Elspeth, however, feeling guilty, was more aware of possible outside interference and pushed him aside at the crucial moment.

"That's James Henry. Oh my God, what's happened?" Elspeth was on her feet regardless of her semi-nudity. "What's the matter?"

The boy saw only her head and her waving arm. By the time he had reached them, running and crying, they were both in a reasonable state of dress.

"It's Teresa. She's trapped on the cliff. You've got to help her, quick!"

"There, there." Elspeth's arms were around him.

Dai struggled with his belt, swearing loudly. "Bugger, bugger, bugger. Where is she? Come on, show me."

Teresa had bravely and sensibly not moved from her position. Dai surveyed the situation calmly. His initial panic had been short-lived and he felt the same feeling come over him now as he had during a battle in the war. Everything seemed to move in slow motion, and yet his brain was working twice as fast as normal.

"Get the rope from the boot of the bus. You know — the rope I use to tie on the heavy baggage. Hurry up now, Elspeth. Take James Henry with you. He's had enough excitement for one day.'

Elspeth rushed off. As she ran, her arm around James Henry, she felt the weight of her guilt at having left the two children to their own devices while she and Dai were being wicked. She found herself sobbing. "I'm sorry God, it won't happen again. I shouldn't have done it."

"Done what?" asked a winded James Henry.

"Never you mind. I was being taken advantage of, that's all."

James Henry, on the run, had a sudden mental picture of his Uncle Dai and Auntie Elspeth in a similar position to a photograph he had seen in his Nana's magazine. It featured two scantily-clad figures in the throes of what seemed to him to be the attempted murder of the lady by the gentleman, who was lying on top of her. Underneath the photograph were the words, *He tried to take advantage of me.* The thought of his Uncle Dai murdering Auntie Elspeth almost unhinged his mind, and his high-pitched whoops, mingled with Elspeth's full-throated cries, brought the miners and their wives rushing to the bus as the couple hurtled down the hillside.

"Uncle Dai was trying to kill Auntie Elspeth," yelled the boy.

"Teresa's stuck on the cliff and Dai's after her," cried Elspeth.

"The dirty devil," said a miner's wife.

"A rope — I want a rope! It's in the boot."

"Now, now. Hanging him isn't going to help." An old miner laid a restraining hand on Elspeth's arm. "Let's have the full story."

Elspeth took a firm grip on herself, and taking deep breaths between each sentence, explained the situation on the cliff face. The rope was produced, and rejecting offers of help, she ran back up the hill to Dai. The others watched her go, and some of them, remembering what James Henry had cried, started asking him questions. But the boy, calmer now, refused to answer them. He wanted to think a while by himself in order to get things right in his mind.

On the cliff face Dai was talking quietly to Teresa. He had decided what he had to do and prepared the girl for what was to come. "I'm going to get a rope and tie one end around that tree at the top of the cliff and the other around my waist and when I come across towards you, I want you to take my hand in your right hand without moving your body."

Teresa bit her lip and nodded.

Dai's position near the clump of bushes was made more dangerous by his sheer weight. More loose earth tumbled towards the sea. He waved to her and started back to the top of the cliff where Elspeth now stood holding the rope. She handed it to him without a word, turning her head away. Dai had no time to wonder why and went about his task of tying the rope to the tree. He tested the strength of the knot and, satisfied with it, fixed the other end around his waist and began the descent towards Teresa.

From her position on the wooden bench, the girl's grandmother, aroused from her sleep by the cries of Elspeth and James Henry, watched silently as Dai prepared his rescue attempt, and crossed herself repeatedly.

Dai lowered himself to the clump of bushes and began his crab-like crawl across the rock face to the girl. More stones rattled down the cliff as he did so, and for one heart-stopping moment the rope snagged on a small outcrop of jagged rock. He freed it with difficulty and edged his way to within three feet of the ledge where the girl trembled with the exertion of holding on. Dai tested the rope once more by pulling hard on it, and then called out to Teresa, "Try to move your feet along the edge, keeping your body tight against the cliff. Then, when I say 'now', stretch your right hand ever so slowly towards mine."

The girl did so and shook violently with the effort.

Dai, whose angle of descent now made it impossible for the rope to carry him any further towards his left, stretched out his left hand as far as it would go towards Teresa's right. Their finger tips were now only inches apart. He strained his considerable weight against the rope and tried to find a foothold with his left boot. A shower of shale cascaded down the cliff and sent him swinging towards the girl. For one sickening moment he was aware of the drop beneath his feet.

"Now, Teresa, now." Her hand came towards his and he realised that she had moved her body away from the security of the cliff face in her attempt to reach his outstretched hand. He gripped her wrist as she began to fall backwards and for what seemed like an eternity she swung like a pendulum in his grasp. On her third swing he managed to pull her to him and he held her tightly. He could feel her heart pumping under his grip.

"Good girl. There's a brave girl. Hang on to me, now, and we'll soon be safe."

Slowly, steadily, he hauled the two of them up the cliff until they arrived exhausted on the top, to fall at the feet of Elspeth.

She rocked Teresa in her arms and crooned brokenly over her as Dai, panting, lay on his back, the rope still around his waist.

The grandmother, her mouth working unceasingly as she prayed, rushed forward. Without a word, she took her granddaughter from Elspeth's comforting arms and folded her own hard ones around the child. She looked at Elspeth and the still prone Dai. Her eyes held no tears or any apparent emotion and she turned away silently to lead the child down the hill to the bus.

Dai got up slowly and untied the rope from around himself and the tree, wrapping it around his hand and elbow to make a nice tidy coil. Elspeth watched him, her eyes bright with tears. She came towards him. Her fiancé opened his arms to embrace her. She slapped him hard across the face.

"Dai Fargo, that's the last time you'll mess about with me. Those children could have been killed because of your — your lust."

"*My* lust!" Dai was shocked and indignant. "You were as anxious as I was to get amongst the ferns. Now it's all my fault." He threw the rope on the floor in disgust. "Women, bloody women! I'll never understand them."

Back at the bus, everyone was making a big fuss of the two children, and accusations of neglect were being levelled at Dai.

"Shouldn't have left the poor dabs alone on the cliff top."

"Aye — and then dragging Elspeth — such a respectable girl, too — dragging her off to do something nasty to her from what young James Henry was saying."

Dai Fargo replaced the rope in the boot, his face grim. "All right then, all aboard."

He swung the starting handle and got into the driver's seat. His passengers filed into the bus, chattering indignantly about what they had heard. Elspeth was greeted with sympathy and the two children nursed to sleep by a relay of clucking matrons.

The return journey was quiet, with no singing, and even the stops at the roadside for calls of nature were silent affairs.

When they arrived back at Panteg, Dai was left in no doubt as to what his passengers thought of him — his rescue of Teresa unmentioned by all except one.

As Teresa's grandmother made to leave the bus, she suddenly turned and patted the disconsolate Dai on the shoulder. "You gooda man. Molto bravo. Save-a Teresa. Grazie," she said, in the longest speech anyone had ever heard her make. Then, unsmiling, she got down from the step, refusing assistance, and headed for the café, Teresa's hand held firmly in hers.

James Henry watched them go as he waited for his Auntie Elspeth to get down. When they had gone ten yards Teresa turned and blew him a kiss. He blushed and began to cry.

"Come on, now, blow your little nose." Elspeth hugged him to her. "Overtired and exhausted, that's what you are."

Dai parked the bus in the garage and came to join his fiancée and his nephew. He was angry and contrite and ashamed in various degrees. Above all, he wanted to settle things with Elspeth before it was too late.

"Now look here, Elspeth," he started.

"Don't 'look here' me, David Fargo. We're finished, that's all. Finished, so there." She walked away quickly, leaving James Henry and Dai together.

"Oh hell!" exploded Dai. "Sorry, James Henry."

The boy avoided his eyes and headed for his Nana's house. His world was being turned upside down and it seemed to him that his Uncle Dai was the one responsible for it happening.

five

It was nearly lunch-time in the offices of the Glanmor Colliery Head Office in Bryn Street, Swansea. In the pay department the three occupants were preparing to leave the green-painted room with its two dirty windows overlooking the main street, its three desks and its ledger-lined walls.

Mr. Huw Lloyd-Price closed his pay ledger and addressed his assistant pay clerk, Elvin Vaughan, who was combing his greasy black hair and studying himself in a pocket mirror propped up against the chipped enamelled tea mug on his desk.

"Get that damned hair cut before Friday. The miners will think you're a damned nancy boy." He snorted through the thick black hairs in his nostrils and leaned back on his high stool.

Glynis Protheroe snickered softly as she removed the carbon from her typewriter. Elvin stopped combing his hair and looked up. He was a tall, loose-limbed eighteen-year-old, unco-ordinated physically except with a billiard cue in his grasp, who nourished secret dreams of Glynis which had him thrashing around in bed at night. A blush spread over his long, normally pale face.

"I had a trim last week, Mr. Lloyd-Price." His voice still held the remnants of puberty and a fresh crop of pimples flared momentarily on his left cheek, lit up by his embarrassment.

"Trim, be damned — sorry, Glynis — barber's taking money under false pretences. If you'd come up before me in France I'd have ordered the whole lot off. Breeds lice, long hair. Unhealthy." Lloyd-Price ran his stubby hand over his own close-cropped hair. He had a bullet-shaped head which sat squarely on top of a pair of broad shoulders. He was a short man with a habit of thrusting out his chin when he talked. When he walked he gave the impression of a man constantly fighting a strong gale. During the war he had been a major in the Welch Fusiliers, a fact which he never forgot to bring up at every available opportunity, as his trembling new assistant was only too aware.

"Friday will be your first trip to the Colliery, won't it?"

Elvin nodded.

"Big responsibility, lad, taking the wages to the miners. When we get on that bus we'll have a lot of money with us. Have to be alert, see what's going on around us. With hair like that you won't be able to see a damn thing — sorry, Glynis."

Glynis smiled forgiveness and plucked at the brooch on the front of her generously-filled blouse with crimson-nailed fingers. It had been a gift from Lloyd-Price after their first torrid encounter during an over-time session when the Chief Accountant from London had demanded to see certain figures which didn't seem to balance. Before the night was over the books had balanced and so had Glynis, precariously, on the edge of her desk, under the heaving figure of Huw, as she called him for the first time in a loud voice which had rattled the windows of the dingy little office. She sat now regarding him, remembering the roughness of his tweed suit and the awkwardness of her position at the time. There had been many times since, more comfortable times, a snatched lunch-hour in the despatch room, a leisurely afternoon session on Fairwood Common. There was only one fly in Glynis's ointment: Mrs. Lloyd-Price.

Huw paused in his lecture to Elvin, saw the look in the typist's eye and warmed to it. Then he thought of his wife and shuddered. She was beginning to suspect him, he knew.

Elvin, unaware of the by-play, was conscious only of the pause in his inquisition and took the opportunity to sidle out of the open door of the office.

Lloyd-Price turned back from the cloying gaze of Glynis and wagged a finger at the space before his desk which had previously held Elvin.

"In my battalion — bloody boy's gone!"

Glynis got up from her desk and put an arm round his shoulder. Instinctively he grasped her waist in both hands and drew her to him. He nuzzled her breasts with his nose. Glynis was a tall girl.

At that moment Elvin, who had left a most necessary part of his equipment — his comb — on his desk, furtively re-entered the office. He stood open-mouthed at the scene before him. Glynis saw him first. She gave a little sharp cry. Lloyd-Price burrowed further into her chest, at the same time pushing her towards his roll-top desk.

"I'll make you squeal louder than that in a minute." His voice was hoarse and muffled.

Glynis thumped him on the back. He looked up at her face, registered her expression, turned his head and saw Elvin. Elvin returned his stare. They stood all three, transfixed for a second.

The elder man made the first move. Whipping his handkerchief out of his top pocket he licked a corner of it. "Got something in her eye," he said.

"Came back for my comb," said Elvin at the same time.

"Dropped my pencil," said Glynis wildly.

They stopped talking abruptly and looked at each other again.

"Your flies are undone, Mr. Lloyd-Price," remarked Elvin with surprise.

"Good heavens, so they are." His superior fumbled with his trousers and Glynis turned away to do up the buttons on her blouse. Elvin picked up his comb and put it in his pocket. Somewhere in the back of his adolescent mind he recorded the fact that he might be able to turn what he had seen to his advantage.

"I think I'll go up to the billiard hall at dinner-time. I may be a few minutes late coming back." He eyed Lloyd-Price warily.

"Certainly, certainly, boy."

"I might even be *ten* minutes late," he said, and then, not wishing to push his advantage too far, left.

Glynis began to cry softly into a small square of lace. Her lover rubbed his face with his own larger handkerchief and blew his nose hard. He patted her back.

"Don't worry, girl, he's too damned stupid to notice anything."

"He noticed your flies were undone. It'll be all over the office now."

Lloyd-Price began to sweat. So far they had always been discreet. For a good reason. The head of Coal Sales was his wife's uncle.

"Leave him to me. I'll have a quiet word with him after dinner."

The billiard hall at the top of the High Street, Swansea, was full of cigarette smoke. Elvin made for a vacant table and looked around for a partner. Sid Jewell, who frequented the place with a view to picking up a few bob from unsuspecting youths, rose from the bench on which he had been sitting in the semi-darkness.

"Fancy a game, buddy?" He twirled his cue in his hands.

Elvin nodded, sizing up his opponent with an expert eye. Whatever his limitations in the office, he was a superb billiard and snooker player. He selected a cue from the rack, handling it clumsily on purpose. Sid's battered spirits rose. He could see the price of a few pints rattling in his pocket.

A half an hour later and thirty shillings lighter, Jewell called it a day.

"Beginner's bloody luck." He spat dejectedly.

Elvin, who felt magnanimous in victory, said, "Tell you what — I'll buy you a drink." The skint Sid readily agreed.

Elvin brought the glasses over to the dark corner of The Bush Hotel saloon bar where Sid insisted on sitting.

"Cheers!" said the pay clerk, lifting his pint.

"Likewise," said the conned con-man, gloomily raising his double scotch.

"Can't be too long. Got to get back to the office." Elvin was determined not to buy another round.

"Office worker, are you? I'm in films myself. Talent spotting mostly." His American accent reasserted itself.

Elvin took out his comb and parted his hair carefully. "Fancy! I do a bit of crooning myself. I came third in the 'Go As You Please' contest at the Scala in St. Thomas." He coughed into his hand. "Where the blue-hoo of the ni-hight meets the gold of the da-hay . . ." he sang.

"Very nice," said Sid rattling his empty glass on the table by way of applause. "I might be able to do something with you. Go over by there by that window and turn round a couple of times."

Elvin, sniggering self-consciously, did as he was told.

Two labourers sitting at a table near the window watched his antics with mouths agape. "Couple of blessed nancy boys, mun," said one in a loud voice. In another corner of the bar a foreign sailor waved and gave him a big wink.

A flushed Elvin returned hurriedly to his seat.

"Get some more drinks up while I think about an idea I've got." Sid sat back comfortably, having hooked his man.

"No, really, I've got to get back to the office."

"What office?" asked Sid. "Surely a film future could be more valuable than any old office job?"

"I'm a pay clerk with the Colliery Head Office in Bryn Street. Important job, too." He leaned confidentially towards Jewell. "On Friday I'm going up to Panteg with the pay for the Colliery."

Sid's eyes glazed over in disbelief. He couldn't credit his good luck. "Ah, yes, well, that *is* an important job, now isn't it? How much will you be carrying when you go to pay out?" He licked his lips nervously as Elvin closed his eyes and made a mental calculation.

"Let me see, now. About, say, two thousand five hundred pounds."

"In cash?" Sid's voice rose.

"Aye, cash. Notes and silver, like."
"Well, that is an interesting job, I can see. Stay there and I'll get the drinks this time. Just a half of beer, is it?"
At the bar Sid's trembling fingers searched his pockets for enough change to pay for two halves. He returned to the table at the run. "There we are. Now then, about this job of yours . . ."
Elvin combed his hair again. "Where the bloo-hoo of the ni-hight . . ."
Jewell patted him on the back. "Very good, excellent. Drink up tidy now."
The pay clerk, unaccustomed to too much drink, drained his half pint in one go. He wiped his mouth with the back of his hand and fumbled in his jacket pockets for cigarettes. "Have a fag, Sid."
Jewell accepted a Woodbine from the crumpled packet, palming another for later.
As Elvin began another search for matches, a cigarette lighter appeared magically before his face.
"I light for you." The sailor from the corner of the bar loomed over them. "You nice boy. Too nice for this old man." He was six foot three in his wellingtons and his huge frame stretched his Nordic-patterned sweater to its limits. With one hand he seized the back of Sid's jacket and removed him effortlessly from his chair. He sat down opposite Elvin and patted his hand. "Sing nice for me."
"Just a minute, buddy," said the thwarted Sid.
Without looking away from Elvin the sailor back-handed Jewell right over the next table.
"Where the bloo-hoo of the ni-hight . . ." warbled Elvin, two octaves up on his previous efforts.
"Lovely." The sailor smiled and squeezed Elvin's knee under the table.
"Mam! Oh Mam!" blubbered the clerk.
Sid Jewell lay under the table at which the two labourers were sitting. He groaned.
"Serves you right, you big ponce."
A heavy boot thudded into his ribs. He abandoned all hope of

getting more information from Elvin and crawled through the sawdust towards the door. As he dragged himself upright the figure of two and a half thousand pounds flashed across his mind. The kicks and blows would be worth it if he could get his hands on the money.

He had only staggered a few yards up the road from the pub when he heard footsteps pounding behind him. Elvin ran past, arms flailing in desperation. After him came the sailor, arms outstretched in invitation. Sid put out his foot and the big man crashed to the ground. Before he could get up, Sid kicked him in the crotch.

"Serves you right, you big ponce," he said with a certain amount of satisfaction.

Elvin, who had reached the end of the street, turned for a fleeting glance at his pursuer.

"It's all right," shouted Sid. "He's out for the count."

The few passers-by, like all good Pharisees, took to the other side of the street, ignoring the groaning sailor and going hurriedly about their business.

The panting pay clerk was joined by his saviour. "Thanks," he said.

"See you again tomorrow," said Sid. "You can tell me more about your job."

"Certainly." Elvin took another look at the sailor, who now showed signs of getting to his feet.

"Same time, then," shouted Sid to Elvin's rapidly retreating back.

"You're half-an-hour late." Lloyd-Price's tone was gently chiding. Yesterday he would have gone purple with fury at Elvin's late entrance.

"Yes, well. Had a drink with a talent scout." Elvin's comb came out and the action of tidying his dishevelled appearance calmed him down.

"Talent scout?" Lloyd-Price's voice rose sharply.

"Why not? He said he might be able to do something for me.

That I had a good voice." The junior clerk sat down and looked at himself in his mirror. "Where the bloo-hoo of the ni-hight . . ." he crooned to his reflection.

Lloyd-Price winced. "Nice, very nice that." He spoke through clenched teeth. "Now Glynis is out of the room, let me explain about the little misunderstanding before dinner—"

"There was no misunderstanding as far as I'm concerned," said Elvin. The violence of the afternoon had affected him and he wanted someone upon whom to vent his new-found spleen.

"That's all right, then." Lloyd-Price heaved a sigh of relief. The boy was, after all, either very good-natured or an idiot.

"You were about to do 'it' to Glynis."

The bald statement drained the blood from the elder man's face.

"How dare you say that?"

Elvin looked in his mirror again and flicked his comb through his hair before replying. "Because your flies were undone and her blouse was unbuttoned, that's why." He sat back and smirked at his sagging senior. "Wait until I tell the other lads."

"You wouldn't dare — would you?" Lloyd-Price was plaintive now. "What do you want from me?" He held out his arms in despair.

Elvin was taken aback by this sudden surrender. He could think of nothing he wanted — except — ah yes, something he'd always wanted since he'd come to work in the office. Something that Lloyd-Price guarded jealously, would almost give his life to keep.

"I'd like to carry the gun when we take the wages."

The other man's mouth opened and closed without any words coming out. At last he spoke in a broken whisper. "The gun? You want the gun?"

Nobody knew how much it meant to him. All the time he was a major in the Army he had never seen a shot fired in anger. He had been in charge of a replacement depot in Calais where he was able to bully the men as he wished, the Smith and Wesson in the holster attached to his Sam Browne belt a visible symbol of his complete authority. He swaggered, he preened, he walked tall when he wore it. Without it he would look nervously around him, feeling naked, and afraid of his charges. He had kept it after his discharge from the Army and persuaded his superiors in the Colliery Office that he needed to carry it when delivering wages. "You never know with those damned miners. They could turn nasty any time," was his argument. He kept it in the safe in the office and carefully oiled it and checked it every pay day. In an increasingly uncertain world — his private life and the desperation of the times — it represented power and comfort to him. With it he was still Major Lloyd-Price, without it he was Half-Price. And now this pimply, greasy-haired lout wanted to take it away from him. His resistance stiffened. He growled deep in his throat.

Elvin stood up quickly. "Mrs. Lloyd-Price wouldn't like it either if she found out, so there."

Lloyd-Price's growl became a groan. His resistance crumbled again. His wife ruled him with a rod of iron. Without her private income and her influence through her uncle in Coal Sales he would be hard-pressed indeed. She had only married him for the hyphen in his name.

"All right! All right, you win." Lloyd-Price's head drooped in defeat.

"Let me see it now, then." Elvin was ecstatic. "Come on, get it out of the safe."

Wordlessly the senior clerk took out his keys and went to the large green metal safe in the corner of the office. He knelt before it as if in supplication, opened the door and removed a carefully-wrapped oilskin bundle. He stood up and brought it to Elvin.

"*You'd* better unwrap it," said Elvin, nervous now.

Lloyd-Price unbound the gleaming gun, the handle immaculately polished, the barrel slick with oil. He flicked open the chamber to check that it was unloaded and held it lovingly. The power it represented flared briefly within him and he pointed it in the direction of Elvin's chest.

"Don't shoot him — he's not worth it!" Glynis came through the door at a run, colliding with both men and knocking the gun to the floor.

"Now look what you've done," said Elvin and Huw in unison.

Lloyd-Price picked up the Smith and Wesson and examined it for damage. Elvin handed him his handkerchief to clean the barrel.

"Silly bitch — could have broken it," said Lloyd-Price. Elvin nodded in agreement.

"Men — stupid ruddy men," sobbed Glynis.

The clerks, absorbed in cleaning the gun, took no notice of her.

six

"Twenty-five shillings and tuppence." Dai Fargo sat back in his chair at the kitchen table in 33 Gwydyr Terrace and looked sadly at the small piles of silver and copper lined up on the table top.

His mother rummaged around in the brown conductor's satchel in a vain attempt to find more coins. "Are you sure that's all?"

"I've counted it five bloody times — sorry, Mam." He checked the tickets left in the ticket holder than tapped the empty bell-punch to see if there were any of the little circular pieces of paper from the punched tickets left inside. The only way he could make a proper tally of tickets sold on each journey was to count the number of different coloured circles — each colour representing a differently-priced ticket — against the cash in Bryn's satchel. "I reckon that Bryn's only fiddled about ninepence today. That shows you how bad we're doing."

"It's your fault we've had a bad day, David. The whole village is talking about you and what happened at the outing. Leaving our James Henry and that little Italian girl to fall over the cliff like that. All because you were trying to take advantage of Elspeth in the ferns. Uch-y-fi. At your age." His mother took out her handkerchief and blew hard into it. This was the most she had spoken to Dai since he had come home Sunday night. "Broke his little heart last night he did, our James Henry.

Sobbing terrible, he was." She rocked to and fro in her chair, dabbing at her eyes.

Dai banged his fist down hard on the table, scattering the money and causing the little dots of ticket paper to flutter in the air like tiny moths. "The whole thing is a bloody misunderstanding. Teresa's granny was supposed to be looking after them. After all, I had to climb down that damn cliff and bring the girl back up again. Nobody's even mentioned that."

"You shouldn't have gone off with Elspeth like that. In broad daylight, too." His mother was relentless. She was glad to have something to blame her son's fiancée for. "She should have had more pride — especially on a Sunday."

Dai stood up, not trusting himself to speak. He kicked his chair away from the table and stormed out of the house.

"My tablets, get me my tablets," wailed his mother.

Upstairs, James Henry sat up in bed at the sound of the raised voices in the kitchen below. It had been a bad day in school for him. The other children had heard about what had happened at the outing and he and Teresa had been the centre of attention in the school-yard at playtime. She was none the worse for her adventure and revelled in telling the tale. James Henry, still shocked by his thoughts of what his beloved Uncle Dai had been doing to Elspeth, refused to join in. In class he avoided meeting Elspeth's eyes and answered all the questions directed at him to a spot six inches above her head. When he came home from school he had gone straight up to bed without any tea, and had pretended to be asleep when his Uncle Dai came in to see him. Now, hearing his grandmother crying out for her tablets, he rushed downstairs to her.

"In the top drawer of the dresser." Mrs. Fargo, having got up to get them herself, sat back gratefully in her chair. "There's a good boy for your Nana. A drop of water in that cup on the table. Thank you." She swallowed a tablet, throwing her head back like a penguin catching fish as she did so.

James Henry crept into her lap and buried his head in her bosom.

"There, there," she crooned. "Never mind that naughty old

Auntie Elspeth. You've always got your old Nana." And she rocked him to and fro in her lap, patting him.

Dai Fargo knocked on the door of Elspeth's terraced house in Thomas Street. "Time I had it out with her," he thought, "this is bloody ridiculous."

Inside the house, Evan Owens was wrestling red-faced with the corsets of Mrs. Wicks.

"Now, now, Evan," she giggled fatly, not resisting, but not helping either.

The door knocker banged again. This time they heard it.

"It's our Jammy." Mrs. Wicks was up off the settee and buttoning up her dress.

"Oh Diawch." The thwarted Evan stumped heavily up the passage and opened the door.

"I've come to speak to Elspeth, Mr. Owens."

"She's not in. Banging on the door like that, you could frighten the life out of decent people." Evan emphasised "decent".

"I don't suppose you know where she is?"

It was unusual for Elspeth to go out on a Monday night without telling Dai, but then he remembered he hadn't spoken to her after she had left him at the bus stop the previous night.

"If you must know, she's gone to have supper with the Reverend Dowler. After what you tried to do to her at Three Cliffs she felt she needed some spiritual guidance." Evan had no real idea of why she had gone, but was delighted to have a dig at Dai.

"I didn't do any bloody thing to her," Dai shouted.

"Mind your language, Dai Fargo. This is a respectable neighbourhood," said Evan smugly.

"Jammy, is that you?" Mrs. Wicks appeared in the passage behind Elspeth's father.

"No, no," said Evan hurriedly over his shoulder. "It's Dai Fargo looking for our Elspeth." He shut the stained glass door behind him, sealing off the passage and Mrs. Wicks.

"Mrs. Wicks just dropped in to borrow half a loaf." Evan scratched himself nervously.

"Well, tell her I called."

"Who, Mrs. Wicks?" Evan was confused.

"No, Elspeth, mun — you've just told Mrs. Wicks I was at the door."

"Of course — so I did. That's it then. I'll tell her you called."

The door banged in Dai's face. He stood there for a second or two looking at the closed door with its familiar brass knocker. Old Evan had never really warmed to him, but he had always allowed him over the doorstep, even when Elspeth was out. He shrugged his shoulders and set off up the road, making for The Bricklayers' Arms.

"Pint of Hancocks." The landlord plonked the glass on the counter in front of Dai.

He paid for the drink and looked around for familiar faces. The public bar was not very full, money being tight, and those who had drinks appeared to be nursing them. It had gone quiet when he came in and now as he turned with his back to the counter, eyes avoided his gaze and conversations began too loudly. Dai turned back again to face the landlord, Albert Matthias. "What's wrong with everybody tonight, then?"

Albert leaned forward. "It's all over the village, boyo. You attacking Elspeth Owens and letting those kids fall over the cliff."

"I never attacked Elspeth, for God's sake! And only one kid fell — oh, what's the use? Give me a scotch, a doubler."

"And a small port and lemon for me," said a voice. "Come in by here and join the outcast's club." Jammy Wicks poked his head around the corner of the Snug and waved to Dai.

"Why not?" Dai picked up his scotch and what was left of his beer and went into the other bar.

"Ooh, what have we been up to, then? Never thought Panteg would turn out to have a sex maniac in its midst. 'Flasher' Roberts will have to look to his laurels." Jammy grinned wickedly.

Dai growled into his beer and Jammy patted his arm.

"Just joking, mun. I know what it's like to be ostracised by the local society. They're all as prejudiced as buggery — if you'll pardon the word — although I rather like it myself."

Dai laughed aloud.

"That's better. Drink up and then tell me what really happened."

When Dai had finished his version of the previous day's events, Jammy sat back and nodded his head a few times. "Just as you said, love, it's all a misunderstanding. James Henry made it worse obviously by telling the miners that you had attacked Elspeth. I should be so lucky, ducky."

Dai blushed.

Jammy laughed and patted his arm again. "Just joking." He took a sip at his port and lemon. "Mind you, I'm not joking when I say that you made a few enemies in Chapel on Sunday. That little speech of yours on your way out was lovely. But the Reverend Jenkins won't forgive you for it and neither will Miss Thomas, the old bitch. I believe she's calling an extraordinary meeting of the Parish Council this week to discuss a new bus service for the village. There's a lot I hear when I'm at my little bacon slicer in the Co-op."

Dai sank deeper in his chair, gloom clouding his normally cheerful face. "A new bus service would ruin me and Mam. I've been trying to save up for a second-hand Leyland from a Gowerton bus company, but it's damned hard to earn money these days, let alone save any."

Jammy Wicks finished his drink. "Well, must get off home. My Mam will be wondering where I am. She's sitting at home waiting for me to give her a first fitting for a new spring frock I'm making for her."

"I saw her at Evan Owens's when I went to see Elspeth. Called to borrow half a loaf, he said she had."

"Half a loaf? I brought a Hovis and a cottage loaf home from the Co-op tonight. She's got enough to make bread pudding for half the neighbourhood." Jammy stopped and thought for a minute. "I wonder if she and Evan are doing a bit of secret courting? Hey — if he marries her and you marry Elspeth, I could be your step-sister." He waved cheerily and left.

Dai choked over his drink. Then he pondered over what Jammy had said. He would be ruined if his bus route was taken away from him. In the past there had been little competition from the big bus companies because the service he provided was adequate for the district. Now there was talk of a new road being built to connect Panteg with its adjoining valleys. This would remove the village from its isolation and make the run more profitable to the bigger bus operators. That fact had been in the back of his mind for some time, but it was something that was going to happen in the future and he was always going to worry about it tomorrow. Tomorrow had apparently arrived if what Jammy was saying about an extraordinary meeting of the Parish Council was true.

Only one little glimmer of light shone in Dai's gloom. Evan Owens and Mrs. Wicks. If they got together it would release Elspeth from her obligation to look after her father and bring marriage a bit closer. Now, if only his mother would see sense. He ordered another drink and toyed vaguely with the idea of finding a partner for his mother.

The dinner table was being cleared in the Vicarage.

"Hope you enjoyed your supper, Miss Owens," said Mrs. Griffiths the housekeeper.

"*Dinner*, Mrs. Griffiths. Dinner." The Reverend Courtenay Dowler lifted a bony hand in protest, smiling at Elspeth as he did so.

"I'll never get the hang of it. Dinner's lunch and supper's dinner. It's enough to make you turn Chapel." Mrs. Griffiths left the room in a huff, bearing away the dishes on a tray.

"You must forgive Mrs. Griffiths. A treasure in her own way, but with a tendency to do things as she wants them done."

"I must say, *we* have always had dinner at lunch-time, too. And supper at dinner-time."

"Of course, of course." The Vicar put his hands together as if praying for her forgiveness.

They sat side by side on a chintz-covered settee before a roaring fire. It was the only really comfortable piece of furniture in the room. The chairs on which they had sat for the meal were hard and upright. On the walls were photographs of past incumbents and a framed illuminated text of The Lord's Prayer. In a corner a tennis racquet in a wooden press lay against a set of golf clubs and a fishing rod.

Elspeth wondered why she had agreed to come here tonight. She had met the Vicar in school that morning. He was there to take the older children in religious instruction. "Come and have dinner with me tonight. We must discuss forming a Girl Guide troop. And you may want to unburden yourself about what happened yesterday. It seems our Lord frowned on the outing after all." He had squeezed her arm. "Why not," thought Elspeth, "Dai Fargo ought to be taught a lesson." And she had assented.

Now, after a badly-cooked meal washed down with a bottle of what appeared to be communion wine, Elspeth felt uncomfortable. The conversation at table had been about generalities — people in the village, the school, politics, Girl Guides and the depressed state of the economy. The wine had been headier than the conversation and Elspeth felt herself breaking out into an unlady-like sweat. She had on a two-piece suit with a blouse underneath.

"Would you mind if I took my jacket off? It's a little warm in here."

The Vicar leapt to his feet. "By all means, my dear." He helped Elspeth to remove her jacket, his bony fingers shaking slightly.

"That's better," said Elspeth, sitting down again. She loosened the top button of her blouse, causing the clergyman's Adam's apple to yo-yo violently.

He sat down a little closer to her. "This Fargo fellow — don't you think he's not quite right for you? I mean, the way he assaulted you yesterday was unforgivable, if what I've been led to believe is true." He wrung his hands, making his knuckles crack in unison with the spitting of the coal on the fire.

"He didn't assault me, Mr. Dowler."

"Courtenay, please." He moved closer.

"Well, he didn't really assault me, Courtenay. It was just that — that James Henry saw us together in the ferns and he got the wrong impression." Elspeth smoothed her perspiring palms over her skirt. She didn't want to discuss what had happened.

"But you're such an intelligent person, and he's so — so *large*. You deserve someone who can match your intellect. And besides, you're so terribly attractive." The last words came out in a rush and Elspeth looked at the Vicar in astonishment. There was a light in his eye which was quite unmistakable and his long legs had twined together. He kept his hands in his lap, the knuckle-cracking increasing in intensity. His head bobbed up and down.

Elspeth stifled the desire to burst into laughter. She arose hurriedly from the settee and walked quickly across the room. Picking a photograph at random, she pointed to it, saying, "Oh look — a minstrel troop."

The vicar untwined himself and joined her.

"No," he said in mild reproof. "That's my father with his church choir in Uganda. He was a missionary there." He grasped her hands. "That's what we could do if you would share my life with me. Take the Gospel to Africa."

"There's the whole of Panteg to see to first," said Elspeth somewhat hysterically.

"Yes, indeed. Ha ha." The Vicar dropped her hands hurriedly. "Perhaps I'm pushing things a bit too far. How about a little drink, eh?" He went to a sideboard and brought out a bottle of Green Goddess and two glasses.

Elspeth looked at the familiar bottle and remembered the night with Dai when her father had gone up for the Cup Final, and she had lost her virginity. "Just a minute," she said firmly. "Supper may be dinner to you and dinner may be lunch, but to me that bottle means only one thing. Good night." She picked up her jacket from the settee and left the house.

"Good Heavens, what have I done?" the Vicar pleaded to the closed door. He poured himself a stiff drink and then examined the bottle carefully.

seven

"Order! Order!" cried Miss Thomas, banging her gavel on the desk in front of her. The noise subsided and the extraordinary general meeting of Panteg Parish Council was under way.

Miss Thomas stood up, full of authority, at home in the senior classroom of the school of which she was the headmistress. She addressed the six members who had been hurriedly summoned to this meeting as she would the children who normally occupied the desks before her.

"I think that we are all agreed that the state of the bus service operated by David Fargo is disgraceful."

"Hear, hear," intoned the Reverend Iorwerth Jenkins, B.A. "The man is ungodly and so are the hours his bus keeps." He looked around for approval.

"Ridiculous," said the Reverend Courtenay Dowler, M.A.

"What do you mean by that?" The Minister's head swivelled around.

"These desks are ridiculously small for adults." The Vicar crouched like a monstrous schoolboy in his cramped position on Jenkins's left. "Why can't we hold these meetings somewhere else?" He sneezed violently. "Chalk gets up one's nose, too."

Miss Thomas banged her gavel again. "Quiet. I've called this meeting here because our usual meeting place is unavailable and because we don't want the Press involved at the moment. Now, let's get on."

There was a murmur of approval from Hughes the Hake who had left a panful of fish and chips and an accessible till in the hands of his incompetent son. Miss Edwina Rice-Morgan from the Big House at the head of the valley nodded, too. She was eighty-five and deaf and attended meetings out of a sense of duty to the community. Her forbears had once owned all the land for miles around, but her father had drunk away his inheritance and all that was left was the Big House where she had been born and where she would end her days, alone except for a maid who was almost as old as she was. She nodded twice more, and then nodded off.

Stanley Pritchard, O.B.E., J.P., looked at his gold hunter and tried to ease his swelling stomach away from the hasp of the desk which imprisoned him. He was anxious to be away to Cardiff where a bottle of champagne and his mistress were going cold together in a suite at the Angel Hotel.

Harold Hardacre, draper, born in Wakefield and resident of Pantcg for the past ten years, fidgeted with the inkwell before him. He didn't always understand what went on at the meetings but was anxious to do whatever was required of him. It was good for business.

Not one of those present could be called a friend of Dai Fargo. Which was a pity.

Meanwhile, in Al Capone's back room, another meeting was taking place. Sid Jewell had come to a momentous decision.

"I have come to a momentous decision," he said, addressing Bryn Williams, who sat hunched over a cup of steaming hot coffee. The bus conductor expressed little interest. He'd had a hard day. Dai had scarcely spoken to him and there had been little opportunity to pocket any small change because they had had so few passengers. And to cap it all Bronwen had been nagging him about a new settee for the front room. "The springs have all gone on this one," she had complained just before he had come out tonight. "You can feel the pattern of the linoleum through the seat — they've collapsed all together. And the stuffing's coming out of the arms. I'm ashamed to bring the insurance man in here on Thursdays." He had stood with his head bowed against the storm of words, saying nothing, promising nothing, longing to be out of the house, out of Panteg, out of Wales and into the South Pacific. Australia — now there was the place for a man to make a fresh start. When his wife had finished her tirade he had turned without a word and left the room. In the passage he kicked the cat hard up the backside and, somewhat relieved of his frustration, went out of the front door.

"You're not bloody listening." Sid was annoyed at Bryn's lack of attention. His ribs still hurt from the pounding they had received in the pub. "I've been getting information about how much is carried in that wages bag. Cost me a few bob in drinks, but it was worth it."

Bryn looked up listlessly. "How much?"

"Two and a half thousand pounds in cash." Sid leaned back on his chair and allowed a smile to flicker briefly under his moustache.

"Two and a half thousand quid?" Bryn was incredulous. "Split three ways that would be, let's see . . ." He was not good with figures. "Sure it's not three thousand?"

"Split three ways," said Jewell, who had a good head for figures and no intention of splitting with anybody, "that comes to £833 a piece — give or take a few bob." He leaned back again to study the effect of his words.

"Fantastic." Bryn saw Australia looming nearer. He started to shake with excitement.

"Sorry I'm late, boys." Tommy Rees opened the door with a crash and knocked Sid off his chair. "Oh, Duw, there's careless of me." He picked Jewell up and dusted him off apologetically.

"Sit down, sit down. Bloody clown." Sid's ribs started aching again. "Where the hell have you been? I called this meeting for eight o'clock."

"I've been practising with the Clydach Zulus. We're going in for the Swansea Carnival."

Tommy's face lit up like a child's as he spoke.

"What the hell is he on about?" Sid turned to Bryn for an explanation.

"He's joined one of those kazoo bands. You know, those tin things you put in your mouth and sort of sing into. There's a whole lot of them about, marching like bloody soldiers up and down the mountains, practising for the local carnivals. Mostly unemployed miners. All dressed up. Some as pirates, some as Spanish bullfighters. Make their own costumes, like, you know."

"My Mam's made me a loincloth and I'm wearing an old leopard-skin rug that my Uncle Joe brought back from Africa in the war." There was pride in Tommy's voice. "And we all black up, and I've got a spear as well."

"A spear? Did your Uncle Joe bring that back from Africa too?" Sid was heavily sarcastic.

"No, it's an iron railing I took from outside the British Legion Hall in Ystalefera."

"Thank you. That's enough goddamn comedy for tonight. Now let's get down to business. I've decided that we'll make the snatch on Friday."

"This Friday?" Tommy and Bryn were equally surprised.

"*This Friday*," emphasised Sid. "We can't hang about too long waiting for a chance like this. People are getting suspicious in Panteg. That farce in the Co-op must have made the coppers start thinking."

"Sorry about that," said Tommy.

"Never mind, better luck next time. And believe me there's no chance of getting away with mistakes on *this* one."

He told them about his meeting with Elvin in Swansea and the information he had gathered.

"They always get on the bus in Christina Street," said Bryn. "This military-looking bloke and an assistant. High and mighty bugger, he is. Always wants change of a ten bob note. Calls me 'my man'. Pick 'em up about twelve o'clock and drop 'em outside the Colliery Office."

Sid nodded agreement. "Right. So we've got to ambush the bus on Cwmgorse Common somewhere around half past twelve. I've picked the spot. It's lonely there and there won't be much traffic on the road at dinner-time."

"That's where we do our practising," said Tommy. "We march up and down there because there's plenty of room at the side of the road if you have to get off quick for traffic."

An idea formed in Sid's head. "Wait a minute," he said. "I think I've got it." He turned to Tommy. "How many of you are there and do you practise on Fridays?"

"There's fourteen of us — fifteen with me, because I'm at the back with the drum. And we never practise on Fridays."

"This Friday you'll bloody well have to. There's five hundred quid in this for you if we can pull this deal off."

"You said eight . . ." Bryn started to speak and Sid, catching his eye, shook his head, winking a warning. He gestured surreptitiously with his finger, pointing first at Bryn and then at himself. Bryn got the message and winked back.

"Something in your eye, Bryn?" asked Tommy.

"No, Tommy, just an eyelash probably." Bryn went through an elaborate pantomime of blinking and rubbing his eye. Sid watched with growing impatience.

"Suppose you tell your band that there's a photographer from the *South Wales Evening Post* who would like to take their picture on Friday."

Tommy beamed. "Hey, that would be great. Fancy having our photos in the paper. My Mam would be thrilled. Mind you, when I was boxing I had my photo in the paper. How much is five hundred pounds?"

"Listen, you bloody twerp. *I'm* going to be the photographer. It's part of the plot to get the money off the bus and into our pockets." Then slowly and carefully he outlined his plan to the other two.

Police Constable Burns hummed to himself in the night air as he strode with a measured tread along Balaclava Street. He liked the honest ring his police issue boots made as they hit the pavement. It's like a proclamation to the citizens of Panteg that all is well, he thought, that they can sleep safely in their beds because the law is on the march. Not that there was much crime in Panteg. There was little worth stealing in the terraced houses and these people weren't the kind to burgle each other anyway. A few drunk and disorderly cases on Friday and Saturday nights, and of course there was the bungled attempt to rob the Co-op. Burns was not happy at the way Sergeant Powell had let Tommy Rees get away with that one. Funny fellow, the sergeant, at times, Burns mused. He dealt leniently with Rees and then he went and clobbered Flasher Roberts's wedding tackle with a great big ruler. Burns winced as he thought of the scream that Roberts had let out, and instinctively put his hand to his groin. Dear God, that must have been painful. He gave a little shudder.

About fifty yards ahead, the back door of Al Capone's café opened and three figures emerged. One was unmistakably Tommy Rees, another appeared to be the bus conductor chap, but it was the last one who attracted the constable's attention. He caught a glimpse of his face in the poor light from the street lamp, but there was something in the way the man looked up and down the street before scuttling off into the alleyway behind the café that aroused Burns's suspicions.

"Hey, you there!" The constable flashed his torch in the direction of the retreating Sid Jewell. Bryn Williams and Tommy Rees, who were revealed in the light, stood uncertainly in place as Burns strode towards them. "Wha's the other feller gone tae?"

"What other feller?" Bryn Williams could see Australia disappearing and Swansea Jail looming up.

"Hello, Mr. Burns." Tommy Rees shifted from foot to foot. "We weren't doing nothing, honest."

"That's right," said Williams, his confidence returning. "Can't a couple of blokes have a game of cards without having the law chase them?"

Burns knew they had a point. He had no business questioning these men. They were not breaking into Al Capone's café but appeared to be leaving quite legitimately. Still, there was something in their manner which wasn't quite right and the face he had seen in the light rang a distant bell. "Who was the other laddie?"

"Oh *him.*" Bryn Williams cast around in his mind for an answer. "He was a bloke from Gowerton I met on the bus. Wanted a game of cards, so Al let us have the back room. Been a regular thing for a few weeks now."

"What game d'ye play?"

"Snap," said Tommy Rees, thinking of the only card game he knew.

"Bridge. Three-handed bridge. Very interesting game." Bryn was gabbling fast.

"His name, man, what's his name?" Burns was getting impatient with the two men.

"Fred something. Never told us his last name, did he, Tommy?"

"Who, Sid? No, he never."

"Well, must be off." Bryn rubbed his hands together briskly. " 'Night, Constable." He set off quickly, sweat prickling his forehead.

"Me too." Tommy did a bit of shadow boxing. "Got to get home to bed early. Still training, see." He hit his hand against the wall and moaned softly.

Burns felt a certain amount of satisfaction in this. "Off ye go, then. And dinna eat any more ping-pong balls." He moved away to the front of the café and knocked at the door.

Al Capone unbolted the door and looked anxiously at the policeman standing outside. "Whassa matter?"

"Sorry to bother ye, Mr. Capone, but I've just seen three people leaving your place by the back door. They say they've been playing cards."

"I don't know whatta they do. But he owe me for renting da room and he don' pay for da coffee."

"Who doesna pay?"

"The man witha da big nose. I don' like him."

"Any idea of what his name is?"

"I don' ever get to know his name, but the others calla him Boss."

"Well, next time they rent the room, let me know. I'd like a word with that man with the big nose. Good night to ye."

"Who was that at the door?" asked Maria in Italian when Al came back into their living-room.

"A policeman. He wants to know about the man with the big nose who rents the back room and never pays."

"That's just like your husband — too weak to demand what is due to him. That man who drives the bus — now there's a *real* man. He saved Teresa's life. That takes courage. Not like your man — he is a man without balls." Maria's mother made an unspeakably obscene gesture in Al's direction.

"Mamma, please don't do that," Maria said gently. She shook her head resignedly and picked up the knitting from her lap.

Behind her back Al and his mother-in-law exchanged age-old Italian signs.

Back at the police station Constable Burns and Sergeant Powell rummaged through the files of people wanted for questioning.

"It's the nose," said Burns. "There's something about the nose."

Sergeant Powell, in a plaid dressing-gown thrown over his pyjamas and his big, gnarled feet barely contained by a pair of old felt slippers, was not too happy about being dragged from bed by his enthusiastic constable. "Can't it wait until tomorrow?" He took a gulp of cocoa from the mug in front of him.

"No, Sergeant. I was always taught that a conscientious police officer should make an identification while the face is still fresh in the memory. The passage of even a few hours can make all the difference."

"Yes, yes," interrupted his superior. "Well, get on with it. I was hoping for an early night." He picked up his mug of cocoa again and slurped at it, watching the activities of the constable with a jaundiced eye.

Burns, unperturbed, continued to go through the files on the desk in front of him, examining a photograph intently and then with a sigh adding it to the pile of discards. Powell sat back in his chair and closed his eyes in thought, cradling his mug of cocoa in his hands. "Big nose, big nose. Man with a big nose," he muttered. He rocked back in his chair and concentrated.

Burns went on picking up photos and putting them down again.

The sergeant opened one eye and spoke. "Try under J. Jewell. Seem to remember a bloke being wanted for something in Cardiff. He's got no form so there's no photo of him, just a description." He shut both eyes again.

The constable looked up from his work, sighed again, and without hope turned to the J file. "Jewell, Sid. Wanted for questioning with regard to suspected arson of a cinema in Splott. Black hair parted in the centre, thin moustache and large nose. Could be him, I suppose," Burns was grudging in his appreciation of his sergeant's fine memory.

The telephone rang on Powell's desk. It was Al Capone. "I remember now thatta I hear one of dem calla this man witha da nose a name — somathing like-a 'Powell'."

"That's *my* name," said the sergeant gently. "Try again — was it Jewell by any chance?"

"Thatsa right, Sid Jewell. That's what one of dem calla him."

"Thank you, Mr. Capone, you've been very helpful. We'll get in touch with you later."

Powell put the telephone back on the hook. "That's our man then. Jewell. Wonder what he's doing with the likes of Tommy Rees and Bryn Williams. He could be behind that cock-up at the Co-op. I *thought* that somebody had put him up to it." He picked up his cocoa again and placed his slippered feet on his desk. There was a gleam in his eye. "Burns, my fine Scottish lad, I think we've got a real crime on our hands at last. Though what it is I've no idea. Something's cooking, that's for sure."

The constable, busy putting the files back in place, nodded vigorously.

Powell put down his mug and picked up the heavy ebony ruler from his desk and began tapping his hand with it. "We have an algebraic equation, butty. A plus B plus C equals HP. That is to say, Rees plus Williams plus Jewell equals Hanky Panky. And we're going to have fun finding out the answer."

Burns looked at the ruler and shivered slightly.

Miss Thomas plumped up the pillows behind her head, adjusted her blue knitted bed-jacket more comfortably around her shoulders, and lay back with a contented smile. The meeting had gone just the way she had wanted it to and there had not been one dissenting voice to her proposal that she should approach the South Wales Transport Company to initiate a service between Panteg and Swansea.

It was disgraceful, the way that man Fargo had behaved last Sunday. All that talk in the Chapel about the sabbath not being a compulsory day of rest and then he goes and neglects to look after a child in his care while he dallies in the ferns with Elspeth Owens. Miss Thomas pursed her vinegary lips in disapproval. She'd have to do something about that girl, too. A teacher should have more respect for herself. She fidgeted in the bed as she tried to stop her thoughts from wandering to the scene in the ferns. The little bobbles on the fringe of her bedside lamp moved in the light breeze from her half-open window, casting dancing shadows on the flower-patterned wall opposite her bed.

Against her will she began thinking of the one man in her life, Richard Neapes, and the dance at which she had met him. Tall, handsome Richard had asked her for a waltz and she had gladly accepted. All the other girls were jealous, she knew, and as they whirled around the floor of the ballroom she could feel their eyes following them. He could dance beautifully, could Richard. Miss Thomas hugged herself and hummed the Strauss tune to herself as the little bobbles spun in the night air. Poor dead Richard Neapes, who had made a woman of her before going off to war. But that was her secret — no-one would ever know that she was not the virgin she appeared to be. She put out the light to stop the whirling dance on the wall and buried her face in the pillow.

Outside her window, standing in the middle of her vegetable patch, Flasher Roberts disconsolately folded his mackintosh over his battered privates. It was a long shot anyway, and his heart wasn't really in it.

Dai Fargo sat in his chair by the fire at 33 Gwydyr Terrace with the *Western Mail* in his lap and the world on his shoulders. On the pages spread out before him were photographs of young children boarding the S.S. Melita. They were young emigrants going to join their fathers in Canada. He looked down at the paper and wondered whether he'd be better off somewhere else in the Commonwealth. Bryn, his brother-in-law, was always on about Australia. Might be an idea at that. Take James Henry to the sunshine where he'd have no more colds. Would Elspeth come, though? Would she *want* to come? His mother was too old to think about emigrating. "The next move I make from Panteg is the cemetery," she was fond of saying.

There were places in Australia where he could operate a bus service, he was sure. In the outback perhaps. Buy a small bus, fit it with kangaroo bars to keep the marsupials off, and do a bit of pioneering between sheep stations. There was a lot to be said for it. There would be a freer spirit for a start — none of this confining 'Chapel' conscience to weigh a man down. He wondered how much it would cost to emigrate and start all over again. The Trustee Savings Bank Book was kept in a little corner cupboard which also contained the two miners' lamps that had belonged to his mother's brothers, killed in the same underground explosion. His mother kept the book there because she knew that to get it out would be almost as sacrilegious as disinterring a corpse. It was a shrine to Mammon whichever way you looked at it. Somehow he didn't think that he would tempt Providence this time. His mother had always kept the books and it would be wrong to pry. Still, it was his money as well as hers and one day he would ask for a reckoning. He folded the *Western Mail*, sighed deeply, and reaching up, turned down the gas mantle.

Before going into his own room he gently opened James Henry's door and looked in at the sleeping boy. He had been hoping to have a little chat with the lad. Still, tomorrow might bring them together again.

He went to bed dreaming of koala bears, kangaroos driving buses, and the Rev. Iorwerth Jenkins standing in the pulpit throwing boomerangs at the congregation, who all had sheep's heads.

Sid Jewell pushed his bike wearily up the street towards his lodgings. It was now nearly one o'clock and he'd been two hours getting back from Al Capone's café. He'd had a puncture coming down the hill past Bethesda Chapel in the Hafod and he'd had to walk his battered bike the rest of the way. Only the bottle of whisky in his pocket had kept him going.

Adding to his general feeling of depression was the fact of his close call with Constable Burns. He had heard the policeman's boots ringing out on the pavement as he left the back door of the café and had made a bolt for his bike before Burns could get a good look at him. At least he hoped he had. He knew that he was wanted for questioning for burning down the Splott Cinema, so a description of him must have been circulated to all the police stations in South Wales. It would be disastrous to his plans to be picked up now to help the law with its enquiries.

He paused for breath before the front gate of his digs and took another pull at his bottle of whisky. The raw spirit gave him the strength to open the gate and shove his bike up the steps to the front door, his mind working furiously. He wondered whether Tommy Rees or Bryn Williams had been questioned by the police constable. Those two bloody clowns were liable to give the whole game away. There was a lot to be said for America where you could bribe the cops to look the other way. At least, that's what Edward G. Robinson always did in his films. He practised the film gangster's slack-mouthed delivery as he pushed his bike into the hallway of his lodgings. "Now listen, you guys," he said addressing a raincoat and a moth-eaten fur coat on the hall stand.

Upstairs, his landlady and her husband sat up in bed, disturbed from sleep by the entrance of their lodger. They heard him talking to himself.

"What the hell is he doing now?" The husband was querulous.

"Must be rehearsing for a play or something." His wife prepared to turn over and go back to sleep when there was a terrible clatter from below.

Sid had caught the handlebars of his bike in one of the pockets of the fur coat and brought the hall stand down on top of him.

"Don't worry, Mrs. Donovan," said Sid from the chaos in the passage way. "Next week I'll be able to afford a mink coat for you, baby." He waved an arm expansively.

His landlady surveyed him coldly from the top of the stairs. Behind her stood her husband, nervously peering over her shoulder. "He's drunk," he observed.

Jewell struggled feebly in the semi-darkness below them, festooned with hats, coats and mufflers and pinned across the chest by the hall stand. Neither his landlady nor her husband made an effort to help him.

"Where are you going to get the money from next week, then?" sneered Mrs. Donovan.

"Big show coming up, lady. Gonna knock your eye out when you read about it." Sid removed a battered bowler hat from behind his head and attempted to sit up.

"What show is this? What are you speaking like an American for?" Mr. Donovan was now more curious than nervous.

"In Cardiff," said Sid, realising he was talking too much. "I'm an impressionist, see. Listen, who's this — O.K., you dirty rats, I'm goin' to give it to yer. Rattatatattat."

"That's, er — Lionel Barrymore." Mr. Donovan was beginning to enjoy the diversion. Nothing like this ever happened at the slaughter-house.

"Not quite. James Cagney, that was. Lionel Barrymore talks like this . . ."

"That's quite enough, thank you, Mr. Garrick." (This was

the name Jewell had given when he had taken the room.) "When you've finished trying on our coats perhaps we can all go to bed." Mrs. Donovan was unamused.

"Parting is such sweet sorrow," intoned Sid through an old school scarf.

"George Arliss," cried Mr. Donovan.

"Ronald Colman, you twerp," muttered Sid, and putting his face in the mangy fur coat fell instantly asleep.

The Donovans went back to bed.

"Wonder where he *really* expects to get some money from next week?" mused Mrs. Donovan.

"More like George Arliss than Ronald Colman, that last one was," said her husband. "I can do as good as that." He slipped out of bed and went into the next room.

His wife hardly noticed him going. She felt that she was on to something with her lodger. There was an air of mystery about him which she had felt strongly when he first applied for her vacant room. She wouldn't be surprised if he was connected with the criminal fraternity. After all, that was something she knew all about — her first husband had been a petty crook who had spent ten years on and off in Newport Jail, and she could see in Mr. Garrick the same shifty characteristics. I'll have a good look around his room tomorrow, she thought. He's planning something.

The door opened and her present husband came in wearing a straw hat to complement his striped flannel pyjamas. "Every leetle breeze seems to whisper Louise," he sang in a ghastly parody of a French accent. She watched him in silence as he attempted a little dance on the linoleum beside the bed. "Who's that then?" he panted as he finished his routine.

"Al sodding Johnson and your dick's hanging out." She turned away from him and pulled the covers over her head.

"Albert Chevalier," she heard him cry plaintively. "That was Albert Chevalier."

eight

It was Thursday morning and Miss Thomas sat at her desk in her room in the school listening to the chanting of children as they recited their nine times table in the classroom next door. She was on edge, waiting for a telephone call to come through.

Outside her window boys and girls from a senior class played handball under the direction of Elspeth Owens — a trim figure in a blue woollen jumper and plaid skirt, a whistle dangling from a ribbon around her neck.

"Come on, Teresa, pass the ball quicker. James Henry, tackle her!"

As Miss Thomas watched she saw the Fargo nephew make a half-hearted attempt to grab the ball from the sturdy Italian girl, who fell rather too readily on top of him. They scuffled on the unyielding asphalt whilst Elspeth's whistle worked overtime.

The headmistress was seized with a sudden fit of unreasonable rage. She rapped the window hard with the pencil she had in her hand, breaking it in the process. "Get up, get up!" she shouted. "Disgraceful behaviour!" She leaned forward to open the window, upsetting a vase of flowers on her desk. Water spilled over the report she had just finished writing to the Swansea Education Authority about the poor quality of the ink provided for the school. The ink now ran in all directions, emphasising the point she was making in the report and producing a fine watered silk pattern on the paper.

The children stood still, frozen by the hysterical quality in their headmistress's voice. James Henry heaved himself off Teresa who had somehow managed to roll underneath him.

"You dirty boy. There's filthy for you."

The boy began to cry, not knowing what he had done to bring about such a barrage of abuse. Teresa, getting to her feet, put her hand in the leg of her knickers and produced a grubby handkerchief with which she began to dry his tears.

"Leave him alone, he hasn't done nothing."

"*Anything*. He hasn't done *anything*," shouted Miss Thomas, correcting her grammar.

"There you are then," said Teresa logically.

Elspeth blew her whistle three times. "Game over." She looked defiantly at the headmistress.

"I want to see you later, Miss Owens," hissed the trembling figure in the window. "From what I've heard and what I have just seen you're not a fit and proper person to be in charge of young children." The window slammed shut before Elspeth could reply.

She turned to the children who watched her carefully. "Come along, back to the classroom." Her voice was steady although her cheeks flamed with the indignity she had endured before her pupils.

Teresa's arm went around James Henry's shoulders.

"Leave us alone, can't you?" he said, shrugging her off, and he ran ahead towards the classroom.

The headmistress mopped her desk with shaking hands. She had no idea why she had lost her temper so irrationally, and yet she felt justified in her outburst. It's time these people were taught a lesson, she thought. Fargo and that hussy Elspeth Owens and that snivelling boy, and that Teresa Capone was too forward by half. Her mind turned to what she had heard had happened on the Sunday outing. They were in the ferns doing you know what. She knew what, but it had been such a long time. She sat down abruptly and tried not to think of thrashing limbs amidst the greenery.

The telephone rang, breaking into her riotous thoughts.

"Glan Hopkins of South Wales Transport here. I've been told you wanted to speak to us." The voice was bland, soothing.

"We had an emergency meeting of the Parish Council last night," said Miss Thomas in her best voice. "And we came to the conclusion that owing to the fact that we are not satisfied with the way that our bus service is being run by Mr. Fargo, we would like to discuss the possibility of your company taking over the route."

"I see," said Glan Hopkins, new to the bus company and not empowered to make decisions on its behalf. "Perhaps you'd like to come down here and have a spot of lunch at the Metropole and we might come up with something."

"This is very urgent, Mr. Hopkins."

"No time like the present — how about today?"

Flustered, Miss Thomas looked at her watch. He had a nice voice, this Glan Hopkins. Half past ten. "Well, if I catch the eleven o'clock bus I should be there by lunch-time, provided the bus doesn't break down, of course, which it frequently does." Miss Thomas gave a light laugh and patted the hair at the back of her head. Have to give it a good stiff brush before I go to town, she thought.

"Right, I'll see you at the Metropole at one o'clock. That should give this Fargo chap plenty of time to get his old rattler into Swansea. Ask for me at reception." Hopkins rang off and sat back in his chair. He was short, fat, fifty and bald. She might be a bit of all right, he thought. Sounds youngish. I'll wear the wig at dinner-time.

Miss Thomas sat looking at the telephone for a long moment after she had hung up the receiver. Lunch at the Metropole indeed. She allowed herself a wintry little smile and her mind went back to ferns.

While Miss Thomas was regarding her telephone with a certain amount of trepidation, albeit mixed with a leavening of excitement, Sergeant Powell was waiting for his to ring.

It was a fine morning and the sun shone brightly on the

"Wanted" posters on the white-washed station office wall. P.C. Burns was on the beat with a stern warning from his superior to keep a sharp look-out for Sid Jewell. Long nose, centre parting, thin moustache. Three salient features, thought Powell, who didn't like to do much thinking. He was an instinctive copper. "I can smell a wrong 'un," he always said. The Military Medal ribbon which led the others on the left breast of his tunic testified that he was a man of action. Deeds not words, that's me. He eyed the ebony ruler on his desk and thought of the lesson he had given Flasher Roberts. Harsh, but in the long run, fair.

He had a gut feeling that Capone would hear from Jewell today. There was an urgency about the way things were happening. Powell's stomach was churning — and it wasn't just the laverbread he'd had for breakfast, although God knew that was enough. "Keeps your bowels down," said his wife, who came from Penclawdd where laverbread and cockles were as constant companions for breakfast as bacon and eggs elsewhere. He remembered the croissants hot from "La Patisserie" and eaten in bed with Marie when he was billeted with her mother in Amiens. By jingo, that was a civilised breakfast — coffee, confiture (jam, that was, in French) and a bit of slap and tickle afterwards, and to hell with the sharp crumbs. His loins stirred uncomfortably in his blue serge trousers.

He reached for the telephone just as it rang, the insane notion in his head that he might call up the baker's department in the Co-op to see if they had such things as croissants. When it rang before he could get to it he was secretly relieved because he could not have spelled croissants if he had been asked to do so. "Sergeant Powell here."

"Ah, sergente. That Mister — eh — Jewell has-a justa phoneda to ask for da room tonight. He'sa coming at eight-thirty." Capone sounded agitated.

"Thanks, Mr. Capone. That's very helpful. I'll be along later to have a chat." Powell was about to hang up, then said impulsively, "By the way — have you any croissants?"

"Excuse, sergente?"

"Croissants - c - r - no, forget it."

"Momento, signor. Croissants — yes. I make-a some for you. Whenna you want?"

Powell was embarrassed. "Sometime soon. I'll let you know." He hung up.

Al Capone put his receiver back on the hook and looked puzzled. "He wants me to make croissants for him," he remarked to his wife in Italian. "I wonder what they've got to do with this Jewell. Perhaps he wants me to poison him with croissants full of arsenic. Mamma mia." He slapped his hand to his forehead.

"He is the one who should eat poisoned croissants," said his mother-in-law to her daughter. She made an incredibly vulgar gesture in the direction of her son-in-law. He returned it with an interesting variation which brought a reluctant gasp of admiration from the old lady.

Dai Fargo was surprised to see Miss Thomas getting on his bus that morning. It was rare for her to be leaving school at this time of day, he thought. Wonder what's up? Only six more passengers got on, even though Dai delayed his departure for five minutes in case there were any more on their way. In his mirror he could see Miss Thomas looking at her watch, her lips pursed with annoyance at the hold-up. Had done something to her hair, too. Must be an important appointment in Swansea.

Bryn rang the bell twice and the engine chugged sluggishly as Dai pulled away from the kerb. He wondered how long he would be able to keep going with the old bus. Seven passengers weren't enough to keep the route alive. Perhaps he'd pick up a few more on the way in to Swansea. Ever the optimist, Dai whistled a tune over the noise of the tappets.

In the back of the bus Bryn Williams was also whistling as he collected the fares. He even smiled as he handed Miss Thomas her change. "Lovely morning, Miss Thomas." He revealed crooked yellow teeth.

The headmistress nodded curtly and stared pointedly out of the window.

Miserable old boot, thought Bryn. Still, not to worry. If everything went well tomorrow he'd be soon on his way to Australia. Fear and excitement gripped him as he walked up the aisle, dispensing tickets. Tonight they were having their last meeting at Capone's, when Sid was going to give Tommy and himself the final briefing. He looked at the size of Dai Fargo's shoulders and shuddered. Thank God he didn't have to tackle him.

The bus made good time into Swansea, mostly owing to the fact that no passengers wanted to alight before the terminal stop in Christina Street, and none wanted to get on. Miss Thomas was up and out as soon as the bus came to a juddering halt.

Dai climbed out of his cab and came around the bus to Bryn, who shifted nervously on the platform as he approached.

"Not much in the kitty today, Dai." He jingled the few coins in his bag with copper-stained fingers.

"There'll be bloody less if you don't keep your hands out of that bag," growled Dai.

"Come on now, Dai, only a couple of coppers here and there, that's all I've ever taken. Perks of the job — you know that."

"I'm watching you, boyo, don't you forget *that.*" Fargo wagged a threatening finger at his brother-in-law and strode off to the nearest pub to relieve himself and sink a pint of Hancocks. Bryn watched him go with narrowed eyes. Dai's attitude had stiffened his resolve to carry out Sid Jewell's plan. "He'll be sorry he said that," he said to himself and, taking a threepenny bit from the bag, he transferred it to his own pocket. He felt better when he had done so.

Miss Thomas found herself with time on her hands. She made a tour of the shop windows of Ben Evans and David Evans stores, clucking at the prices of some of the items. Patent shoes — one bar — for twenty-nine shillings — disgusting. She looked at her own reflection often, patting her hair into position under her hat and smoothing her skirt with her hands. Perhaps I should have gone home to change, she thought. Mind you, it's a sensible suit for a business lunch. Because that's what it is — it is not an assignation. It just happens to be the first time I have been asked out to lunch with a man since poor dead Richard Neapes. She always thought of him like that — a four-word description of her one and only lover — "poor dead Richard Neapes". Glan Hopkins, the name bobbed up in her mind tantalisingly. There was something about his voice and manner on the telephone that had set a little pulse tingling where no pulse had tingled for years.

"I'm expecting a Miss Thomas," said Glan Hopkins, giving his card to the girl at the reception desk of the Hotel Metropole in Wind Street. The girl nodded, unable to speak in case she laughed outright at the little man standing before her. He was wearing a dark blue suit with a watch chain dangling from his waistcoat, and a bright yellow wig which sat unevenly on his head. Sensing the girl's amusement, he took a furtive look in the mirror behind the desk. The damned thing had slipped again. He coloured with embarrassment and went into the Gents, heading for a cubicle. It was a good job he was not known in the hotel. He'd only been in Swansea for two weeks, having come to the South Wales Transport as a minor executive after the big firm had bought out his own small bus company in Llanelly. They had provided him with a little office and let him deal with complaints and awkward customers like Miss Thomas. He had no authority and had been given the job because of the soothing quality of his voice on the telephone. Tell them anything but don't promise them anything, were his instructions.

A bachelor, he was invariably unsuccessful with the ladies in the flesh, even though he sounded so attractive on the telephone. Desperate, he had read an advertisement in a gentleman's magazine which he thought might alter his life. "Buy a Prescott hairpiece — guaranteed to take years off you. Money back if not satisfied." There were two photographs accompanying the advertisement. One was of an unsmiling bald man and the other was of the same man wearing a wide grin and a Prescott wig. The wig had arrived that very morning and he had brought it to work with him in its box. Locking his office door, he had anointed his head with the glue supplied and then, with a pounding heart, he had put on the hairpiece. The transformation was, to him, miraculous. Using the pocket mirror, also supplied, he tried smiling — raising his eyebrows as he did so. The glue was unequal to the muscular effort involved and the piece came away from his head in front as if a Red Indian had performed on it with a tomahawk. Eventually he thought he had got the hang of it, and not sure whether to wear it that day, he had put it back in the box. Then, when Miss Thomas had telephoned, he had decided to take a chance with it at lunch-time.

In the toilet of the Metropole he now worked to get the wig back on straight.

At the reception desk, Miss Thomas, with heart a-flutter, was enquiring as to the whereabouts of Mr. Glan Hopkins.

"He was here just a moment ago. Are you Miss Thomas?"

The headmistress nodded primly.

"Of course, Miss Thomas, Panteg," said the girl looking closely at her. "I'm Mavis Johns. You were my headmistress. I left three years ago."

"Indeed?" said Miss Thomas with a false smile that vanished immediately it had formed. She had little interest in her ex-pupils unless they were successful in life, and she did not consider being a receptionist a tremendous step up the ladder to success.

"Well, here's Mr. Hopkins now," said Mavis, stung by the rebuff. She deserves him, she thought, suppressing a titter as she saw the look of horror on her former headmistress's face as her lunch date advanced towards her from the Gents.

Glan Hopkins walked towards Miss Thomas with an outstretched hand which wavered as he got closer. "Miss Thomas?" He hoped he was mistaken.

"Mr. *Glan* Hopkins?" She couldn't believe her eyes. The man's hair! There was something wrong with it, not just the colour, the way it lay on his head. Heavens above, it's a wig! He's wearing a dreadful wig! And he's so short.

God, she's older than I am. That face looks as if it's never smiled. Aloud he said, "I have a table booked. Shall we go in now, or would you like to have a drink first?" He raised his eyebrows in an enquiry and the front of his wig came away from his head again.

Miss Thomas gave a little shriek which she half stifled with a gloved hand. Hopkins — thinking that the sound meant acquiescence — headed her towards the bar. The breeze in the corridor rippled his wig like corn in a field.

Before she realised what was happening Miss Thomas found herself seated in a dark corner of the bar.

"What will you have to drink?" The dreadful wig flapped in concert with Hopkins's eyebrows and even though she never drank except at Christmas-time, she heard herself ordering a sherry. Anything not to have to look at his head.

He brought the drinks, carrying both glasses in one hand. He had seen in the mirror behind the bar that his Prescott piece had come adrift, and so he now hoped that by pressing hard on his head with his other hand he might adjust the balance.

Miss Thomas closed her eyes and swallowed almost half the glass of sherry. He took a good pull at his whisky.

"About the bus route. I am sure that we can come to some kind of arrangement with your Parish Council. I am not actually in a position to make a decision, naturally, but . . ."

As his voice went on, she recovered some of her composure. It really was a nice voice, mellifluous, seductive even. She took another drop of sherry.

He paused and had another sip of whisky. She looked quite elegant in the half gloom. Her clothes were neat and when she crossed her legs they weren't bad. "Another drink before lunch?" His hair piece elevated again.

"Take that thing off," said Miss Thomas, suddenly, fiercely.

Hopkins gulped, then, reaching up, tore the offending wig from his head and stuffed it in his pocket. His bald pate was slick with sweat and glue.

"That's better." The headmistress examined his face for the first time since they had met. It was not a handsome face by any means; it was jowly and not too well shaven, but there was a kind of despair in his eyes even in the bad light that she felt a sympathy with. This was someone she could mould to her pattern; perhaps a short, fat, living Richard Neapes. She'd had pupils like him. She began to talk, persuasively, sure of herself, and in command of the situation.

"You don't need to wear a wig, your features are quite strong. Wipe your head with your handkerchief — it's all messy. Now, what we want in Panteg is a proper bus service, not one that breaks down every five minutes and is run by a — a philanderer. It might be an idea if your company let us have a trial run in one of your buses. Perhaps a free trip in to Swansea and back so that we could see what kind of service you would provide." She paused for breath and straightened Glan Hopkins's tie.

He cleared his throat. He wanted to prove that he, too, was capable of action. "Tomorrow you can have a bus in the morning. I happen to know that three new buses have been delivered. It might be a good bit of publicity for the firm."

The head waiter came up to them with menus. Miss Thomas chose for Mr. Hopkins. Over lunch it was decided that Mr. Hopkins would produce a bus — a brand new bus — at the bus stop in Panteg at 9.10 a.m., twenty minutes before the Fargo bus was due to depart. This was Miss Thomas's idea, to deprive Dai of custom and humiliate him as much as possible. The bus would stay in Swansea for about an hour and leave for Panteg at twelve.

"How will you let people know that the bus is giving a trial run tomorrow? It *is* a little hasty perhaps." Glan Hopkins was getting uneasy over his rash promise. He hadn't thought before he spoke.

Miss Thomas was not going to let him off the hook. "I'll telephone my friends this afternoon. We'll make it strictly a ladies' outing. Don't worry, you'll have a full bus tomorrow."

Will I have a bus tomorrow? was the thought in Hopkins's mind as he sat at his desk after lunch. There was no getting away from the fact that Miss Thomas was a very formidable character. She had impressed him more than he dreamed possible when he first met her at the reception desk. He realised as the lunch progressed that he rather liked being bossed about. There was solace in being scolded. She reminded him of his Auntie Emily who had brought him up after his parents were killed in a railway accident when he was seven.

They had parted, promising to meet the next day. "I shall bring the bus personally — what you might call a personally conducted tour — with no tickets to pay for, of course."

But now the effects of the whisky and wine had worn off and he wondered where the bus was coming from. There were, as he had told Miss Thomas, three new buses in the depot, but he had no idea where they were destined for.

He picked up the telephone reluctantly and asked the switchboard for the Transport Manager's Office.

"Hello, Evan — Glan Hopkins here. Hopkins, late of Llanelly Traction Company. That's right. Yes, 'new boy' as you might say. I was with Miss Thomas, headmistress of Panteg School and Chairman of the Parish Council at lunch today. It seems they're pretty dissatisfied with the service they're getting from the Fargo Bus Company on the Swansea route, and I thought that perhaps we could take it over . . ." He passed his free hand over his head and had difficulty freeing his fingers from the lingering glue.

Evan Pitchford, the hard man of S.W.T., put his hand over the mouthpiece and looked around at his colleagues, with whom he had just had an hilarious lunch at the Mackworth. "It's that fat little twerp from Llanelly we bought out a few weeks ago. Trying to muscle in on my territory, as they say in the Westerns." He winked heavily at his companions. "What have you got in mind, then, Mr. Hopkins?" Pitchford held the separate receiver high in the air so that the rest of the company in his office could hear the reply.

"Well, I thought, perhaps, to encourage new business it might be a good idea if we put on a new bus — one of those new buses we've just got in — for a free trial run tomorrow morning."

Pitchford stared at the receiver in his hand with amazement. Around him his colleagues snorted with laughter. "You mean those three Leyland Tigers which arrived yesterday? You want one for a trip up to Panteg and back?"

"No, from Panteg, then back to Panteg. That means from Swansea to Panteg — Panteg to Swansea; Swansea to Panteg and then back to Swansea." Hopkins was sweating now.

"For nothing? All that way for nothing?" Pitchford's mates rolled around his office with laughter. "Not a bloody chance, mate," said the Transport Manager, coming down hard on the new man. "Unless you want to charter it for yourself. We could come to terms that way." In his office two of his friends had to relieve their hysterics in the corridor.

Hopkins was not in the mood to be put down. He felt his honour was being impugned. He had quite a bit of money from the sale of his company, he was a bachelor, and above all he couldn't face Miss Thomas again if he had no bus for Panteg the following morning.

"How much if I drive myself? I drove my own bus, Evan. I know the way to Panteg."

"I'll come back to you, Glan. Let me think about it." Evan put down the receiver with a bang and exploded into laughter. The thought of this little upstart chartering a bus was hysterical. Especially a *new* bus. He routed his lunch-time friends from his office. "Off now — there's work to do, boyos," he said, clapping his hands and shooing them out of the door.

When they had gone, he sat at his desk and wondered whether he could make a few bob out of this Hopkins fellow. The three new buses were not scheduled for service for another two weeks. They were all ready for the road and he could easily release one of them for a day's run on the pretext of running it in, or trying out a new route. He made a few telephone calls to various cronies within the company and then rang Hopkins's number.

"I think we can come to some agreement about this bus. You realise, of course, I've had to grease a few palms."

At the other end Hopkins nodded wordlessly, knowing he was about to be clobbered.

"Are you there? Ah — yes. Well, I think if you let me have fifty quid in cash tomorrow morning — leave it in a plain envelope on my desk before you pick up the bus — we have a deal." He waited tensely for the reply, heard eventually a whispered "Yes", and hung up. Pitchford rubbed his hands together in delight.

Dai Fargo was surprised to see the difference in Miss Thomas when she boarded the bus for the journey back to Panteg. She only just made the platform as Bryn Williams pressed his soiled thumb on the bell. There was a light in her eye when she got on, but Dai saw in his mirror, to his amazement, that she was asleep by the time they had got to Treboeth.

She awoke with a splitting headache as the bus rattled noisily into the Panteg bus stop. She had been dreaming of erotic romps with poor dead Richard Neapes — until his face changed to that of Glan Hopkins, who took her by the hand and led her into a forest of ferns, talking to her all the time, bewitching her with his rich voice and then, just when they were both lying down ready for the hot encounter, the top of his head came off. No more wine for me, or sherry for that matter, she thought as she pushed past Bryn Williams, who wrinkled his nose in surprise when he smelled alcohol on her breath. As the headmistresss made for the school Dai came out of his cab and joined the conductor at the rear of the bus.

"Been drinking," remarked Bryn, nodding in the direction of the retreating Miss Thomas. It was a sufficiently unique occurrence to override his reluctance to engage his brother-in-law in conversation.

"*Her*? Miss Thomas, drinking?" Dai Fargo was amused. That'll be something to tell Elspeth when I see her — whenever that will be, he thought.

"Aye, drinking. Could smell it on her breath, mun."

"Miss Thomas taking a drink is about as likely as the Reverend Iorwerth Jenkins farting in Chapel."

The conductor snickered at Dai's remark, regretting briefly what was going to happen tomorrow.

"Well, come on, let's get this banger back to the garage. I'll have to do something about the bloody tappets before I take it out on the next run at five o'clock. And I hope you've been keeping your hands out of that bag."

Bryn looked forward to tomorrow again.

Back at school Miss Thomas sipped a cup of strong coffee she had prepared for herself on the gas ring in what she liked to call her "study". There was a note on her desk saying that Miss Owens had been in to see her as requested, but had found that she was out. The headmistress had no heart for a confrontation with the younger teacher at the moment. Too many strangely unsettling things had happened to her that afternoon, and besides she had quite a few telephone calls to make.

There would be no time to call another extraordinary meeting of the Parish Council so she would have to inform the important members of what was happening tomorrow morning. She made a list of the ones she would ring up. The Reverend Jenkins, Miss Edwina Rice-Morgan from the Big House — she might like a trip on the bus tomorrow — Stanley Pritchard, O.B.E. The Reverend Courtenay Dowler she did not consider important, being Church of England, and Harold Hardacre the draper would say yes to anything she suggested anyway.

First she rang Mr. Jenkins, who was highly delighted at the news which he was sure would mean the end of the Fargo Bus Company. Miss Rice-Morgan raised some minor objections.

"He's a dear man, I always thought," she said, her voice as faint as if she were a thousand miles away and not in the house on the hill behind the school.

Miss Thomas was very firm with her, telling her that it was in the interest of the whole community that the bus service changed hands and would she like a little free outing tomorrow morning in a brand new bus.

"If you think I should, Miss Thomas. I have a duty to perform, I suppose."

There was a long pause after that in which Miss Thomas was not sure whether the old lady had nodded off. "Are you there, Miss Rice-Morgan?"

"I was wondering what I should wear for the outing tomorrow. What colour is the bus?"

"Red, I believe."

"Then I shall wear red, too."

"Silly old fossil," fumed Miss Thomas as she hung up. She was about to ring Stanley Pritchard when there was a knock on the door.

"Come in," she said crossly.

Elspeth Owens entered, grim-faced, and came and stood, hands behind her back, facing her headmistress. "You wanted to see me."

Like all bullies, Miss Thomas was a coward at heart. "Yes, well, couldn't it wait until tomorrow?" she blustered.

"You asked *me* to see *you*."

"It's about the ferns — no! the fighting in the yard this morning." Miss Thomas tried hard to sort out her thoughts.

Elspeth put her hands firmly on the desk before her and leaned forward, eyes blazing. "You accused me in front of my class of being unfit to be in charge of children. And I think that is a very serious charge." She stood back and folded her arms, waiting for the other woman to reply.

Miss Thomas shuffled the papers on her desk, playing for time, keeping her eyes down to avoid the burning anger in those of the teacher before her.

"It was brought to my notice that last Sunday when Mr. Fargo — your fiancé — arranged that ill-fated outing, you and he, but particularly *you*, because you are supposed to be a responsible person where children are concerned, left a young girl and a young boy in a situation where one of them nearly lost her life. And all the time you and that Fargo man were closeted together amongst the *ferns*." Miss Thomas began to warm to her subject. Her hatred was coming back — the "hwyl" was upon her, and her voice rose in an ecstatic denunciation. "You were rolling in the ferns with him. Dallying with a man to whom you are not married. Giving yourself to him in the bracken while that child was on the point of falling from a cliff. Close to death because of your negligence — saved only in the nick of time . . ."

Elspeth broke in on the tirade. "By Dai Fargo and his nephew. Both of them risking their lives to save her. And I never gave myself to him in the ferns, so there. That was all a misunderstanding." Elspeth's voice rose to match Miss

Thomas's in decibels, a sense of guilt about being alone with Dai and a sense of self-righteousness because she had resisted Dai's efforts at love-making mingling with each other and making her more vociferous in her own defence. "Teresa and James Henry ran off when we weren't looking."

Miss Thomas stood up and pointed her finger at Elspeth, hating her for her youth and for being loved. "And *why* weren't you looking? Answer that, my girl."

"Because Teresa's grandmother was with them, for one thing." Elspeth suddenly went too far. "And don't *you* wish you could have been in the ferns with a man's arms around you? Isn't that half your trouble, you jealous old . . ."

"That's enough," shouted Miss Thomas, wide-eyed with fury. "You can give in your notice now and I shall report your behaviour to the Education Authority. You'll never get a job again in this part of the world. And after tomorrow that vulgar fiancé of yours will also be looking for another job."

"You'll have my resignation in the post tomorrow morning," said Elspeth, quietly now, suddenly wondering what was in store for Dai from this malignant woman. She turned and left the room, closing the door carefully behind her. As she went down the corridor towards her classroom for the last time, she passed Mildred Fairbrother, the large unflappable senior maths teacher.

"I'm going to ask for tomorrow off," she said to Elspeth. "Got an aunt coming down from Chepstow. Is the old girl in a good mood?"

Elspeth, unable to speak for unshed tears, shook her head.

"Thanks for the advice," said Miss Fairbrother, mistaking the direction of the shake. She barged into the headmistress's room. Seconds later Elspeth heard the crash of breaking crockery and the maths teacher came back down the corridor, brushing her skirt and blouse with her hands.

"Picked the wrong time, obviously. Threw a cup of coffee at me. First time she's done that."

nine

"Yes, went straight up the stairs to bed when he came in, did James Henry. Didn't want any tea or anything — Eynon's pie and chips, it was. You know how much he likes that when he comes home from school on Thursdays."

Dai's mother chattered away as she poured her son a cup of strong brown tea at the kitchen table. He put milk in and added three spoonfuls of sugar, stirring noisily while he considered what to do about the lad. There was no doubt about it, James Henry was getting to be a bit of a problem. All that misunderstanding with Elspeth was really to do with the boy thinking he had seen something he had not.

Mrs. Fargo added another piece of cake to the nearly finished slice on Dai's plate.

"Have to have a word with Elspeth about him," he said. "Perhaps the other kids are taking it out of him because of — you know — what happened last Sunday." Dai was reluctant to mention the subject to his mother. He didn't want to start another argument.

"That's another thing," began his mother.

Her son held up both hands. "No more about what is supposed to have happened on the outing, Mam. I've told you the truth. Al Capone's mother-in-law was supposed to be keeping an eye on the kids. Dammo du." He pushed his chair away from the table.

"You haven't finished your cake."

"I don't want any more cake or any more insinuations from you or anyone else."

The telephone rang in the little passage.

"I'll answer it — you'll probably be wanting to take another tablet," said Dai, taking his jacket from behind the door as he left the kitchen.

It was Elspeth, and the sound of her voice washed away some of the sourness from Dai's day.

"Sorry for all the fuss about Sunday," he said contritely.

"Never mind that now, Dai. I've resigned from the school."

"You've what?"

"I've resigned from school and if you want to marry me, say so quick, because otherwise I'm leaving this place for good."

Dai made up his mind fast. "Of course I'll marry you. This long engagement business is killing me. I don't care what Mam's going to say or what your father's going to say or whether we're getting married in a church or a chapel or a synagogue for that matter."

"Oh Dai," sobbed Elspeth.

"Oh David," cried his mother to herself as she listened behind the door.

"And Dai — Miss Thomas is up to no good. She said something about you being out of a job soon. The old bitch was awful to me. And keep an eye on James Henry, too — she made him cry in the yard today. I'll tell you the rest when I see you."

"I'm off to Swansea now, on the five o'clock run. See you when I get back. God, I've missed you, love."

There was a jauntiness in his step as he strode towards the bus after shutting his front door. He punched Bryn Williams playfully on the shoulder before climbing into his cab.

"Come on, boyo. Let's hit the trail," he called out of the window as the surprised conductor rubbed his arm.

The bus rolled away with a burst of the *Hallelujah Chorus* from Dai which was immediately taken up by the seven passengers — three miners off to the pictures; Muriel and Gwen, off to find sailors; Donald Hughes, son of Hughes the Hake, off to spend what he had taken from his father's till, and Jammy Wicks on his half day from the Co-op off to pick up what Muriel and Gwen left behind.

The only one not singing was Bryn. He was tone deaf and knew better than to join in. There had been numerous occasions earlier on when, new to the job, he had been physically attacked by passengers with perfect pitch. It was said that he could not even ring the bell in tune. He contented himself with thinking about Australia and Bondi Beach.

In his bedroom, James Henry thought about running away from home.

Downstairs, his grandmother was contemplating what she could do to keep her son from marrying Elspeth and gradually coming to the conclusion that there was nothing. She made for the dresser to get her pills and then, changing her mind, went to the little corner cupboard where the Trustee Savings Bank Book was kept. There was something else in there that she never let Dai know about. She put her hand inside the top of her dress and pulled out the key which she kept on a ribbon around her neck. Inside the cupbard, covered with a tea cosy, was a bottle of gin which she withdrew and took to the kitchen table along with the Savings Book. Taking a cup down from the dresser she poured a generous amount of gin into it. She couldn't risk drinking from a glass in case anyone came in, and she quickly covered up the bottle with the tea cosy again.

Sipping the gin, she opened the Bank Book and looked, as she had done for the past few months whenever Dai was out and the coast was clear, at the balance standing to her and her son's credit. Dai would have been greatly surprised and perhaps even amused to learn that his mother was a secret — albeit moderate — gin drinker. He would, however, have been shocked beyond measure at the total amount of money they shared in the Trustee Savings Bank. The princely sum of four shillings and twopence lay between them and penury.

Dai's mother had had to draw constantly from their account over the past two years; a fact she had kept from her son, knowing that he had enough trouble keeping the bus route going. But the bills had to be paid from somewhere and a steady drain on their reserves had reduced a reasonable capital to practically nothing. Her tippling had risen in direct proportion to the falling bank balance.

There was a knock on the back door, and before Mrs. Fargo could do more than slide the bank book into her pocket, Ceinwen Rees came into the kitchen, carrying an empty bowl in her hand. She was ready for trouble.

"Brought your sugar bowl back, Mrs. Fargo. Although when you lent it to me it was full of salt. Can't think how you made a mistake like that. Can I smell gin?" Her beady eyes swept over the kitchen looking for the bottle and the tell-tale glass.

Mrs. Fargo swallowed what was left in her cup and dabbed her mouth with her handkerchief, putting it back in her apron pocket before deigning to reply.

"Gin, indeed. Herbal tea for my nerves, Ceinwen. Nerves torn to shreds by people coming in to my kitchen without waiting to be asked and not returning sugar bowls borrowed days ago."

Her next-door neighbour was unmoved by the accusations. "Smells like gin to me."

"I wouldn't know what gin smells like," replied Mrs. Fargo haughtily, spoiling the effect by hiccuping.

Ceinwen Rees's eyes flew to the tea cosy and back to the old lady's face. She saw the guilt there, and moving forward, whipped off the cosy, revealing the gin bottle.

"Herbal tea, my arse," she cried in triumph. "Wait till the Sisterhood hear about this."

"I don't care what you say to anybody, you nosy bitch. And don't you swear in my kitchen. Go on, get out!" Furious, Mrs Fargo rose from her chair and made towards Ceinwen.

"I'm going. It's all right, don't you worry. And by the way, your luxury bus service to Swansea is being taken over by South

Wales Transport. It's all over the village tonight. There's a free trip into Swansea in the morning for the ladies of Panteg. That let's *you* out for a start."

"Well, while you're in Swansea you might give my regards to Tommy's father. Not the one in the picture on your mantelpiece. His *real* father — lives in Dan-y-graig, I believe?"

Ceinwen Rees went white as she backed, shaking, towards the door. "How do you know? That's not right. You've got no proof."

Mrs. Fargo followed her to the door, calm now. "We all have our little skeletons, Ceinwen, so perhaps it's better we keep our cupboards locked. Good night." She shut the door in her neighbour's face.

It had been a shot in the dark. There had been rumours about Tommy's real father years ago, but nobody had ever before accused Ceinwen to her face. At least that'll keep her quiet about the gin, she thought.

She sat back at the kitchen table again, her heart pounding. Perhaps another little spot of gin would help while she tried to work out the implications of what Ceinwen Rees had said about the South Wales Transport bus going into Swansea tomorrow morning. And, of course, the idea of David marrying Elspeth — that needed a drop of gin, too.

Sergeant Powell stood in the Capone's living-room. He had removed his helmet but he still towered over Alberto and his wife. For once the mother-in-law was absent. She had had pains in the stomach for the past few weeks and, not trusting the doctor — especially an English one — she was off scouring the hills around Panteg for plants to boil. There were few of the exotic herbs of her native Sicily, but there were some she thought she knew and could use for her self-cure.

"About this Jewell fellow. Now, I understand from your phone call to me that he is having a meeting here tonight. That right?" The police sergeant was referring to his notebook as he spoke.

"Thatsa right." Al was agitated by the presence of a policeman in his home. In Italy the carabinieri were always on the look-out for trouble or a hand-out. Here he wasn't sure, since the sergeant's phone call asking about croissants, whether there was a more subtle approach in Panteg which ultimately led to the same thing.

"Sitta down, please."

The policeman sank thankfully into an armchair, only to rise again quickly when he found Mrs. Capone's knitting, along with her needles, beneath him.

"Sorry, sergente." Al was sweating in case Powell thought that it had been deliberately placed on the chair. Italian police would think so. His wife smiled slowly and removed her knitting.

"Three of them meeta here at da same-a time — notta da same-a time of day or evening, but together. Yes, that's whatta I mean, together."

With an effort Sergeant Powell took his eyes off Mrs. Capone. He had never noticed before that she had the same calm Continental quality and colouring as Marie, the girl he had dallied with in Amiens. The girl with whom he had eaten croissants in bed. He was seized with a completely irrational desire for the second time in twenty-four hours.

"Croissants. Have you made any for me?"

Al ran his fingers through his hair. "Notta yet. I don' know what kinda filling you want."

"Make them plain. I'll fill them myself."

Al breathed a sigh of relief.

Powell got back to the business in hand. "Now, I want you to listen to what goes on in that room tonight. Is it possible to hear what's being said in there — through the wall, perhaps?"

The little Italian looked mystified.

"Show me the room and let's see what we can sort out."

They went along to where Sid held his nocturnal meetings. Powell surveyed the room, tapping the walls with his pencil.

"What's in the room next to this wall?" he asked, discovering a pipe which ran along the top of the wall near the ceiling and disappeared into a corner.

"Thatsa da toilet," said Capone.

"All right. Can I borrow a glass — a tumbler, say, for a minute?"

The café proprietor was back in a flash with a glass, cleaning it on his apron as he came into the room. He handed it to the sergeant.

"Can you sing?" enquired Powell.

"Me? A leetle — yes, why?" Capone felt as if he was losing control of his mind.

"You stay here and sing something and I'll go into your toilet and put this glass against the wall and see if I can hear anything through it. Savvy?"

The other nodded dumbly.

"Wait until I bang on the wall and then start singing."

The sergeant went out, glass in hand, leaving Al standing bewildered in the middle of the room. There was a bang on the wall and he launched uncertainly into a tenor version of *O Sole Mio*. He had managed a half chorus, warming to the task, when the policeman came back in.

"Try singing a bit softer. After all, they'll be talking not singing, won't they? Do a bit less of the fortissimo and a bit more of the pianissimo." Powell smiled at the Italian and left the room again, and a few seconds later banged on the wall.

"O sole mio," began Capone, very sotto voce. "Stan froute a te."

The door opened again. "Couldn't hear a bloody thing that time. How loud were you singing?"

"Softly, like-a this . . . O sole mio . . ." Al gave his second version.

"Too quiet, mun. Bring the voice a bit further forward. O sole mio." Powell sang a rather nice baritone.

Capone joined in with a tenor harmony. They stood together in the middle of the room and sang the song together all the way through.

"Bravo. Bravo," cried Mrs. Capone from the doorway, clapping her hands in appreciation.

"Thank you," stammered Powell, pleased and embarrassed.

"You gotta nice voice, sergente," said Al, who had enjoyed the duet.

"Well, back to business. Suppose you and your wife chat in a conversational manner and I'll listen to find if I can pick up anything of it. Wait until I bang on the wall."

Dutifully Mr. and Mrs. Capone waited mutely until they heard a bang, which was not on the wall, and was followed immediately by an oath and a tremendous crashing of porcelain ware.

They spoke then in unison. "Jesus!" they said in Italian, albeit in a conversational manner. "He's fallen through the toilet seat." They hurried to help him.

Sergeant Powell lay in his sitting-room, his leg heavily bandaged and his ego sadly dented.

"Nasty gash on the shin bone — worst place an injury like this could happen," he explained to P.C. Burns and Mrs. Powell, both of whom stood regarding him from a suspicious and respectful distance. Respectful on the part of P.C. Burns — full of suspicion on the part of Mrs. Powell. "The flesh on and around the shin is very thin. Makes it all the more painful when it suffers a blow," he went on.

"Fancy dressing you had on it when you got home. That Mrs. Capone must have had your trousers off to bandage you that far up your thigh." Mrs. Powell was naturally cynical from a lifetime of hearing excuses why her husband was late home from work and similar apparent indications of unfaithful behaviour. Her suspicions were unfounded in all cases, except one. A few years ago a postcard had arrived for her husband from a Marie in Amiens, saying things in French which when translated had made the Vicar's face burn with embarrassment. Sergeant Powell had yet to see it. And so he had given up dreams of breakfast in bed with croissants stuffed with jam, followed by a roll in the hay. His own hay now formed a prickly straw mattress upon which he performed with a reluctant roll once a week.

"Let's say it was a very embarrassing experience and leave it at that." Powell was anxious to get the subject of his stupid accident at the Capone's café out of the way and to concentrate Burns's mind on more important matters. "It is now seven-thirty precisely," he announced from the settee where he lay, his leg resting high on the arm. "At eight-thirty there is going to be a meeting of these idiots, Sid Jewell, Tommy Rees and Bryn Williams — which could possibly mean a felony is about to take place. Burns, get down there to Capone's and keep a look-out on that back room. But for God's sake don't stand on the toilet seat."

P.C. Burns smiled weakly at his sergeant's attempt at jocularity and then allowed his natural seriousness to settle on his brow again.

The bell rang in the passage outside and Mrs. Powell went to answer it. She returned seconds later with Elspeth Owens.

Elspeth was distraught with her news. "James Henry's missing — gone out of his bedroom window. Duw, what are we going to do?"

ten

Elspeth had gone to meet Dai at his house the moment she had heard the bus chugging its way up the street. He had climbed out of his seat and hugged her, happy that the decision to marry had finally been taken and apprehensive about the forthcoming scene when he told his mother. Together they had entered the house and whilst Dai hung up his coat in the passage, Elspeth went on into the kitchen.

"I'll put the kettle on, Dai," she called over her shoulder. She practically fell over the prone form of Mrs. Fargo before she saw her. "Dai, come quick!" Elspeth was on her knees as she called. She leaned over the old lady who was snoring loudly.

"Her heart, that's what it is." Dai was behind her, his face creased with anxiety. He made for the dresser.

The smell of gin coming from Mrs. Fargo's open mouth assaulted Elspeth's nostrils. She could hardly believe her own nose. Mrs. Fargo, leading light in the Sisterhood of Ebenezer Chapel, sworn enemy of strong drink — drunk! Dai obviously had no idea that his Mam was a secret imbiber, and Elspeth hesitated to tell him.

"Where are those damn pills?" He was still rooting around in the drawer of the dresser.

Elspeth wondered what to do, then Mrs. Fargo slowly opened her eyes and looked into the face of her prospective daughter-in-law. Realisation dawned in her mind and she made a mute appeal to Elspeth not to tell her son.

"Get a glass of water for your mother, Dai, and open the kitchen window. She's just fainted, that's all. A bit of fresh air she wants." She took the glass from Dai and, lifting up the old lady's head, put it to her lips. There was gratitude in the look Mrs. Fargo gave to Elspeth, and something more beside. The younger woman knew now that she was at last accepted, that the battle for Dai was over. "That's better," she said, as she smiled into the old lady's face. "Get the kettle on, Dai — don't bother about the pills." She helped Mrs. Fargo into her chair.

The big man stood looking down at the two women in his life, anxious about both of them. There was a hint of command in Elspeth's voice he had not noticed before, and his mother seemed strangely subdued. He scratched his head in puzzlement and went to fill the kettle.

"The teapot — not under the cosy." The hoarse words slurred from Mrs. Fargo's tongue along with a blast of White Satin gin. There was urgency in her voice.

Elspeth looked at the kitchen table, saw the tea cosy and guessed what was hidden there. She worked swiftly, removing the gin bottle, stuffing it into the pocket of her coat, which she had not yet had time to take off, and was replacing the tea pot under the cosy when Dai turned back from filling the kettle and putting it on the stove.

"I think it's time we told your Mam that we're going to get married," Elspeth said gently but firmly.

Dai shook his head out of his mother's eye-line, trying to stop her. "Well, let's wait until Mam's . . ."

His mother interrupted him by holding up her hand. "S'aright" was all she managed to get out.

Dai's nose wrinkled. "I swear I can smell gin. Thought I smelt it when I came in. Funny, we don't keep gin in the house."

Elspeth produced the bottle from her coat. "I brought this along to celebrate," she said calmly. "It must have leaked a bit in my pocket. Get some glasses will you, Dai?"

He nodded, hugely relieved at the way things had worked out.

She smiled again at Mrs. Fargo. "Hope you don't mind, Mam," she said, using the word for the first time to her mother-in-law to be. A tear rolled down Mrs. Fargo's cheek.

Dai took the bottle and poured a generous portion into two glasses. He was about to pour out a third glass and stopped. "Hey," he said, with a big laugh, "I was going to pour one out for Mam. Fancy Mam drinking! The Reverend Iorwerth Jenkins would have a fit." He laughed again and shook his head at his forgetfulness. "Sorry, Mam. Never mind, perhaps you can have a tiny drop at the wedding reception. But you must have something to toast the future bride with before we get down to picking a day for the wedding. Have some dandelion and burdock?" He reached into the pantry and brought out a flagon of dark brown liquid. As he filled his mother's glass with it, he had a sudden thought. "Let's get little James Henry down to join us in the toast. Poor little lad needs a bit of cheering up."

He ran up the stairs to his nephew's bedroom shouting, "Come on, James Henry, we've got something to tell you." Moments later he came back down again. "He's not there. His bedroom window's open and he's left a note on his mantelpiece."

"What does it say?" Elspeth's mouth was dry with fear.

" 'Dear Uncle Dai and Nana,' " Dai began reading from a piece of lined paper James Henry had torn from one of his school exercise books. " 'I have run away from home because nobody seems to love me any more and I seem to have caused a lot of troubble—' " Dai looked up. "He's spelt it with two 'b's'." He read on. " 'Don't come looking for me because I am going to sea. Yours sincerely, James Henry Fargo.' "

Mrs Fargo, suddenly sober, rocked to and fro in her chair, tears running down her face. "It's God's judgement, that's what it is,' she wailed. "I'm a wicked woman."

"Hush now, Mrs. Fargo — Mam." Elspeth cradled the old woman's head in her arms and looked wide-eyed at Dai, who was still staring at the note in his hands.

"Poor little dab," he said at last. "We'd better start looking for him. Go and tell Sergeant Powell what's happened and I'll see if I can find him myself. Stop crying for a minute, Mam, and tell me the last time you saw him. He might not have gone too far."

James Henry was half way up the mountain behind the school. He had passed the Big House where Miss Rice-Morgan lived and taken the path that wound up the side of the Bryn and led out of the valley into the next one. His resolve was already weakening and he sat down near a clump of gorse. Panteg sprawled below him and he could see his grandmother's house quite plainly.

He reviewed the reasons which had driven him to leave such a warm haven. It had all started with his Uncle Dai and Elspeth in the ferns and Teresa making him climb down the cliff. The thought of Teresa made him feel funny again and his head spun with strange, unmanageable thoughts which were all mixed up with the things he had read in his Nana's *True Confessions* magazine. And then Miss Thomas had shouted at him, and his easy relationship with his Uncle Dai seemed to have been shattered since the outing. He still loved his Nana, though, which was why he had climbed out of his bedroom window and down the drainpipe instead of going downstairs and out through the front door. Had he seen her he might have changed his mind about leaving home.

But he had left for good, he assured himself. The sun had nearly gone down behind the mountain on the western side of the valley and as a cool wind stirred the gorse bush behind him, he wondered whether he had enough warm clothes. He opened the mouth of the pillow-case he had brought along and checked the contents. Pyjamas, dressing-gown, change of under-pants and vest; that should be all right until he got to Swanse Docks and signed on as a cabin boy. He wasn't quite clear how he would go about signing on, but it was the thing that boys did when they ran away from home. And then when he got to Africa or somewhere he'd send a postcard to his Nana and they'd all be sorry for making him so unhappy.

He put his hand in his pocket and felt the three and sixpence he had taken from his money box on the mantelpiece in his bedroom. He had been saving up for a Hornby train set, but now he'd need the money for the fare into Swansea. There was a railway station over in the other valley and he'd buy his ticket there — single to Swansea, he'd say. One way — no return.

The wind began to whine across the mountainside as the sun began to disappear. No return, he thought, looking down at his Nana's house. I'd better rest a bit here in the shelter of the gorse until first thing in the morning and go on in daylight. They'll be sorry, he thought, as he took his dressing-gown from the pillow-case and put it on over his clothes. Perhaps I'll die of pneumonia. He sniffed back a tear and huddled against the unwelcoming prickles of the gorse bush. They'll be sorry.

"Get your bike out and go and look for the lad." Sergeant Powell was decisive. "If you move fast enough you can still be back in Al Capone's by eight. He's not a marathon runner, he's a twelve-year-old kid."

Burns was reluctant to take out his B.S.A. motor bike from its shed other than for week-end trips into Swansea. It was polished with loving care three times a week and shone like glass. The thought of tearing round Panteg, which had more than its share of unmade roads, in a frantic search for a bairn who was probably hiding two or three doors away from home, he found irksome. He began to protest and then, seeing Elspeth's evident distress, nodded at his sergeant. "Aye, all right. But it's verra important that we find out what — y'know — is happening elsewhere, if ye get my meaning."

"I know that. If you're not back in time I'll sort something out." Powell dismissed him with an imperious gesture and settled back against the cushion of the settee, careful not to move his damaged leg.

"What's the matter with your leg, Sergeant Powell?" Elspeth, in spite of her anxiety over James Henry, was nonetheless curious.

"Injured it in the line of duty, Miss," said the sergeant uncomfortably.

"Hurt his shin and some kind lady bandaged his thigh for him as well. There's first aid for you." Mrs. Powell added her footnote to her husband's cryptic remark with deceptively honeyed tones.

"Go on, take Miss Owens into the kitchen and give her a cup of tea while I make a telephone call."

The two women exited and the sergeant painfully made his way to the telephone. He rang the Italian's number. "Listen, Mr. Capone. We have a bit of an emergency on here at the moment. Lost child, see. Now, it's important that somebody listens in to that conversation in your back room tonight. If P.C. Burns can't make it in time, I'd like *you* to listen through the toilet wall with the glass tumbler like I did and write down what they say. Got that? Don't trust to memory. Write it down."

On the other end of the line the café proprietor nodded dumbly. "I try," he said at last and hung up.

His wife looked up from her chair where she was knitting and reading a book at the same time. Teresa was serving in the café to give her parents a break.

"That was Sergeant Powell." They spoke now in Italian.

His wife smiled softly. "Nice legs he's got. Policeman's legs. Not hairy at all."

Al looked at her in surprise. "How do you know that a policeman doesn't have hair on his legs? When did you see any other policeman's legs anyway?"

"Don't you remember — my mother used to be a seamstress before you married me. You must have forgotten that she used to do the alterations for the carabinieri's uniforms in the village. She used to shorten or lengthen the trousers while the men waited for them." She put down her knitting and looked into space, a little wistful smile on her face. "They used to stand around the kitchen waiting for their trousers. Fine legs — like marble some of them. Not hairy like yours."

Once again Al began to think that he was losing his mind. The sergeant asking for croissants, then falling down his toilet, and now his wife had a fixation about policemen's legs. "I'll shave them then, if that will make you feel better. But in the meantime I have to listen through a glass in the toilet to find out what those men will be saying in my back room and I have to write it down. I can't write very well in English. What do I do?"

"I'll relieve Teresa in the café and you can tell her what they are saying and she will write it down." His wife, having delivered the solution, left the room to implement it.

Al watched her go with narrowed eyes. He hadn't liked the way she had bandaged the sergeant's leg — her insistence on his removing his trousers. In Sicilia that would have been enough reason for a Capone to remove more than the policeman's trousers. Perhaps his mother-in law was right. They should go back home before the family was completely corrupted by these foreign ways. He wondered where his mother-in-law was and then remembered that she was off in the countryside looking for herbs. A witch, that's what she was called in her own village. A *strega*. He hoped she'd fall over a cliff.

She was at that moment, black-garbed like a large wingless crow, walking down the mountain in the twilight. At her side swung a kerchief she had taken from her head and now used to carry the various herbs she had collected with which to make her medicine. The gorse bush attracted her attention merely because she thought that under its branches she might find some grass or flower she could use. Then she saw the white pillow-case and beside it the sleeping form of James Henry.

She bent down and touched his cheek. Her hand was cold and the boy woke immediately.

"Nana," he said, forgetting where he was, and then remembering, burst into tears.

The old Italian woman gathered him to her flinty breast and crooned to him in a cracked voice. James Henry unleashed all his worries and tears in a torrent of words whilst the Sicilian, understanding the emotion if not the speech, soothed him with an old lullaby which had its origins in the time of the Greeks. Half an hour later she wiped his tears away and together, hand in hand, they made their way down to Panteg, stumbling now and then in the dark.

Sid Jewell pedalled the last few yards of the hill up into Panteg and got off his bike with a sigh of relief. He carried the bike with him into the seclusion of an alley between two rows of back-to-back houses and turned off his light. It was safer now that he was in enemy territory to use the back way into Al Capone's. He mopped his sweaty forehead with a grubby handkerchief and remounted his bone-shaker. His mind was so full of thoughts of the money he would soon have at his disposal that he was careless about which side of the unmade road he was on.

A hundred yards away, P.C. Burns, having scoured the streets for James Henry with no result, decided to come down the alley which Sid Jewell had just begun to ride up with no light on. The sudden noise of the motor cycle brought Sid back to earth, and finding that he was on the wrong side, he pulled across the alley. Burns, who was coming at a fast pace, became aware, too late, of the bike crossing his path. To avoid Sid he turned his handlebars towards the opposite wall of the alleyway. At twenty-two miles an hour he was still going fast enough when his front wheel hit the back door of number 23 Garfield Terrace to be precipitated over the wall and into a cucumber frame. He groaned and lay still, his face buried in manure.

Sid, completely unscathed, did not wait to see what had happened. Adrenalin pumped through his veins, and in the due process of the blood's circulatory system, into his feet, which pumped the pedals of his old bike like they had never been pumped before. He flew like a bird over the rough roads and pulled up at Al's café in what could have been an Olympic record for the distance, taking into consideration the state of his bike, his varicose veins and his all-round physical condition. He had to lean against Al's back door for a full five minutes before he was able to breathe properly. The sight of the policeman's helmet, the spike of which had gleamed momentarily in the light of the crashing bike's headlamp as its wearer soared effortlessly over the wall, was enough to have powered him from Lands End to John o' Groats.

The meeting had to be short. There was no time to indulge Bryn's and Tommy's slow-wittedness. He was going to give them their instructions and leave Panteg as fast as he could. The law was after him, that was for sure, and for a brief moment he felt like James Cagney in *Public Enemy*.

His lip curled over his teeth as he entered the back door of the café. Tommy and Bryn were already in place around the table; so was Al, tumbler at the ready, stationed in the toilet, a tense Teresa at his side with pencil poised to take down the conversation in the other room.

"Phnerrgg," said Al.

"What?" said Teresa.

"Thatsa what he justa said — 'Phnerrgg'."

"How do you spell it?"

"How do I know? I don' write English."

After Sid had done his Cagney snarl he addressed the other two in his natural voice. "Look, there's not much time. I had a bit of trouble with a copper down the road — he finished up in somebody's back garden."

"Not Powell," said Tommy, aghast. "You didn't hit Sergeant Powell? He likes me."

"Shut up, Tommy. Could have been him or the other bloke."

"Burns," said Bryn.

"What does?" asked Sid.

"That's his name — the other copper — Burns. Didn't hit

him, did you?" Bryn saw Australia disappearing fast.

"No. His bike hit a wall and he flew over it. For God's sake let's get down to business. Tommy — have the Zulus already marching up and down for a photograph by the time the bus arrives."

"Right," said Tommy. "What tune do you want them to play for the photo. *Men of Harlech*?"

"Any bloody thing — it's supposed to be a picture, not a record," snarled Sid. "The important thing is to stop the bus. When it's stopped, Bryn, you nip out and let down the air in the tyres, right?"

"All of them, or just the front ones?"

"All of them. We can't risk Fargo being able to chase me with the bus. We'll give you plenty of time." He lowered his voice. "Tommy will go on board and explain that it's all a publicity stunt for the Carnival and ask the passengers if they'll co-operate by pretending to be attacked. I will already have explained to your Zulus that I think it would make a good picture. But I have to keep off the bus in case the young pay clerk recognises me. Then, Tommy will grab the bag off the other clerk pretending that it's all part of the stunt. He passes the bag to me, keeping the two clerks from following. I get on the motor bike and side-car and make a break for Swansea. Simple." Sid spread his arms wide and smiled.

"Yes, but when do we get our share?" Bryn was anxious to get his hands on the money as soon as possible. He wasn't too sure about Sid — he didn't seem to be playing much of a part in the robbery. It was himself and Tommy who would be doing all the work.

"We'll meet on Sunday at the Middle Market Gate in Swansea and we'll do the share-out at my digs."

"What time?"

"Let's say three o'clock." Sid hoped to be somewhere off the Lizard in a banana boat by then. "Look, you two will be in the clear. Bryn only has to be sure that no-one sees him letting the air out of the tyres and Tommy can always say that he thought it really was a publicity stunt."

"When will the pictures be in the paper, Sid? I don't have to hit anybody, do I?"

"Perhaps just a friendly tap with your spear on the pay clerk's head, that's all. Make it look like an accident. And there won't be any pictures, you twat, because there won't be any film in the camera."

"Ah, what a shame," said Tommy. "My Mam would love a picture of me dressed up."

"Yes, shame. Still, we'd better split up now and don't forget — not a word to a soul." Sid pushed back his chair in a gesture of dismissal and the other two stood up. 'We'll leave separately. Me first." Sid bent and fixed his bicycle clips and straightened up. As he did so, Tommy hit him on the head.

"Is that hard enough to pretend to hit the pay clerk?"he asked.

"Christ Almighty!" Jewell shook his head to relieve the pain. He stared hard at the ex-boxer, looking for malice and finding only innocence. "Yes, that's hard enough."

"O.K., Sid."

Sid gave Tommy another searching look and left, rubbing his head.

"What did you want to hit him like that for?" asked Bryn.

Tommy grinned sheepishly. "Because he called me a woman's you-know-what."

"What do you mean?"

"You know — a," Tommy's brow creased with the effort as he spelled out "T-W-A-T."

In the toilet a very confused Al called out to an equally puzzled Teresa the last word of the conversation he had imperfectly overheard, then, realising what it meant, stopped after "A".

"'Twa', what does that mean, Dad?"

"Whatta any of it mean?" He had been unable to understand most of what had been said, especially when Sid had lowered his voice to deliver the main part of his plan. "Why thatta policeman notta turn up?"

Burns was recovering in the front parlour of 23 Garfield Terrace. Considering the fact that he had fallen through a cucumber frame at twenty-two miles an hour, he wasn't in too bad shape. A gash on his forehead would need a few stitches, his uniform was badly torn, and the smell of manure clung to him. He sipped a cup of hot, sweet tea, made for him by Mrs. Melinda Jackson, a widow of not too mature years, who now sat rather close to him on the sofa, undeterred by the aroma he was giving off. Indeed, her dear departed husband had been in charge of the pit ponies in the Colliery and the smell had an aphrodisiac effect on her.

'Nice of you to drop in, Mr. Burns," she said, all California Poppy and mothballs.

"Yes, well, I must get back to the station. There's a boy lost, you see, and duty to be done." He struggled to his feet and, glancing at the clock on the mantelpiece, saw that the meeting at Capone's café would be well in progress by now — if not over. And his bike; he wondered what the damage was. He managed to escape from Mrs. Jackson's clinging presence by promising to return and pay for the damage done to her cucumber frame. His bike, though badly dented and its headlamp broken, started after a few tries and he set off gingerly for the police station, his helmet sitting uneasily on the temporary bandage Mrs. Jackson had fashioned from one of her old nighties.

It was Elspeth who answered the knock on the door. Dai was not yet back from his search for his nephew and Elspeth had returned as soon as possible from the police station to be with Mrs. Fargo. When she saw James Henry standing on the doorstep she grabbed him to her and burst into tears. The old Italian lady remained in the shadows long enough to see that all was well and disappeared silently into the night.

By the time Elspeth had recovered some of her composure she looked in vain for the boy's Good Samaritan. "We'll thank her tomorrow. Come on in now and see your Nana. She's been going frantic with worry."

There was another tearful reunion with his grandmother until Dai arrived breathless from running around Panteg.

"Thank God he's back." Dai collapsed into a chair and breathed a deep sigh of relief. "I thought I might have to go all the way to Peoria, Illinois to fetch him."

"Where?" Elspeth asked, looking at James Henry, who was blushing and smiling behind a curtain of tears.

"It's a secret between the boy and me. Got to have some secrets from the womenfolk haven't we, boy?" Dai patted his nephew on the head. "By the way, have you told him *our* secret, Elspeth?"

"Not yet."

"Well, tell the lad."

Elspeth turned to James Henry and folded her arms, looking into his face with a slightly anxious smile. "Your Uncle Dai and I are getting married next month," she said.

"Next month, is it? That's news to me," laughed Dai. "I suppose Mam and you have fixed that between you."

"That's right." Elspeth wrapped her arms around Mrs. Fargo and James Henry. "And we'll all live happily, ever after."

"It will be a wedding that Ebenezer Chapel will never forget," said Mrs. Fargo.

Elspeth's hand stiffened on the other woman's shoulder. "I thought we'd be having a Church wedding." There was a hint of steel in her voice.

"That's something we'll talk about later on," Dai interposed hurriedly. "Let's get this young man to bed."

"First we'd better let Sergeant Powell know that James Henry's back," said Elspeth.

"Thanks for telling me," said the sergeant. "All's well that ends well, or something." He replaced the receiver on the hook and limped back to the settee. "Where the hell has Burns got to?" He directed the question at his wife.

"Probably out getting his leg bandaged by some obliging lady." She shook the pages of the *South Wales Evening Post* she was holding by way of emphasis and settled back reading again.

Before Powell could think of something stinging in reply the doorbell rang. His wife put down the paper with a snort of annoyance and went to answer it. She returned with the white-faced and shaken Burns in tow.

"What the devil has happened to you?"

"Some fool on a bike was coming up a back alley on the wrong side, and when I tried to avoid him I ran into somebody's back door and found myself flying through a cucumber frame." He took off his helmet and Mrs. Powell tut-tutted with concern at the bloodied bandage.

"Let me take that off for you. Sit down by here, there's a good boy."

"There's no time, Mrs. Powell, there's the little laddie to find and I'll have tae get down tae the café."

"The boy's already back home and I told Capone to listen in to the conversation in his back room. God knows what he'll make of it. Sit down and let my wife change the dressing. She'd like that."

Burns did as he was bidden and allowed the sergeant's wife to remove the makeshift bandage. "Hello," she said sharply as she began to unwind it. "There's lace on this — somebody's torn up her nightie by the look of it."

Burns went scarlet. "It was Mrs. Jackson's. It was her cucumber frame, y'see."

Mrs Powell pulled away the last piece of linen from his wound with an unnecessary force. As Burns winced, Sergeant Powell, who was watching from the settee with a great deal of amusement, burst into laughter.

"It's no laughing matter. There seems to be something about a policeman's uniform in this village that drives women to do very strange things. You'd better send for the doctor, this wound needs stitching." Mrs. Powell gathered up the bandage and, holding it between two disdainful fingers, left to dispose of it in the kitchen.

Powell dabbed at his eyes with the back of his hand. "Duw, that's the best laugh I've had for years. Wasn't wearing it when she tore a piece off it, was she? Didn't tear off a piece yourself, did you? Mrs. Jackson's got quite a reputation for chasing the fellers."

"I think I'll awa' tae the doctor's tae get this thing stitched up." Burns was anxious to leave the station and Powell's unseemly levity.

"All right, but don't be too long. I want to know what went on down at the café. It's no good talking to Capone on the phone — that rhymes, Burns. There's something about to happen on our patch and I want to find out what it is." Powell watched his constable take his welcome departure and then lay back, his hands folded on his stomach and his injured leg supported by the arm of the settee. He chuckled again at the remembrance of his wife's face as she found the lace on the bandage. And Burns's face, too, had been a picture. Bit straight-laced, the lad was. Probably to do with his Scottish upbringing. He wouldn't know what to do if Mrs. Jackson *had* been wearing her nightie. Now, *I* would, he thought. By God, I would. He thought of croissants again, and Marie and Amiens, and dozed off.

Burns, his head stitched and re-bandaged by the doctor, went to Al Capone's before reporting back to the station. His main objective was to get to bed as soon as possible, but after only two minutes with the Italian he realised that he had a long night ahead of him.

"Now start again, more slowly, Mr. Capone. We don't seem to be making any sense."

"Looka, Constable. These-a notes were made by my Teresa. She take-a down what I hear. But I don' hear too much."

"I only put down what my Dad said — but it was very hard because he doesn't speak English very well." Teresa sat at the table in the Capone's living-room with Burns and her father on either side of her. Her notes lay on the green chenille table-cloth. The constable picked them up and studied them again.

'Phnergg. Something about policeman on fire, flying. Lulu's letting hair down for a photograph on the bus. Taking bag away for publicity. Not hit hard. Christ Almighty. Twa."

"I canna make head nae tail o' this lot." Burns's head throbbed from his recently stitched wound and the effort of trying to work out what the conversation in Al's back room was all about. He just wanted to go home and lie down.

"Sorry, Constable. They talka too fast for me. I keepa changing ears and I miss a lot." Capone was apologetic. At the same time he too wanted to get to bed.

"And I dropped my pencil twice. I'm sorry." Teresa was also ready for bed.

Burns got to his feet, aware that his presence was becoming unwelcome. "I'll take these notes wi' me if I may, Miss Capone."

"I see you out," said Al, ushering the policeman towards the door. As he opened it he turned to Burns and said, "Twat."

"What was that?" Burns could hardly believe his ears.

"Thatsa whatta the last word was. TWAT. The man spell it out, but I don' like-a to tell Teresa. Is a bad word." Then, leaning forward, he asked the question that he had been wanting to ask the policeman since he had come in. "You gotta smooth legs or hairy legs?"

"I dinna see what it's got tae do wi' you, but I happen to have fairly smooth legs," stammered the bewildered Burns, exiting swiftly.

"She's-a right then, my wife." Capone clapped his hands to his forehead. "They all gotta legs like-a marble."

"They're a funny lot, those Italians," said Burns to Powell when he got back to the station. "He actually asked me whether I've got hairy legs or not. Not a homosexual, is he?"

"If he were, Jammy Wicks would have smelled him out ages ago." Powell gave a short laugh. "No, definitely not. Come on, let's have one more go at this Chinese puzzle we've got here." He spread the notes on the table and considered them. "Phnergg — that's weird, that is. No idea what that is. Something about policeman on fire — flying. That should mean something to you."

"What d'ye mean, Sergeant?"

"*Policeman on fire* — that's you, BURNS. Al doesn't know your name, does he? After all, you're pretty new here. And flying — you went flying over the garden wall tonight."

"That's right." The other was excited now. "There was something vaguely familiar about the laddie on the bike even in the dark. The head and nose. Jewell — it must have been him." He touched his forehead gingerly, where the stitches had been put in. "That's one thing I owe the blackguard for when we get him."

"The rest of it doesn't make any kind of sense at all." Sergeant Powell flipped his forefinger over his lower lip as he always did when he was perplexed. "There's a bus involved in whatever's happening, and a bag and a photograph. 'Not hit hard — Christ Almighty — Twa".' Powell resumed his lip fiddling.

"Twat," said Burns.

Powell stopped playing with his lip and looked at Burns with smouldering Welsh eyes. "That's not a nice thing to call anybody."

"I know," said Burns hastily. "That's what somebody called somebody else in Capone's. That's what 'twa' stands for. Al told me as I was leaving that he hadna wanted Teresa tae know what was said, which is why he left the 't' off in the original." He was sweating. "The last 't'."

"I see," said Powell slowly. "You weren't getting nasty about the way I play with my lower lip?"

"No, no' at all." The constable's voice hit the top treble register.

"Don't like being made a fool of, you see." Powell held the other policeman's gaze until the younger man looked down at the desk to avoid his eyes. He found himself looking directly at the ebony ruler the sergeant had used with such devastating effect on Flasher Roberts.

"Look," he said, trying to subdue the rising hysteria he felt. "I think we're both verra tired. We're both injured and it might be a good idea if we looked at this whole thing in the morning when we're fresh and our minds are working properly."

"Perhaps you're right." Powell leaned back in his chair and tried to straighten his bad leg. "Obviously it's something to do with a bus — which, in Panteg anyway, can only mean Dai Fargo. But there doesn't seem to be anything in this information to give us any sense of urgency. Lulu, whoever she may be, can let her hair down without causing us much hardship." He stifled a yawn. "At least the Fargo boy got back safe and sound. Thank the Lord for small mercies, as Flasher might say."

"Ha ha." Burns's laughter was inordinately generous for the slightness of the sergeant's sally. He thought it was a good time to take his departure. He continued laughing as he backed out of his superior's presence, and even up to the time that he tried to kick-start his bike for the fourth attempt. Then he felt nearer to tears as the extent of the damage done to his B.S.A. became more apparent. Suddenly he was filled with the desire to get the man who did it; who had made him crash into the cucumber frame. Sid Jewell was building up a fine legacy of hatred for himself.

The object of Burns's venom was safely back in his digs in the outskirts of Swansea. After the fright of the policeman's accident it seemed now that everything was coming together for him. He had pedalled back to Swansea in record time and had arrived at a pub near the docks by ten o'clock. There he had engaged in conversation with two men and a girl and had come to a satisfactory arrangement. He was now talking to Mrs. Donovan, his landlady, in the hallway.

"Thank you for the loan of the motor bike and side-car tomorrow."

"The *hire*, Mr. Garrick, the *hire* of the motor bike and side-car."

"Of course. And you'll get the money when I get back tomorrow afternoon. It's a publicity stunt I'm organising, you see." Jewell gave her a Ronald Colman smile and tapped the side of his considerable nose with a nicotine-stained forefinger. "We show-business folk have to take whatever comes along. There's something big brewing for yours truly."

"Where's all this money coming from, then? All this talk last night about mink coats and things." Mrs. Donovan had made a thorough search of her lodger's room but had found nothing to substantiate her suspicions that he was about to commit some kind of felony. She was still convinced, however, that he was up to something. He had suddenly asked her that morning whether he could hire her husband's motor bike and side-car for Friday and they had settled a price with surprisingly little haggling. Three pounds, they'd agreed on.

"All in good time, my little chickadee. All will be revealed in the fullness of time." Jewell was now W. C. Fields.

"I know who that is," said Mr. Donovan, who had joined his wife in the hall for what he cheerfully expected to be another impromptu cabaret. "That's Harpo Marx, of the whatsaname Brothers."

"Close, pretty close," said Sid, climbing the stairs and disappearing into his room.

"Ah, he's gone, and I wanted to show him my Chevalier impersonation." Donovan was crestfallen.

"Tomorrow morning you can do an impersonation of a man walking to work, because he's borrowing your bike and side-car. And no arguments — he's letting us have a couple of quid for our trouble." Mrs. Donovan stood, staring up the shabby linoleum stairs, deep in thought, oblivious to the protestations of her husband who faced a dawn walk of three miles. There was something afoot, and she was determined to get her share of whatever came out of it.

Dai Fargo drove his last trip of the day back from Swansea in a reflective mood. His mother had told him what Ceinwen Rees had said about the South Wales Transport bus giving a free ride for the Panteg ladies in the morning. It looked like the beginning of the end for the Fargo Bus Company, he thought. He looked in his mirror and saw his seven passengers; the same ones that he had taken in earlier on. Muriel and Gwen were in the back seats with the three miners; Donald Hughes, son of the fish and chip proprietor, was trying not to be sick — the beer and whisky he had consumed was too costly to lose without a struggle. In the aisle next to him sat Jammy Wicks, a secret smile on his face. He'd had a good night but he wasn't telling anyone.

Dai changed gear abruptly to avoid hitting an Austin Ruby saloon badly parked on a hill, and Donald Hughes lost his battle with the booze in his stomach.

"There, there," said Jammy Wicks, holding the boy's head.

"Here, here!" shouted Bryn from the platform as the tide of vomit swept back down the bus towards him.

Dai drove on. There was nothing he could do except hose the bus down first thing in the morning. It reminded him of a song, and he began to sing it. "Hello, hello — hose your lady friend," he sang, and they all joined in except for Donald, who heaved in rhythm, and Bryn, who was wondering how he would have time to let down all the tyres on the bus without being noticed.

By twelve midnight, Panteg was almost asleep. Only a few bedroom windows shone in the darkness. Behind one Mrs. Capone waited patiently for her husband to come to bed. He seemed to be taking a long time in the bathroom.

Al knocked on the door. "Put the light out," he said.

Obediently his wife did so from her side of the bed and he entered the room cautiously. In the dark his legs glowed with an unnatural whiteness.

"My legs, too, are like marble, Maria," he said hoarsely.

"Come to me, my love," she said and drew him down to her. They made love with an intensity that Alberto had not experienced since their early married days.

Afterwards he went to sleep almost immediately, heedless of the blood still oozing from the countless nicks he had made on his legs with his cut-throat razor. Maria listened to his snores and smiled enigmatically at the ceiling.

James Henry cuddled up to his grandmother. He had deserted his own bed for hers, and the old lady welcomed his company. She lay awake now, pondering over the events of the day. So much had happened in the past twenty-four hours. She appreciated what Elspeth had done in covering up her drinking bout from David, and she was resigned to the wedding taking place next month. But she was going to put her foot down about where it would be held.

Elspeth lay in her bed making plans for the wedding. She was sure she could overcome Mrs. Fargo's objections. The only thing she wasn't sure about was whether Dai could get married in Church. Perhaps if he was baptised and took a quick course of confirmation classes. . . . Anyway, she'd ask the Vicar tomorrow — there'd be plenty of time now that she had resigned from the school. She fell asleep to dream of being chased by a giant Miss Thomas, who kept changing into Mrs. Fargo, who became a tea cosy, which in turn became the Reverend Courtenay Dowler.

Miss Thomas dreamed of poor dead Richard Neapes and living Glan Hopkins fighting a duel for her hand. Their weapons were scalping knives and the duelling ground was knee-high in ferns which kept growing taller and taller until they blotted out the sun.

Tommy Rees made the springs of his bed creak and groan as he saw himself in the largest ring he had ever set eyes on. He was dressed as a Zulu, complete with spear, and when his opponent entered the arena everybody gasped. It was the biggest lampshade in the world. He felt he was in for a bad night.

Bryn Williams moaned in his sleep as he wrestled with the gigantic tyres of a fifty-foot-high bus. Beside him his shrewish wife fended off his flying elbows with increasing annoyance.

P.C. Burns kept sailing through the air and falling through cucumber frames in which predatory ladies in lace nighties lay in wait for him.

Sergeant Powell fell asleep with the jigsaw puzzle of the conversation in Capone's back room foremost in his mind. He found himself chasing a hairy "Phnergg" down a back alley whilst some painted lady called Lulu took photographs of him from the back of a bus. Croissants and Marie and Amiens failed to make an appearance.

Dai Fargo, having put away his bus, locked the garage and headed for his bedroom. He undressed slowly, grunting with the effort, and when he eventually pulled the blankets over himself he fell into a dreamless sleep. His was the last light to go out that night.

And so, one by one, the worthy and unworthy citizens of Panteg went to sleep, unaware that the day ahead of them would be one they would remember all their lives.

eleven

Friday dawned bright and clear, but Glan Hopkins, sitting at his lone breakfast table in the little bungalow he'd recently purchased in the Mayals with the proceeds of the sale of his bus company, viewed the morning with considerable gloom. On the table next to the toast rack lay a plain brown envelope containing fifty pounds which he was shortly going to hand over to Pitchford for the sole purpose of satisfying his ego. It wasn't as if he was going to get anything out of it personally. A pat on the head from Miss Thomas, perhaps. He felt his bald pate for traces of glue from the previous day. There was none, thank God, but the whole of his scalp was still tender from the scrubbing he had given it.

He was tempted to forget the whole thing. After all, there was no contract — nothing written down on paper. And yet he had promised Miss Thomas and if he called it off now, Pitchford would never let him forget it. There was no getting out of the situation as far as he could see. He would have to grit his teeth and go through with this elaborate gesture. There was one tiny gleam of light. If the trip was successful and the South Wales Transport did take over the route, it might elevate his status within the firm. He might be regarded as a trail-blazer. Yes, that was the way to look at it. It was an investment in his future. He smiled for the first time that morning.

"Can I have some more blacking, Mam?" shouted Tommy Rees to his mother from the kitchen. He stood there, monolithic in appearance, naked to the waist. He had already applied a tin of Cherry Blossom boot polish to most of his upper half and he still had his legs to do.

"Good God, Tommy — look at you!"

All the rehearsals of the Clydach Zulus Jazz and Kazoo Band had been conducted in ordinary clothes with just spears, shields, kazoos, snare drums and bass drums. But now, today, because they were having a photograph taken, they were going the whole hog. Five miles away in Clydach, corner shops had a run on black boot polish.

"Turn around and let me do your back."

Tommy turned dutifully and his mother rubbed hard at his skin with a tin of brown polish, the only colour she had left. He would have to be a two-tone Zulu.

It took a good half an hour to finish his make-up, but the overall effect was quite startling. With his boxer's physique and the accoutrements of a Zulu Impi Warrior, he was an extremely frightening sight. Even his mother backed away. Excited by his appearance in the mirror of the hall stand, Tommy let out a yell.

"Walla Walla Walla," he cried, shaking the spear-shaped railing he had removed from outside the British Legion. The moth-eaten leopard-skin rug assumed a fresh dignity across his wide shoulders. He just couldn't wait to have his photograph taken. All thoughts of the bad thing that he and Sid and Bryn were about to do that day were forgotten in his newfound joy in his make-up. He felt lucky. He went into the front parlour and took a swing at the heavy Chinese lantern which hung there, brought home from Hong Kong by his Uncle George who served in the Glory's Garrison Artillery. The lantern swung back at him. He ducked and it missed.

"Walla Walla," he shouted in triumph. It caught him squarely on the mouth with its return swing. Still, one out of two wasn't bad.

Elvin Vaughan stood next to Lloyd-Price in the manager's office of Barclay's Bank, Wind Street. He watched with awe as the bank clerk deftly counted the notes. Lloyd-Price, to whom the whole procedure was a mundane affair, leaned languidly against the back of the chair. At his side lay the bag in which he would carry the money to the Colliery. It would be attached to his wrist with a strong steel chain when they set off to pay out the miners. He yawned elegantly. Two and a half thousand pounds took a long time to count. When the clerk had finished it would be his and Elvin's turn to check the notes and silver.

He watched his junior's face as the money piled up. Long-haired oaf, he thought. This was the idiot who was going to be carrying the gun today. And I am the idiot who made it possible for him to do so, by being caught with Glynis.

"Will you please check the money now?" The clerk was anxious to get back to his ledgers.

"Certainly, certainly. Mr. Vaughan, you check the copper and silver." Lloyd-Price felt a little better at the thought of Elvin having to plough through so many heaps of half-crowns, florins, shillings and sixpenny pieces. To say nothing of all those piles of pennies and halfpennies. He damped his finger on the sponge provided and pulled a wad of pound notes towards him.

Elvin bent to the task of piling copper and silver in separate columns prior to placing them in the blue bags stamped Barclays Bank in large black letters. This was not a job for a man who would one day be a singing star.

Dai paused in his effort to hose the vomit from the inside of his bus. The smell was pretty bad and he sprinkled more Jeyes fluid on the floor. He applied the hose again, walking backwards through the bus, directing the jet of water at every nook and cranny. At least he'd have the old banger shining as well as he could make it. The South Wales people were sending a brand new bus along today, so the gossip went. He'd go down fighting anyway.

To his surprise, Bryn turned up in the garage. He usually reported for duty with about four seconds to spare. Today he was an hour early. Dai threw him a chamois leather.

"Make yourself useful now you're here. We've got to have this old bus spotless to meet the competition. Start shining up those headlamps."

Bryn caught the leather and smiled uneasily. "Right ho, Dai. Want me to give the wheels a once over?" He was most anxious to examine how to let the air out of the tyres.

"Aye. But make sure those lamps are nice and clean first."

Bryn went to work with an energy that surprised Dai. He was unaware of the conflict which was raging within the other man. Since the meeting with Sid last night there were doubts in Bryn's mind whether the plan would work. It seemed simple enough, but how in the hell was he going to let out the air from all the tyres unobserved — and even if he did, wouldn't he be a suspect anyway? Burns had seen Tommy and himself leaving Al's back room a couple of nights ago and surely he would put two and two together. Meeting Sid at the Middle Market Gate on Sunday didn't seem a clever thing to do either. The news of the robbery would be all over South Wales by then and the police were certain to be watching him and Tommy. He was beginning to lose faith in the whole scheme.

Sid Jewell checked the camera he had bought with his dwindling resources from a second-hand shop near Swansea Station. He had been looking for one ever since he had had the idea of taking photographs of the Clydach Zulus as a ruse for holding up the bus. It was important that the camera looked authentic. A Press photographer wouldn't use a box Brownie for the job. He had been getting desperate about finding the right-looking machine when he had seen the very thing he wanted in the shop window. A large, battered Press camera.

The proprietor explained to him that the camera was useless for taking photographs because a football had been kicked at it during a match at the Vetch Field, Swansea. The opposing centre forward, after missing an open goal, blamed the flash that the cameraman on the touch-line used at the crucial moment for making him shoot wide. The next time he came near the photographer he had let him have the ball straight into the lens.

"However," the shopkeeper had said, "it looks good. You just can't take pictures with it, that's all."

Jewell declared a passing interest in it and eventually they arrived at the reasonable price of four shillings and sixpence. He left the shop with the camera under his arm and the aged proprietor was left rubbing his throat where Sid had seized him during their bargaining.

Now, in his room, he turned it over in his hands as he prepared for the job which was going to change his life-style. Putting the heavy camera to his eye he pretended to take a shot of himself in the cracked mirror over the wash-hand stand.

"Señor Sidney Jewell, playboy and gambler, was seen last night at Rio de Janeiro's night spot, the Copaca thingummy. On his arm was, as usual, a beautiful blonde." He lowered the heavy machine and winked at his reflection in the spotty glass.

Tonight he would be tucked safely away with a pretty female companion in a cabin on a banana boat heading for South America. It was going to cost him money, but there would be plenty left out of the two and a half thousand. All he had to do was to be at the gangplank of the *S.S. Heracles* and on the receipt of three hundred pounds in cash he would be taken on board with no questions asked. The girl had certainly looked worth every penny, and the two blokes had seemed reliable enough, though the quiet one was a bit of a nancy boy by the look of him. What was his name again? Something Wicks, that was it. Wicks.

He looked around the room to see if he had left anything behind which the police could follow up. His pitifully few possessions were now packed in a small brown case which he had secured with a leather strap. There was no point in coming back here after he'd got the money. He would drive the motor bike and side-car down to the docks, park it in one of the empty warehouses and lie doggo with the money until the time came to board the ship. As he closed the door he wondered how long Bryn and Tommy would wait for him at the Middle Market Gate. Bloody idiots would probably still be there when he was in Rio.

"Hasta la vista," he said in his Ramon Novarro voice to Mrs. Donovan, who came out to meet him in the hall.

"We don't speak Welsh, I'm afraid, Mr. Garrick. And where are you going with your suitcase?"

"These are props, Mrs. Donovan." Sid patted the case and held up the camera. "It's all in the fair name of publicity."

"Yes, well, I'd like the three quid in advance for the hire of the bike and side-car."

Sid began to sweat under his heavy overcoat. He now had only three pounds and about three bob in loose change left. He made a swift decision. "How about me giving you two quid now, in good faith, and, because I shall be getting well paid for the little stunt today, I'll let you have another two this afternoon? O.K.? That makes four."

Mrs. Donovan was reluctant but, deciding that a bird in the hand was worth two in the bush, agreed.

Sid handed over the two notes with a flourish. Mrs. Donovan counted them and put them in the pocket of her pinafore.

Jewell picked up his case again and tucked the camera under his arm. "Would you please open the door for me?"

His landlady did so with an ill grace, muttering something under her breath as she manipulated the various locks which held her front door in place.

"What did you say?" Sid had caught only part of what she had said.

"Good luck with your silly stunt."

"Oh — yes. Thank you and goodbye — for the er, present." Sid hurried out to the motor bike and side-car which stood at the kerb. The side-car leaned away from the bike part at an alarming angle, but when he threw his case and camera in it, the balance appeared to be redressed. He kicked the starter several times before the engine coughed into life and he left in a cloud of blue exhaust smoke.

Moments later he returned for the side-car which he had inadvertently uncoupled with the extra weight he had thrown into it.

Mrs. Donovan watched him from her front door, a cigarette dangling from the corner of her mouth, as he struggled to put the recalcitrant side-car back together with the bike. "Never mind, love. Next week you'll be driving a Rolls Royce." Her cigarette bobbed up and down as she spoke.

Jewell restrained himself from comment until he had completed the remarriage of the frequently divorced component parts of the machine he had borrowed. It was only when he had safely started the bike again and was astride the saddle that he gave vent to his feelings.

"Piss off, you old bitch!" he shouted in triumph, then his heart gave a lurch as the engine spluttered again. He had only two seconds to spare as his landlady launched herself at him from her position at the front door.

The bike surged forward as she came for him, fingernails at the ready. As he finally putt-putted his way up the street he gave her a two-fingered salute which Al Capone's mother-in-law would have applauded for its sheer bravura.

"I hope Pitchford knows what he's doing," the garage foreman had said to Glan Hopkins when he went along to pick up the bus he had hired. "If there's anything wrong with it when it comes back, I'm not going to be responsible. You'd better sign this form."

Hopkins had done so with a flourish. The rationalising about his situation which he had gone through that morning still held him on a steady course. An investment in his future — a trail-blazer. He hummed to himself as he drove the brand new, gleaming bus into Panteg. He was looking forward to meeting

Miss Thomas again. This would prove to her that he was a man of his word — a chap to be reckoned with.

At the bus-stop in Panteg, Miss Thomas had more than she could handle. Somehow, the news had got around about the free bus ride into Swansea and back for certain ladies in Panteg, and nearly every woman in the village had turned out.

Muriel and Gwen jostled for position in the queue with little Miss Rice-Morgan, who was in a bright red dress with a cloche to match. Mrs. Powell fought a genteel battle of elbows with Ceinwen Rees, and Mrs. Melinda Jackson, trying to work her way up to the front, encountered the unexpectedly steely muscles of a veiled lady in a smart black two-piece.

"Please, ladies, please," cried Miss Thomas, trying to bring order to chaos. "This is a private trip and only those who were invited can be allowed on board."

The only trouble was that no-one had a printed invitation to the bus trip. It had been arranged so hurriedly that there had been no time to issue any. Miss Thomas was acutely aware that the way things were, there was no possible chance of limiting the admittance to her cronies. She looked frantically about her for some kind of assistance from a policeman. You can never find one when you want one, she thought.

The reason why neither Panteg policeman was available was because they were locked in earnest conversation at the police station.

"I've been thinking about that garbled bloody conversation Capone's daughter wrote down." Sergeant Powell sat behind his desk, dressed in his uniform again, with his leg held out straight before him. It was still painful but he was able to walk on it.

Burns nodded. "It was on my mind last night too." His head buzzed under the bandage and his ribs ached from his flight over

Mrs. Jackson's wall and the landing in the cucumber frame. "I hav'nae been here all that long, but I know quite a few people in Panteg and I've never come across a Lulu."

"Neither have I. Sounds French to me, like croissants." Powell sat back and allowed himself a quick flashback to Marie and Amiens. A little smile flickered under his moustache.

"What are they?" asked Burns.

"They're sort of pastry things the French have for breakfast with butter and jam on them, and a lovely big cup of coffee to dip them in." The sergeant licked his lips reflectively.

"Never heard of them. Scones — now that's what I like. Fresh cream and home-made jam spread on them and a nice cup of tea with plenty of milk and sugar." Burns closed his eyes in ecstasy.

Both men sat silently for a while staring into space, remembering past breakfasts. With a little sigh Powell refocused his eyes and returned to the job in hand.

"Perhaps we'd better get young Tommy Rees in and ask him what it's all about."

"We canna really bring him in, sergeant. We dinna know what tae question him aboot. After all, the three of them hav'nae done anything wrong — well, not yet, anyway."

"I suppose you're right. Unless we can crack this code that Capone's presented us with we've got nothing to go on." He flicked the notes which Teresa had written.

Burns crossed his legs and linked his hands behind his throbbing head. He looked out of the window into the street. Outside, the normal life of Panteg went on. A horse and cart clattered past, the driver flicking his whip over the beast's rump. A paraffin van lumbered by on its solid tyres. Across the street a large black savage carrying a spear and wearing a leopard skin climbed into a lorry alongside the driver.

"Dinna see that in Panteg verra often," said Burns.

"Don't see what?" Powell looked up sharply.

"A black feller in a leopard skin carrying a spear." Burns was still in a trance-like state. "He's just got intae a lorry."

Powell looked out of the window and saw only the back of a

truck carrying builder's materials as it drove off up the street.

'You sure it wasn't a miner with a fishing rod?" Powell was afraid that Burns had received a harder knock on the head than was first believed. The lad might have a delayed concussion.

"Something familiar about him, too," said Burns, coming alive now after his initial shock.

"Perhaps you'd better go and lie down for a bit on the settee. There's nobody in the sitting-room. The wife's gone off on the free bus trip into Swansea." Powell was solicitous.

"Bus," said Burns. "That's it! It was Tommy Rees, I'm sure. Just caught a glimpse of him side face as he got intae the lorry." He was excited as he grabbed the notes from the desk and examined them. He pointed a finger in triumph. "If I'm nae mistaken that's nae Lulu — it's Zulu!"

Powell looked at Burns with increasing alarm. "Why should Tommy Rees be dressed up as a Zulu? It doesn't make any sense."

Glan Hopkins heartily wished that he had never met Miss Thomas as he watched the pushing, yelling mob of women invade his borrowed bus. The headmistress had been elbowed aside as she tried to organise a queue. She now stood at his side.

"I had no idea so many people would turn up," said Miss Thomas lamely.

"Neither did I. If I had, I would never have agreed to this charade." Hopkins's mellifluous voice had acquired overtones of hysteria. The bus rocked with the battling women inside and it was obvious that there would be far more left behind than there was room for on board. "I'll just have to drive off. The longer the bus stays here the more chance there is of it being wrecked. And it's brand new, you know." There was a sob in Glan's throat as he walked back to the bus and climbed into the driver's seat.

He drove off, heedless of the fighting women on the platform, and as he gathered speed he looked in his driving mirror and saw Miss Thomas running behind waving her arms in the air. He thought of stopping and then changed his mind. "Serves her right," he said to himself, savagely changing up into top gear. Behind him on the bus the fighting ceased and those without seats clung desperately to the upright poles and each other. In a back seat, crushed up against the window, Miss Rice-Morgan adjusted her red cloche hat and went to sleep.

Gwyneth Pugh, the lady who had battered Tommy Rees to a pulp, daintily pulled her skirt down over her massive knees and fixed her hair. Next to her the smartly-dressed lady in the black two-piece arranged her veil carefully to hide her face. Jammy Wicks was enjoying himself in his perverse way.

Dai drove up as Glan Hopkins drove away. He pulled into the kerb and climbed out of the cab. There were fifteen ladies left behind from the free trip who now eyed him with hostility. Miss Thomas, still panting from her chase, leaned against the bus-stop sign for support. She wagged an accusatory finger at Dai.

"This is all your fault, Dai Fargo. If you provided a decent bus service this fiasco would never have happened."

"What fiasco am I responsible for?" The big man stretched his arms wide in exaggerated surprise. "If you ladies are so anxious to get a free ride into Swansea on somebody else's bus it's not my fault if there aren't enough seats to go around."

The headmistress started to speak and then suddenly began to cry. The humiliation had been too much for her. The plan she had prepared had gone so badly awry that she had even been prevented from boarding the bus herself. The other women fell silent, embarrassed at the sight of the woman they had always thought was as hard as nails dissolving into tears. They watched uncomfortably as she clung to the bus-stop sign, her shoulders heaving.

Dai was nonplussed. He went up to Miss Thomas and patted her tentatively on the back. "There, there," he said. Her reaction was to wail louder than before. Dai looked at the women and shrugged helplessly. He came to a decision. "Tell you what," he said. "I'll take you all into Swansea for nothing. If the South Wales Transport can do it — so can I. All aboard the Skylark."

He ushered the unresisting Miss Thomas on to the bus and the other women followed with cries of "Good old Dai", "Who needs the South Wales Transport?" and "Why don't you do this every Friday, Dai?"

All this time, Bryn was taking the opportunity to examine the tyres. When Dai had gone back into the house to clean up after hosing down the bus, Bryn had conceived the brilliant idea of removing the spare tyre. He reckoned that if he could actually puncture a tyre with a knife it would be a quicker job than running around letting the air out of all of them, and, to make absolutely certain that Sid could get away, the absence of a spare would be essential. It would be relatively simple to slash the rubber, he thought now. He ran his hands over the off-side front wheel. The tyre felt harder than he had expected. He fingered the pocket knife he always carried. Perhaps a little cut on the side now when nobody's looking and then when the time came a quick thrust into it would finish the job. By the time Dai had put Miss Thomas aboard Bryn had hacked away a reasonable portion of rubber.

"Bryn, come on! Can't keep the good ladies waiting," shouted Dai from the driver's seat, refraining from saying what he actually felt about his brother-in-law's non-appearance.

"Sorry, Dai." Bryn sidled round the bus and jumped on to the platform. He felt more confident about his part in the robbery, though faint alarm bells still rang in his head about Sid's plans after the job was done. Perhaps he could leap into the side-car with him and to hell with being found out. It would be far better to be with the money when it left the bus. "Hold very tight," he called out as he pressed the bell. Dai noted the unaccustomed light-heartedness in Bryn's tone, and trundled away on his momentous journey, shaking his head in wonder at his conductor's changes of mood.

Miss Thomas sat alone in the front of the bus, her head held down as she stared into her lap. She had stopped crying and was now wondering what she was doing on the Fargo bus. She would have to change to Glan Hopkins's bus to come back from Swansea. This time she would make sure who was in charge. Fargo had been very kind to let her and the others travel free of charge, but it did not alter the fact that she was going to have him removed from the route.

P.C. Burns knocked on Ceinwen Rees's door. He was tingling with excitement. Powell had at last been convinced that there was something in what he had said about Tommy Rees being a Zulu and that this was the potential code-breaker to the incomprehensible conversation in Capone's. He banged the knocker again, harder this time. There was no reply. Burns, frustrated, looked across the tiny weed-covered patch that served as a front garden for the terraced house towards the next-door neighbour's front parlour window. The curtains twitched to one side as Mrs. Fargo peeked out at the police constable.

She opened her front door and waited for Burns to make his way out of Ceinwen's rickety gate and around to her own wrought iron one.

"Mrs. Rees in, Mrs. Fargo?" he enquired.

Mrs. Fargo sniffed disdainfully and drew her woollen shawl more closely around her shoulders. "I'm afraid she's gone off to Swansea on a free trip. Fat lot of good it will do her I can tell you. The Fargo family has provided transport for Panteg for thirty years and it's scandalous the way people around here . . ."

Burns cut her off in mid-sentence with an apologetic wave of his arm. "This is important, Mrs. Fargo. Now listen carefully, does Tommy Rees dress up as a Zulu for any reason ye can think of?"

"A Zulu?" Mrs. Fargo hit a top C. "Zulu?" she repeated.

"Have ye ever seen him dressed up like — y'know, an African with a spear and a leopard skin over his shoulders?"

"You must be mistaken, officer." Mrs. Fargo was suddenly afraid of the constable before her. There was a funny look in his eyes and he had a bandage around his head.

"Oh, dear God," said Burns taking off his helmet and rubbing his hand over his face. He was at once vulnerable and pathetic and Mrs. Fargo's heart reached out to him.

"Come on in and have a cup of tea. We'll have a chat and perhaps then I can understand what you want to know."

Burns accepted the idea thankfully and entered the house. He made himself comfortable in a chair in the kitchen whilst the old lady put the kettle on. She talked all the time she was preparing the tea.

"I don't know what things are coming to. This old South Wales Transport giving free rides into Swansea and back. What next, I ask you? My David has been doing the best he can with the bus he's got. Times are hard and money tight but we've never put up the fares — not since 1929." Mrs. Fargo bustled around the kitchen, setting out a cup and saucer for the policeman and putting the tea in the teapot. She paused with the black and gold coloured caddy in one hand and a teaspoon in the other. "Like a Welsh cake? They're very tasty with a cup of tea."

Burns nodded uneasily. He was conscious of time going by rather quickly and something about to blow up in his and Powell's faces very soon.

Dai's mother reached into the pantry and brought out a biscuit tin full of small round flat cakes made of flour, fat, sultanas and currants, sugar and eggs, and took out half a dozen. She put them on a plate and placed it before Burns. He picked one up tentatively.

"Yes, as a matter of fact if it weren't for the regular contracts we have with some of the local industries we'd be in a bad way." She poured the boiling water into the tea pot and put the lid on it.

Burns took a bite of his Welsh cake and to his surprise was overwhelmed by the taste. "These are lovely," he said through the crumbs as he pushed a second one into his face.

"Nice, aren't they?" Mrs. Fargo was warming to the Scottish

policeman. What he wanted was somebody to look after him, poor dab. "As I was saying, if it wasn't for things like the Colliery giving us a weekly contract for taking their clerks with the wages from Swansea to the mine and back every Friday, we'd be far worse off than we are." She poured milk into Burns's cup and followed with the tea. "How do you like it, Mr. Burns?"

"As it comes, thank ye, Mrs. Fargo." The constable accepted the proffered sugar bowl and helped himself to four spoonfuls. He stirred his tea carefully and took another Welsh cake. He had a mouthful of cake and was gulping at his cup of tea when he realised what the old lady had said. He choked helplessly, and it was nearly five minutes later, after being struck heavily between the shoulder blades by the alarmed Mrs. Fargo, that he recovered his breath. "Say that again please, Missus," he gasped when he was able.

"Say what?"

"That bit aboot your bus carrying the wages frae Swansea tae the Colliery every Friday."

"You've just said it, boy bach," said Mrs. Fargo. "Every Friday at twelve o'clock Dai picks up the pay clerk and his assistant and brings them with the bag of money to the pit. It's been going on for ages. Don't make a song and dance about it, of course, it wouldn't do."

"Then there will be a bag of wages on the bus today?"

"That's right, love. Every Friday. Leaving Christina Street at twelve."

"Thank ye, Mrs. Fargo." Burns rose hurriedly. "I'll have tae get back tae the station." He paused and looked at the cakes left on his plate.

"Take them with you, love. I'll put them in a bag." Mrs. Fargo was flattered that he liked her baking.

"There's no time, I'm afraid. I'll take them in my hand." The constable scooped up the Welsh cakes and left for the station.

"I'm right!" he called in a flurry of crumbs to Sergeant Powell as he entered. "There's money for the Colliery on that bus today."

"Is there, be damned?" Powell hit his desk hard with the flat of his large hand, making the contents leap into the air. "What about Tommy Rees? Did Mrs. Rees tell you where he's gone and why he's all blacked up?"

Burns shook his head. "She wasn't in. She's awa' on that free bus trip intae Swansea. Nearly all the women have gone on it. And Mrs. Fargo had no idea what I was talking aboot when I asked why he's pretending tae be a Zulu."

"Well, we still haven't got much to go on. I suppose I could telephone Swansea and tell them that we believe that the Colliery wages are going to be snatched off the Fargo bus by Zulus, but I don't think they'll take very kindly to the idea. They'll think we've gone bloody potty. And besides, if there is something in it and we handle it ourselves we'll be one up on those toffee-nosed buggers down there at Swansea Central." Powell was not too keen on the Swansea police. They had sent him up here to Panteg when he was expecting promotion in the town force.

"I suppose you're right, Sergeant." Burns was not too sure whether they were doing something which could land them in trouble.

"Of course I'm right. Now, let's have a look at those notes again. The answer's in here somewhere."

Tommy Rees was enjoying himself in the front of the lorry.

"For God's sake stop shouting 'Walla Walla' out of the cab window," complained Ben Walters, who was already regretting giving him a lift into Clydach.

"Sorry, Ben. I'm excited that's all. Big day for us Zulus, see. Having our picture taken." He was still convinced that Sid would actually take a photograph.

'I never knew that there was a Clydach Zulus' Jazz and Kazoo Band. How long have you been going then?"

"Oh, about three weeks, that's all. I met some fellers at the Labour Exchange and they were talking about forming this band, like, and they asked me to join. This is my spear." Tommy waved his stolen railing at Ben.

"Look out, mun. That thing's lethal," said Ben, alarmed by the antics of the large man beside him. The sooner he dropped him off the better.

Elvin handled the gun lovingly. He had unwrapped it from its oilskin covering under the glowering gaze of Lloyd-Price. Only the threat of his dalliance with Glynis being revealed to his wife kept him from snatching it back from the pimply clerk.

"Feels great in the hand." Elvin lifted the as yet unloaded Smith and Wesson and pointed it at an imaginary target. "Bang Bang!" he cried, pressing the trigger as he spoke.

"Don't do that," shouted Lloyd-Price. "You'll ruin the mechanism."

"You don't have to shout," pouted Elvin.

Glynis observed the two men from her desk near the door. Like little schoolboys, that's what they are, she thought. She regretted ever allowing Lloyd-Price to touch her. He was obviously too afraid of his wife ever to leave her and the snatched love sessions she'd had with him had usually left her unsatisfied. Until Elvin had caught them canoodling she fancied she might have a good chance of binding him to her with her over-ripe body. But since then, Lloyd-Price had taken hardly any notice of her. The feeling of injustice grew in her ample bosom as she listened to the two men making preparations for the trip to the Colliery. She wondered how she could humiliate her erstwhile lover.

Lloyd-Price was going over the details again with Elvin. "Don't forget, now. Make sure that the safety-catch is on before you put the gun in your shoulder holster, understand? I don't want to be responsible for you shooting your damned foot off." He stole a glance at Glynis, intending to apologise for his bad language, but she looked away disdainfully.

'When do I load the gun then?" Elvin was trembling with excitement.

"There's plenty of time for that — and I'll load it. We'll leave the office at 11.45 to proceed on foot to Christina Street." The older man assumed a military manner as he went through the routine. "Before we leave I shall attach the steel bracelet and chain from the bag containing the cash to my wrist and you will keep the key to it on your person in case anyone tries to steal the money. The key opens the bracelet and the bag." He put a small key on the table.

"Why don't *you* carry the key, then?" asked Elvin.

"Because," said Lloyd-Price with slow emphasis, as if talking to a child, "if anyone tries to steal the bag they couldn't unlock it and neither could I. The reason being that *you* have the key. And so the thief would have to take me with him whether he liked it or not."

Glynis, listening intently, suddenly had an idea.

Dai bowled along Cwmgorse Common, the old bus creaking and sighing. Won't be long before she packs in, he thought. No chance of a replacement either, although Mam must have a bit of money put away. Still, there's no hope of keeping the route now S.W.T. is going to put new buses on. They're bound to be more comfortable than this old thing. Still, she's been a good old loyal servant over the years. Her time's up, that's all. How can you fight a big combine like South Wales Transport? He changed down into third gear as he came off the common and began the slow descent into Swansea. Not too bad, he thought, sneaking a look at his watch. Twenty past ten. Should be on time for a change.

Suddenly his off-side front tyre burst and he went into a skid. His strength and experience were equal to the occasion, although his passengers were not. He swung the wheel with the skid and slowly the bus responded to his skill. It came to rest alongside a hedge in the last remnants of countryside before the Swansea suburbs took over.

Dai climbed carefully out of the bus. He had finished up on the wrong side of the road and he had to negotiate part of the hedge which was trying to get into the cab with him. "Nothing to worry about," he said cheerfully to his anxious passengers. "Come on, Bryn, give us a hand. Looks like we've got a puncture. Get the spare wheel out."

Bryn, white-faced, shrank into a seat and tried to think of an excuse.

Ahead of him, Glan Hopkins was already pulling into the bus-stop. He could not wait to discharge his unruly cargo. After the initial shock of his speedy departure the passengers had settled down to raucous singing. Some of the words they sang made him blush like a schoolgirl. These weren't his kind of people at all. God, if only he had not returned Miss Thomas's telephone call yesterday morning. He came into position at the kerb as the Panteg ladies were getting to the end of "She's got hairs on her dicky dido right down to her knees" sung to the tune of *The Ash Grove*.

"Come on. Come on." He banged on the side of the bus with his hand, not wishing to leave his seat and risk being trampled by the exiting ladies. "Leaving sharp at twelve. Can't hang about."

Chattering like magpies the women of Panteg descended from the bus and dispersed with an amazing rapidity in the direction of the Market and the Oxford Street and High Street shops. Jammy Wicks, in his black two-piece, minced off in high-heeled shoes to a different destination. Miss Rice-Morgan, unperturbed by the row, sat fast asleep in her seat.

Glan Hopkins, waiting until he thought everyone had gone, climbed out of his cab and boarded the bus to see what damage might have been done. He was relieved to find that apart from a few smouldering cigarette ends there was nothing to worry about. Miss Rice-Morgan whimpered in her sleep. Hopkins, surprised to find a passenger still aboard, shook her gently by the shoulder. "Swansea, madam. We've arrived at Swansea."

The fragile lady opened her eyes and smiled up at him. "What a lovely voice you have," she said.

"Thank you very much," said Glan, pleased at the compliment.

"My father had a voice like yours. All milk and honey. Could charm the birds off the trees with it. Unfortunately most of them turned out to be vultures." She smiled up at him and fell asleep again.

Hopkins was uncertain whether to wake her or let her sleep. He decided on the latter course and went in search of a toilet and a stiff whisky.

". . . Photograph on the bus. Taking bag away for publicity. Not hit hard. Christ Almighty. Twa." Powell stopped playing with his lower lip as Burns read out the notes that Teresa Capone had made.

"We both know what 'twa' means, and we also know that for 'Lulu' we read 'Zulu'. Taking bag away is obviously the bag of money from the Colliery Head Office, and not hit hard refers to the feller with the bag." Powell ticked off the points they agreed about on his thick spatulate fingers.

Burns looked down again at the notes. "Suppose there's a photograph being taken somewhere of the bus for publicity?"

Powell shook his head. "Can't imagine anybody taking publicity pictures of Dai Fargo's bus. The bloody thing's falling apart. That's why they're all complaining about the service he's been providing. I like Dai myself. Nice bloke. Good soldier, Dai." The sergeant was prepared to reminisce again. "I remember one time outside Neuve Chappelle . . ."

His constable cut him off before he could get going. "Look, why don't we ring the *Evening Post*? If there's a publicity picture being taken, they'd be the ones to do it."

"Not a bad idea," said Powell, dragging himself back from France with an effort. "Get 'em on the telephone."

Burns dialled the newspaper's number and whilst it rang ran his tongue round the crannies in his teeth, searching out particles of Welsh cake. "Hello, *Evening Post*? Constable Burns of Panteg here. I'm enquiring aboot a publicity picture ye might be taking of a bus. Fargo's bus. Right. I'll hold on."He looked over at Powell who sat back in his chair, leg stretched out before him. "He's gone tae find out," he said, needlessly.

Powell, playing with his lower lip, nodded.

Burns turned his attention to the telephone again. 'Ye've nothing on your schedule about photographing a bus? Thank ye."

"Wait a minute." Powell held up his hand. "Ask him if he knows anything about any Zulus."

"My sergeant wants tae know if ye know anything aboot Zulus." Burns felt foolish asking the question. "Yes — Zulus. Y'know, people dressed up like African savages." He turned towards his sergeant again. "He's . . ."

"Gone to find out." Powell finished the sentence for him.

Burns searched his pocket for the Welsh cake he had placed there. He brought it out and examined it, picking bits of navy blue fluff from its surface. He was about to take a bite when the voice at the other end interrupted him. "The what?" The constable dropped his Welsh cake on the desk, concentrating on what the other man was saying. "The Clydach Zulus' Jazz and Kazoo Band." Burns wrote the words down on the blotter before him. "Are they well known locally? I see. Thank ye." He hung up and looked at Powell, his eyes shining. "There's a band, only formed a few weeks ago apparently — y'know, a kazoo band, not a proper one. And we're lucky because one of the blokes in the *Evening Post* office has a brother in it."

"That's all very well," said Powell, getting up from his chair and moving stiffly around to Burns's desk, favouring his injured leg. "But where does that leave us?"

"Well, they must be practising somewhere today, otherwise

Rees wouldn't have gone tae all that trouble blacking himself up, Sergeant."

"Aye. But *where* would they practise?"

"It would have tae be somewhere along the route that Fargo's bus takes," said Burns. "I'll bet it's aboot here." He stood up and put his finger on the map of the county which was pinned to the wall behind his desk. His finger traced the main road leading out of Panteg and down into Swansea. It stopped at the green area marked "Cwmgorse Common". "It's got tae be here. It's quiet and there's never much traffic and it's nice and flat for marching on."

"How do *you* know what's good for marching on?" Powell realised that Burns had probably hit on the right answer to the problem. At the same time he resented the fact that the younger man had done so. "If you'd been in the army like I was . . .'

"Sorry, Sergeant. I didna mean tae upset ye. But I dinna think we've got much time left if we're going tae catch them at it."

"That's all right," said Powell, mollified by Burns's deference. "Now, as I said, we have to keep this to ourselves. We don't want to look idiots if we're wrong in our assumptions — at the same time, if we can pull off an arrest we'll be sitting pretty." He picked up the Welsh cake Burns had dropped on his desk and began to eat it. "We'll nip down to Cwmgorse Common on your bike. The two of us will have to go in case we need to overpower them. We'll take the shotgun as well, as extra protection." He masticated slowly as his mind slipped into gear. "No good using my Austin Ruby, it's leaking oil like the clappers. I'll ask old Arthur Bracknell, the special constable, to watch the shop while we're away. He can answer the telephone and take down any complaints. Crime in Panteg will have to mark time, boyo, bigger villains are abroad." He sucked his teeth. "Where'd you get this Welsh cake from?"

"Mrs. Fargo gave me a few when I went tae see Mrs. Rees." Burns had watched his superior eat his cake with some annoyance.

"Nice. Very nice. Wonder if she can make croissants?"

"I'll start the bike," said Burns hastily. He wasn't sure whether his beloved machine was capable of carrying both of them after his accident the previous night, but transport in Panteg was hard to come by.

"Right ho." Powell squared his shoulders. This was like the old days. Over the top. Show 'em what you're made of. He walked to the cabinet where the shotgun was kept, forcing his leg to move naturally. The polished stock and gleaming barrel drew a sigh from him. There was something about a firearm that always attracted him. He put the gun to his shoulder and peered along the barrel at the picture of his wife which stood in a silver frame on his desk. "Bang, you're dead," he said to himself, thinking of Marie and Amiens again.

Sid Jewell parked the motor bike and side-car off the road leading across Cwmgorse Common. He chose a clump of yellow blossoming gorse about ten feet off the highway. It was near enough for a quick get-away and provided sufficient cover for the machine. He looked at his watch. It was ten past eleven. Fine, he thought. The Zulus are due here at about eleven-thirty and the bus is due at twelve-thirty. He picked up the Press camera he had brought and practised holding it in a professional manner. He had seen enough American films in his career as a projectionist to know how Press photographers were supposed to behave. In his pocket he had a card on which he had written in large black letters "PRESS". From the side-car he produced a battered trilby which he had acquired for the purpose of the disguise he had worked out for himself. Using the wing mirror of the bike he donned the trilby, having already placed the Press card in the mildewed ribbon which encircled the hat. Not too bad, he thought, looking this way and that, changing angles so that he saw himself the way he wanted to see himself. Satisfied, he sat on the seat of the bike and waited for the Zulus to arrive.

They came in dribs and drabs, in various kinds of transport:

most of them on pushbikes, a few relying on lifts from neighbours going into Swansea. Sid watched in amazement as Cwmgorse Common was slowly transformed into the veldt of South Africa. Some of the Zulus had effected a very good likeness to their counterparts, others by nature of their lack of height and bandy legs looked exactly what they were — poor undernourished Welshmen looking for a reason to keep themselves occupied and feeling very embarrassed. There were white patches here and there where the blacking-up process had been overlooked, and some of the footwear was very un-African. They formed a cluster around a tall ex-R.S.M. of the Welsh Guards who was responsible for their formation. Berwyn Llewellyn, standing six feet six inches tall, was a very imposing figure. He stood in the centre of his men, commanding silence. Immediately the noise abated.

"Where's Tommy bloody Rees?" asked Berwyn in his deep Paul Robeson voice.

"He's just coming now, Berwyn," said a voice. "He's had to walk down from Cwmscwt. There he is, look." The figure of Tommy Rees had appeared on the skyline, magnificent in his get-up and waving his spear-railing.

"Damned idiot's always late on parade," said Berwyn. He raised his own assegai and pointed it to the sky, uttering an age-old Zulu war cry. The others shivered at the sound. Even Sid in his clump of gorse fifty feet away felt his blood curdle. By God, that bloke looks authentic, he thought. And sounds it.

Tommy Rees put on a spurt as he heard the war cry and ran panting down the road to join the group. "Had to walk from Cwmscwt," he said by way of apology.

"All right. Where's this photographer bloke?" asked Berwyn, eyes flashing.

Before Tommy could answer Sid emerged from where he had hidden the bike and was walking towards him. "Hello, fellows," he cried, waving a friendly arm. As he did so the Press card fluttered from his hat. He picked it up and held it in his hand as he approached the band. "Press — like it says on the card," he said, putting the card away quickly.

Berwyn Llewellyn towered over him. "From all I've seen of it, it could say 'LIFT', 'PULL' or bloody 'PUSH'. We've come a fair distance today to have this picture taken and I just want to make sure that we're not wasting our time."

"What do you think this is then?" said Sid, indicating the Press camera.

"O.K., O.K." said the big man, lifting his hands and revealing pink palms.

"That's a great make-up," said Sid, trying to ingratiate himself.

"It should be," replied Berwyn, resplendent in his real leopard skin, his real induna headband, and his real black skin. "My mother was a great grand-daughter of Chaka the Zulu King."

"Oh yes?" Sid smiled weakly.

"Walla Walla," shouted Tommy, not looking so magnificent next to the real thing.

"Shut up," said Sid.

"Come on, then. Let's get fell in," said the half-Welsh Zulu, and like magic, his men came into position on the road.

"There's no hurry yet for the picture." Sid was anxious that the band shouldn't get too tired before the bus arrived. "The idea is that I take the photograph of your lads attacking the bus, like. Sort of Indians attacking the Wells Fargo coach — only this time it's Zulus attacking a bus. *Welsh* Fargo, eh?"

Berwyn snorted down his dilated nostrils at Sid. "Any more jokes like that and *I'll* attack *you*."

Glynis eyed the small silver key that Lloyd-Price had left on the desk. Both he and Elvin had gone next door to the café for a cup of coffee and a bun before leaving to catch the bus. She knew that the key was the one which locked the bag and also the bracelet which would be affixed to Lloyd-Price's wrist. It was the first time she had heard him going over the routine with an assistant. If only she could switch keys, Lloyd-Price would find himself very embarrassed when he got to Panteg and discovered he couldn't open the bag. She examined the key carefully. It looked very much like one she carried in her purse. The one that locked the drawer in her desk at home, the drawer that held her love letters.

She took out her bunch of keys. Side by side on the desk there was clearly a difference in size and shape, but seen separately they would look very much like each other. She hesitated whether to switch them or not. There'd be a terrible row — still, she thought with a wave of anger, he's got it coming to him. She slipped the real key into her purse and left the other one in its place. Lloyd-Price might know which was which but Elvin never would.

Footsteps down the passage heralded the entrance of the two pay clerks. Glynis hurried back to her own desk, her heart pounding.

Dai was sweating with anger and frustration as he wrestled with the inner tube. Bloody Bryn *would* leave the spare wheel behind. God knows why he had to take it out of the boot to clean it. Whoever heard of anybody cleaning a spare wheel? There must be another reason, and when they got back to Panteg he'd shake it out of him. For the moment he had his work cut out trying to repair the hole in the inner tube made by the nail he had picked up. He wondered, too, why the tyre itself had such a hole in it.

While he sat on the floor of Jenkins' Garage, putting a large rubber patch over the damaged inner tube, his passengers were seated before cups of coffee prepared for them in the little café next door, compliments of Dai.

The air was blue with condemnation of Dai Fargo and his dreadful bus service. In a corner on her own, Miss Thomas sat seething. There was precious little chance now of getting into Swansea in time to pick up the Glan Hopkins bus. It was well past eleven and that fool Fargo was nowhere near being ready.

She looked across at the bus which sat forlornly by the side of the road, jacked up and deserted except for the conductor, Bryn, who stood smoking morosely alongside it.

He puffed away with his head down, looking at his cracked boots. No chance now of replacing them with sandals for treading the white sands of Bondi Beach, the shimmering vision of Australia had dissipated completely and he wondered what Sid would do now the robbery was off. He thought how stupid those Zulus would look prancing up and down Cwmgorse Common, waiting for a bus that never came, or when it did come, would be too bloody late to carry any wages on it. There was nothing to worry about with Dai, he thought. He can't really prove I did anything to the tyre and he's already swallowed the excuse about the spare wheel. At least I think he did. Bryn gave a little shiver as he thought about what Dai might do to him if he found out.

"Pull in over by here," Powell shouted in the ear of Constable Burns as they got to the approach of the Common. His leg hurt from the journey on the bike from Panteg. He had never been a good pillion passenger and Burns was too flashy a rider for his liking. Apart from that the bike wasn't behaving too well. The crash the previous night had affected it more than Burns had thought and the steering was rather erratic.

Burns was glad to stretch his legs too. His sergeant had gripped him around the waist with arms of steel, and his head ached from the combined effect of his accident and the assault on his ears made by his passenger as they had taken the bends on some of the narrower roads. He pushed his bike off the road and put it on the stand.

Powell stamped the ground painfully, trying to get the circulation moving in his legs. "You drive like a bloody maniac, Burns," he commented angrily.

"It's not my fault, Sergeant, the handlebars need straightening out."

"So do you." Powell gave his constable a glare and got down to the business in hand. In the mid-distance they could see the Zulus marching up and down the road. The sergeant stood looking for a moment. "Somebody's drilled those fellers well," he remarked, his soldier's eye admiring their precision. "Now, cover up that bike with some gorse and let's get a bit nearer on foot, so that we can see what's going on.'

Burns grunted with the effort of removing pieces of gorse bush and making a rough hide for his bike. The prickly thorns hurt his hands and he cursed under his breath. The excitement of the chase had abated somewhat and his head was banging away again.

Powell waited until Burns had finished, standing with his shotgun at the ready. In his mind he was back in France again. The Zulus up front were the Germans and he was leading a patrol. "Come on, lad," he said briskly as the constable plucked thorns from his hands and his uniform. "The enemy are only yards away. We'll have to get down and crawl forward under the cover of the bushes. Do exactly as I do."

He threw himself on the ground, wincing as the pain from his injured leg jolted through him. He started crawling towards the marching men in the distance. Burns watched in amazement. "Sergeant," he called. "They canna see us frae here."

"Down, lad, down," hissed Powell over his shoulder. "They may have posted a sentry."

Burns, shaking his bandaged head in utter bewilderment, got down on his hands and knees and started to follow. He's gone mad, he thought, not for the first time that day.

Lloyd-Price checked the contents of the Gladstone bag which held the money. He rearranged the blue paper bags of silver to suit his mania for neatness and patted down the piles of notes. Elvin watched from the other side of the desk, impatient to be given the gun. The shoulder holster which Lloyd-Price had personally strapped on him felt tight where his superior had used rather unnecessary force. He saw the key lying on the desk and picked it up.

"I'll put the key in my pocket," he said.

Lloyd-Price nodded without looking up, still fussing with the money. "Be careful you don't lose it."

Elvin pocketed the key, and Glynis felt the tension leave her.

At last the senior clerk declared himself satisfied with the way the bag was packed and snapped the lock shut. "It's self-locking," he said to Elvin. "And so is this." He snapped the bracelet, which was attached by a length of chain to the bag, firmly on his wrist. It snapped shut with a solid clunk which brought an unseen smile to Glynis's face. "Works like a policeman's handcuffs. Only you can release me now, Elvin." He allowed himself a short bark of uneasy laughter.

Elvin sniggered, fingering the key in his pocket. "Can I have the gun now, Mr Lloyd-Price?" His eyes were bright, like a small boy's.

"All right. All right." Lloyd-Price heaved a sigh of resignation and, with great reluctance, withdrew from the drawer of his desk the gun he cherished so much. His movements were restricted by the chain and bracelet. "I've put this damned thing on too soon. You'd better unlock me while I load it."

Even before Elvin could put his hand in his pocket for the key, Glynis had leapt forward from her desk and was at his side.

"Let me load it," she said, her heart thumping. She turned a smile on Lloyd-Price which made him forget his determination not to have anything more to do with her. "Let me put it in," she whispered coyly, handling the little magazine and looking deep into his eyes.

He began to sweat. "God, I wish you would," he said huskily.

"Just a minute, Mr. Lloyd-Price, you wouldn't let me put it in, why should she be allowed to?" Elvin, missing the by-play, was indignant.

"Shut up you little whipper snapper," snarled his senior, now thoroughly aroused.

Elvin sat down at his own desk and sulked.

"I'll get rid of him for a minute." Lloyd-Price contrived to whisper in Glynis's ear.

Yes, she thought, about a minute is all it takes you. "When you come back," she murmured. "Now show me where this goes," she said loudly, for Elvin's benefit. She loaded the gun with more dexterity than Lloyd-Price had expected and handed it back to him with a sultry smile. "Slipped in nice and easy, didn't it?"

"Just let me put the safety-catch on," he said, his throat constricted with passion.

"I hope *your* safety-catch is on," she murmured slyly.

Elvin, anxious to get the gun, got up from his desk. "Come on Mr. Lloyd-Price, let's have the gun. We'll soon have to catch the bus." Glynis was glad of his approach. The older man had a look in his eyes which signalled that he was about to seize her in his arms, bag and bracelet and all. She moved away from him thankfully now that her little ploy had worked. The key remained in Elvin's pocket.

"Open your coat then, damn it." Lloyd-Price was savage with frustration as he rammed home the weapon in his junior's shoulder holster. He didn't even allow Elvin the brief satisfaction of handling the firearm. "Now button it up again and let's get down to Christina Street."

Elvin led the way out of the office, too thrilled with the excitement of being armed to notice the tender, longing look and the blown kiss which Lloyd-Price gave to Glynis.

She waited until the sound of their footsteps had receded down the corridor before she burst into helpless laughter.

Dai Fargo bustled into the little café where his passengers had all finished two cups of coffee each and had ordered biscuits. The café proprietor had also provided them with pastries and jam the like of which most of them had never tasted before.

"I've repaired the puncture, ladies. Sorry for the delay. We should get to Swansea about ten minutes past twelve."

To cries of "So you should be" and "Disgusting service, that's what it is" the ladies left the café led by Miss Thomas, grim-faced and silent. Only Mrs Powell remained at the counter talking to the café proprietor.

"You're French, aren't you?"

The pretty, rosy-cheeked lady nodded animatedly. "I am, yes. Married to a Welshman I met in the war."

"Could you let me have a couple of those pastry things we had. They were lovely. I'm sure my husband would enjoy them. He was in France during the war. Served in Amiens."

"Did 'e?" said Marie.

Powell had reached a gorse bush near to the marching men which was big enough to conceal himself and Burns. He pulled himself painfully to his knees and unslung the shotgun from his shoulder. Burns, a good fifty yards away, panted towards him, his uniform a sorry mess from his progress on all fours from where they had left the bike. By the time he got to his sergeant he was exhausted. He lay flat out, gasping for breath.

Sid Jewell stood twenty feet away, camera poised, pretending to take pictures of the Zulus as they paraded up and down the road, marching and counter marching to the music of their kazoos. Tommy Rees's part appeared to be a pretty menial one. A big bass drum was strapped to his back and a little Zulu in a towelling loincloth walked behind him banging it with sticks. He was the comedy element of the band, at the back of the formation.

The man who impressed Jewell and caused icy fingers of fear to clutch at his heart was the real black man, Berwyn Llewellyn. He carried himself like the R.S.M. he had once been, hurling his heavy assegai in the air as a signal for the band to change direction or cease playing. He was not a man to trifle with, and Sid began to wonder whether his plan would work if this big fellow refused to cooperate at the crucial moment. He cursed Tommy Rees for not telling him that he would be encumbered with a big bass drum throughout the hijack. How the hell would he get on the bus to get the bag with that lot on his back?

As the band marched up the road to where Sid was standing, Berwyn lifted his spear high and the men came to a halt with a precision which would have done credit to the Brigade of Guards.

"How many more times do we have to do this before that bus arrives?" Berwyn left his men at ease and came on to the grass verge where Sid shifted awkwardly from foot to foot.

"Shouldn't be too long now." Jewell looked at his watch. "The bus leaves Swansea at twelve and should be here about twenty-five past."

Mickey Mouse's yellow gloved hand moved jerkily under the almost frosted glass. "Coming up to twelve o'clock — give or take five minutes." Sid Jewell held up his wristwatch for inspection.

The other man gripped his wrist with a hand like a bunch of over-ripe bananas. "O.K. But when the bus gets here, take your pictures quick. I've got to be back at work at three. I'm on the afternoon shift at Panteg Colliery. We get paid today."

Glan Hopkins sat disconsolately on the wall of a house near the bus-stop in Christina Street. He wondered why he had been so stupid as to hire this bus. All his earlier self-delusions had left him and he faced the reality of knowing that he was a man who would never make lasting friendships with women, and that men would always take advantage of him. There was a basic flaw in his nature which prevented him getting close to anybody — except on the telephone. He wondered if there would be any future for himself on the wireless. Perhaps as an announcer. Everybody said how nice his voice was. Even that little old lady whose head he could just make out reclining against the corner of the back seat of the bus.

"This is the British Broadcasting Service," he said aloud, practising. "Here is the weather forecast."

"Going to piss down this afternoon from the look of it."

Hopkins looked up guiltily, not aware that he had been within anyone's earshot.

Pitchford sat down beside him, first dusting the stone wall with his handkerchief. He tapped the front of his jacket with his hand. "Thanks for the money in the envelope," he said, his eyes darting from side to side. "Thought I'd nip along and see how the trip is doing. Got to keep an eye on the bus, d'y'see. Brand new, that Tiger is." He nodded towards the vehicle standing proudly by the bus-stop. "Make sure nothing happens to it, for God's sake. Otherwise your head will be on the block, old man. Done you a favour, so don't let me down. You'll have to take the responsibility if anything goes wrong with it, mind." Pitchford was uneasy about the deal he had done with Hopkins and had come up from his office in Oxford Street to reassure himself that the bus was still in one piece. There would be Hell to pay if there were as much as a scratch on it before it went into service with South Wales Transport. He'd had to bribe the men at the garage to let Hopkins have it, but they would be the first to tell if anything did happen to the bus. Pitchford had a particular reason for not wishing anything to go wrong today of all days.

"Don't worry," said Hopkins, with a forced smile. "It will be back in the garage as good as new by half past two." He crossed his fingers as he said it; so far only four ladies had boarded the bus.

'It had better be, that's all I can say." Pitchford got up from the wall, carefully adjusting the creases in his trousers. "See me back in my office when you've put the bus away." He turned and walked quickly away on his expensively shod feet. On his way down Christina Street he passed two men, one carrying a Gladstone-type bag and the other walking slightly ahead moving his head from side to side in an exaggerated manner as if surveying the street for possible trouble.

"For Christ's sake, man, act natural," said Lloyd-Price for the umpteenth time. Elvin, glorying in his role of bodyguard, ignored the other's protests. He walked with his arms held away from his sides as he had seen many a Western gunman do in the films. He was enjoying himself.

Hopkins watched the pair approach from his seat on the wall. To him it appeared that the young lad in front was a bit simple and his father was taking him for an outing.

Lloyd-Price sat down heavily alongside him and, trying to conceal the chain around his wrist, put the bag on the wall at his side. He was sweating from the walk from the office and the antics of Elvin had not helped his temper.

Elvin took up a position at the bus-stop and resumed his watch, this time switching from cowboy to gangster. He chewed a non-existent wad of gum as he leaned against the sign, his hand half in, half out of the inside of his jacket.

"Pity," said Glan Hopkins, inclining his head in the direction of the apparently demented clerk. "Born like it, was he? Or a nervous breakdown, perhaps?"

"Boy's an idiot," snorted Lloyd-Price. "Born like it certainly — he hasn't got enough damned brains to have a nervous breakdown."

"I'm sorry." Glan Hopkins was surprised that a father could be so forthright about his son. He got up and looked at his watch. "Coming up to twelve o'clock. Have to get my ladies together for the trip to Panteg. Sort of goodwill mission I'm performing for South Wales Transport. We're hoping to take over the route from the Fargo outfit."

"About time, too," said Lloyd-Price. "That bus is rarely on schedule and it's not a very comfortable ride either." He looked around before continuing. "Got the wages for the Colliery in here. My firm uses Fargo for the journey because there's no-one else. Every Friday I have my insides battered all the way to Panteg and back. Not a very enjoyable experience at the best of times, and today I've got that blasted boy with me as an assistant."

"I see," said Glan. "He's not your son, then?"

Lloyd-Price almost spat at the thought. "No, he's supposed to be my bodyguard, but God help us all if he has to fire that gun he's carrying."

Hopkins was appalled at the thought of the irresponsible youth carrying a weapon, but at the same time was intrigued by the news that Fargo's bus conveyed the wages to the Colliery every week. He saw a way of redeeming himself slightly in Pitchford's estimation.

"Why not come along with me? Most of the women I brought down don't seem to want to finish their shopping in time for the journey back." The bus was only half full and a church clock nearby began to count midday. "There's no sign of Fargo. He should have been here ages ago."

Lloyd-Price thought quickly. The bus looked extremely comfortable and he didn't want to hang about waiting for Dai's banger. "All right, thank you. I'll personally recommend the S.W.T. takes over our little Friday jaunt when they begin operating." He called to Elvin and together they boarded the bus, picking the seats right behind the driver. Elvin took the one near the window.

Hopkins got into his cab, wondering whether or not to wait for the rest of his passengers. If they missed this bus they could always get back with Fargo. As for Miss Thomas, he was delighted that she had missed the bus in Panteg, and if she was coming with Fargo there was no chance of her getting here in time for the return journey. And anyway, she was really responsible for his hiring the bus in the first place. He started the engine and fingered the gear lever in an agony of indecision. Just then there was a commotion at the bottom of Christina Street as a gaggle of women carrying shopping bags turned the corner and came towards the bus like a band of marauding Amazons.

Hopkins's nerve broke, and gibbering with fear, he let in the clutch, took off the hand brake and spurted up the street in a shower of gravel, leaving behind a trail of yelling, frustrated ladies.

Some goodwill mission, thought Lloyd-Price as he clung desperately to the pole alongside him.

The two buses passed each other as Dai was turning right to Swansea High Street Station, and the sight of the gleaming new vehicle again filled his heart with despair. The women pointed and waved angrily at Glan Hopkins who kept his face averted. Miss Thomas was near to tears again. She thought that at least he might have waited for her to make the return trip.

When they arrived at the Christina Street bus-stop Dai was besieged by the angry women left behind by Hopkins. Bryn tried vainly to stem the tide of would-be passengers.

"Let the others get off first, please," he shouted.

Dai came around to the platform and added his weight to the proceedings. "Hold it!" he shouted with all the power of his enormous lungs.

The women who were pushing and shoving each other inside the bus slowly quietened.

"Listen, let the people off who have just come in with me and then we'll see how many of you I can take."

It took about five minutes before order was formed out of the chaos and the bus was filled up. Dai looked around for the two pay clerks from the Colliery Office and came to the obvious conclusion that they had travelled with Hopkins.

Miss Thomas stood uncertainly at the kerb side. She couldn't make up her mind whether to stay in Swansea or get back to Panteg and the school which she had been neglecting these past two days. There'd be a few questions asked at the next Council meeting if she took too much time off. She felt that her world was being turned upside down.

"There's just room for one more, Miss Thomas. Are you coming or not?" Dai's voice was cold as he addressed the headmistress.

"Yes." She turned her head away from him as she spoke so that he would not see the hatred in her eyes, and climbed the step on to the platform. The only seat available was at the back, where she found herself wedged between a mysterious lady in a black two-piece with a heavy veil and Mrs. Powell, who had decided that she had better go back straight away rather than do any shopping in Swansea. The police sergeant's wife clutched the bag of croissants in her lap. They'd be a nice little surprise for him, she thought. She was sorry she had been so unfeeling over his bad leg.

Quarter past twelve, said Dai to himself, as the chimes of the church clock mingled with the noise of the engine as he swung the handle. Looks as if I've lost the Colliery contract and I've got a full load of passengers for the first time for weeks and I can't take fares off them. Large spots of rain began to splash against his windscreen as he drove away. And to cap it all it's going to piss down. "What a friend we have in Jesus," he sang recklessly, avoiding a horse and cart by a hair's breadth.

"We'll make a bonfire of our troubles," blew the Clydach Zulus into their kazoos as they turned, about turned and right and left wheeled at the command of their magnificent drum major. Sid Jewell ran alongside taking action photographs with his filmless camera. The rain had started in earnest now and he was desperately trying to show that he was doing a good job for the *South Wales Evening Post*.

The boot blacking was beginning to run and the plumed head-dresses some wore drooped at sad angles. Even two-tone Tommy Rees was looking a sorry sight. Only Berwyn Llewellyn, who revelled in his job, kept the men marching, throwing his spear high in the air and catching it as it came down without so much as an upward glance.

Burns, his sodden uniform trousers rubbing his knees raw, tapped Powell on the shoulder. "How much longer do we have tae stay on our knees in the gorse bush?"

Powell turned, his eyes blazing with a wartime zeal. "Until we've captured the buggers."

"Captured who? We canna arrest Jewell for taking pictures and it doesna look as if they'll stand much more of this marching in the rain."

As he spoke, Berwyn held up his spear high above his head

and halted his men. He came over to Sid Jewell, who was kneeling on the road pretending to take an unusual angle shot of the band.

"That's it," said the black man with an air of finality. "No more pictures — we're going home."

"But you can't! You can't! You haven't attacked the bus yet. That's the picture that can give you nation-wide publicity," pleaded Sid, the rain pouring off the end of his long nose in a miniature Niagara.

Glan Hopkins's bus suddenly came into view.

"Here's the bus, boys," shouted one of the band, anxious to get the picture taken and be off home.

Sid and Berwyn turned together.

"That's the wrong bus," cried Sid. "Fargo's bus is the one we want."

"You'll have to make do with this one." Berwyn's tone brooked no argument. "All right, lads," he called. "Stop the bus and pretend to attack it and then we can all sod off."

"No, no, not that one!" Sid was sobbing with frustration, as the band broke ranks and headed for the bus.

In the gorse bush, Burns and Powell stiffened, ready for action.

In Hopkins's bus, Lloyd-Price was almost asleep, lulled by the smoothness of the ride and the comfort of the seat. The bag in his lap caused erotic fantasies to ferment in his mind, stirring his loins warmly. He was brought back to earth by Elvin's elbow in his ribs.

"We're being attacked by natives," he said, his voice yodelling.

"Don't be so bloody stupid, boy."

Glan Hopkins brought the bus to a halt, petrified by a huge negro who stood firmly in his path clad only in a leopard skin and pointing a lethal-looking spear at his head. Around the bus he could see other, less convincing but no less menacing black men leaping up and down in the rain.

"What do you want?" he shouted through the small space he created by winding his window part way down.

"A photograph," came the unexpected reply. "The *Evening Post* just want to take a picture of my lads pretending to attack your bus. Won't take long — we're soaking wet and we don't want to hang about in this lot. That O.K. with you?"

Hopkins, relieved that it was only a publicity stunt and that he wasn't losing his mind, shouted his acceptance out of the window. He switched off the engine and, hesitating whether or not to leave his seat, decided that if a photograph was going to appear in the *Evening Post* he would be better off as an out-of-focus figure behind the wheel.

Sid Jewell, seeing his dream of a life of luxury in South America running away down the drain along with the rain that pelted across his face, abandoned the idea of the robbery of the century and slopped forward with his camera to finish the charade of picture-taking.

Tommy Rees, the drum still strapped to his back, entered into the spirit of things. With shouts of "Walla Walla" he started to board the bus, brandishing his iron spear. The size of the instrument prevented him making a clean entrance and the startled ladies screamed at his appearance as he scrabbled in the doorway.

Lloyd-Price and Elvin, immediately opposite him, stared blankly at his antics. Only one person on the bus seemed to have any initiative.

Gwyneth Pugh rose from her seat, umbrella raised, her big face contorted. "It's you, Tommy Rees, you bastard," she cried, bearing down on the unfortunate ex-boxer who was now firmly jammed in the doorway. "Where's the maintenance for my Elvira?" She hit him with all the strength of her massive frame, using her sturdy umbrella as a club, and when that broke, she seized the iron railing that Tommy had dropped as he lifted his hands to ward off the blows, and hit him with that. At last, mercifully, Tommy fell backwards out of the bus and, governed by the drum on his back, rolled several feet down the road.

Jewell, appalled at the sight of his strong-arm man being pulverised, came to the door to see what was happening. It was then that he saw Lloyd-Price and the bag of wages. All is not lost, he thought wildly, ignoring Gwyneth who pushed past him and continued her attack on the feebly resisting Rees. He could still do it. He waved his camera at the ladies on board, giving them one of his smarmiest smiles. "All out for a photograph, it's for a good cause. Come on, a little rain won't harm you."

The passengers were confused by the events of the last few minutes. They weren't sure whether the fight between Gwyneth and the "black" man was real or not. They were in a state of shock, and Jewell's appearance with his camera gave their minds something to hang on to. It's a put-up job, they thought thankfully, and began to leave the bus as the cameraman directed them. With a lot of good-humoured shoving and giggling they started to line up outside. As Lloyd-Price and Elvin rose to join them, albeit reluctantly, the younger clerk pointed his finger at Sid.

"I didn't know you were a photographer," he said. "I thought you were a talent scout. When am I having my audition, then?"

"All in good time, boy," Sid was grinning mirthlessly.

Lloyd-Price sat back again, not liking the look of this strange fellow.

Outside the bus the women and the Zulus were exchanging rough banter, the cries of Tommy Rees had ceased and Gwyneth stood over him panting with exertion.

Sid shut the bus door. "Is this the bag you were telling me about, Elvin?" He lifted the article in question, assessing the weight of its contents.

"Here, put that down." Lloyd-Price was highly indignant.

Sid, in a sudden violent effort, tried to pull the bag away from him, not realising that it was attached by a chain to the other's wrist.

"Help!" shouted Lloyd-Price, tugging the other way and succeeding in rescuing the bag. In a quick movement he swung it several times around the pole at the side of his seat until the chain bit into his wrist.

Elvin, galvanised into action at last, went for his gun, pulled it from his holster and waved it unconvincingly at Sid.

"Look out!" yelled Jewell, using the oldest con trick in the world.

"Where?" said Elvin, looking over his shoulder.

"There," cried Sid, knocking the gun to the floor.

He picked it up and made his mind up fast. On the road outside the Zulus and the Panteg ladies were still chatting, but the rain was getting heavier and they were calling for him to take their picture. Using the muzzle of the gun he tapped on the glass separating the passengers from the driver's seat. Hopkins turned round, saw the weapon and froze.

Jewell, calm now and knowing the scenario after the countless gangster films he had watched from his projection room, pointed the gun at the driver. "Drive on," he said with his best Cagney impression.

Glan Hopkins, losing a spurt of urine into his trousers, did just that.

Sergeant Powell and Constable Burns, hampered by the rain, were not able to see too clearly. They had seen Tommy Rees getting jammed in the doorway of the bus, but as they were expecting Fargo's bus to be the one to be attacked, they held back. They only moved forward when Jewell went aboard. The time they took to get to the bus from where they had been concealed was too long. The vehicle passed them with a roar as Hopkins put his foot on the accelerator in his panic to do as he was told. Powell lifted the shotgun to his shoulder and fired both barrels into the back of the receding bus. It skidded on to the grass of the Common, where it demolished the gorse-covered bike which Burns had loved so dearly, and then found the road again.

"Christ Almighty!" pleaded Powell to the grey skies.

Around him Zulus and Panteg ladies milled in utter confusion.

In the back of the speeding bus, Miss Rice-Morgan stirred fitfully in her sleep.

"What the hell's happened here?" Fargo pulled up his bus with a jerk as he found himself surrounded by the Panteg ladies and a mob of Zulus. He had made good time from Christina Street and was only ten minutes behind Glan Hopkins.

Powell came to Dai's window. "There's been a robbery. They've stolen the Colliery wages and we've got reason to believe that your brother-in-law is in on it."

"Good God!" Dai was shocked. "Those clerks should have been on my bus, but they'd gone when I got to Christina Street. Had a puncture on the way in, and my spare wheel was missing."

"Aye. Well, there's no time to stand here bloody talking. Get your passengers off the bus and we'll try and catch the bloke. I'm commandeering your vehicle." Powell waved his shotgun wildly, furious that he'd been unable to stop the robbery.

"All right, Sergeant. Although I don't think this old banger of mine is in any shape for chasing a brand new South Wales Transport bus."

Powell went round to the back of the chugging vehicle. Bryn, white-faced and anxious, was the first to greet him.

'What's going on?"

"You know bloody well what's going on. You and that poor idiot lying over by there." Tommy Rees had been removed from Gwyneth's clutches by a couple of the Zulus and now lay unconscious with his drum still attached to his back.

"It was all Sid Jewell's idea." Little bubbles of saliva appeared at the corners of Bryn's mouth and he was ready to tell everything.

"We'll hear all about that later. Get the passengers off."

Behind Bryn the ladies were buzzing with excitment. Nothing like this had ever happened to them before. They could see out of the windows men dressed up as Zulus and the sight of

Sergeant Powell carrying a shotgun added to the feeling of unreality. They left the bus in a rush to find out from their neighbours already on the common what was going on, carrying the conductor with them.

Bryn seized his chance and set off like a hare through the chattering crowd outside, his money bag flapping as he ran. Powell, temporarily unsighted by the flood of ladies, yelled "Stop, thief!" at the top of his voice and made after him, his bad leg temporarily forgotten.

P.C. Burns, who was questioning Berwyn Llewellyn about Sid's activities with the camera prior to the robbery, did not notice his superior's abrupt departure. He looked across at the bus, which had now discharged all its passengers, including Miss Thomas, who stood to one side, overwhelmed by the noise and confusion. Near her, Mrs. Powell, clutching her bag of croissants, watched her husband chase the conductor over the Common with a look of disbelief. This was when Burns took matters into his own hands. He had been increasingly alarmed by the way Powell had been behaving on the Common, with his wild talk of 'sentries' and the 'enemy', and he was beginning to suspect that his sergeant was losing his mind under the stress. Seeing Powell's frantic figure now in the distance, waving his shotgun in apparent pursuit of someone — Burns had not seen the conductor take flight — convinced him. Obviously the most important thing was to get after Jewell. Too much time had been wasted already. Burns jumped aboard the bus shouting, "Let's go!"

Dai, not waiting for any further instructions, did just that. He let in the clutch with a bang and started off in the direction of Panteg. If his old crate had to go to the scrap heap soon, he'd make sure the old girl went down fighting. Free of the weight of the passengers, the decrepit vehicle almost flew along the road on what was to be its last journey.

twelve

Sergeant Powell halted, panting for breath, the pain in his leg fierce again. His quarry, more nimble and motivated by fear, was a speck on the horizon, too far to be caught. No-one had answered Powell's call for "Stop thief!" because everybody knew Bryn Williams and there was no reason to suppose that he was a thief. A fiddler perhaps, but a thief — never.

The sound of Dai's bus starting off swung the sergeant around in alarm. Where was the man going without him? He started to limp back to the Common which seemed to be a seething mass of shoppers and Zulus. He arrived amongst them waving his shotgun for silence. "Who sent that bus away? Where's Constable Burns?"

"On the bus with Fargo," said Miss Thomas, reasserting a little authority.

"Why didn't the fool wait for me?" Powell was beside himself with rage. Everything was going wrong.

"Hey, Sergeant." Berwyn Llewellyn came up to the fuming policeman, his face set. "Is it true that the Colliery wages have been stolen by somebody on that S.W.T. bus?"

"Yes," said Powell, eyeing the coloured man with some respect.

"My money's in that bag, then. First time I've worked for weeks and some bugger's pinched the wages." He waved his spear high above his head, uttered a terrible cry, leapt on his push-bike and set off after the two buses. Other Zulus with bikes followed suit.

Powell looked around in despair for some method of transport that would enable him to join in the chase. Fate came to his rescue for the first time that day.

"There's a motor bike and side-car hidden in this gorse bush," shouted a small bandy-legged Zulu who had been taken short and found to his surprise that he was relieving himself all over a vehicle.

Powell ran to him and started to pull the machine from its hiding place. "Anybody here ride a motor bike?" he called to the watching crowd.

The mysterious woman in the black two-piece and the veil stepped forward without hesitation and, hitching up her skirts, got on to the saddle. Everybody watched open-mouthed and silent as she kicked the bike into life.

Powell, as startled as the rest of them, hesitated for a moment before climbing into the side-car. His wife came forward from the crowd and pressed the bag of croissants into his hand. "These will keep you going," she said. He nodded his thanks and put the bag in his lap. Then he waved his shotgun imperiously. "Forward!" he cried.

Jammy went forward with all the speed the old bike could muster. Unfortunately, the side-car had become uncoupled again when Powell climbed into it and it remained where it was. The on-lookers stifled their laughter as the elegant lady wheeled the bike in a full circle and came back. Willing hands had the machine together again in short time and soon it roared away in one piece.

On the South Wales Transport bus Sid Jewell was still tugging away at the chain that linked Lloyd-Price to the wages bag. Elvin, completely subdued, watched the struggle from his seat by the window.

"Come on, where's the key?" shouted Sid, losing some of his calm.

"I haven't got it." Lloyd-Price was red-faced with the exertion of trying to hold on to his precious bag.

Jewell waggled the gun in his face. "The key, buddy. Let's have the key."

"I haven't got the key, man." Lloyd-Price, fearful now for his life, but determined not to tell where the key was, looked at Elvin to warn him to keep quiet.

Jewell caught the look and turned his attention on the wilting junior clerk. "Have you got the key, sonny?"

Elvin shrank into his seat and looked piteously back at his senior.

"Look, if you don't tell me, either of you, who has the key, I'll put a bullet in your head." Sid put the muzzle of the gun against Lloyd-Price's temple. "I'll count up to five. One . . .'

"He's got it in his pocket," yelled Lloyd-Price, the veins standing out on his forehead like bunches of grapes.

"That's better!" Sid took the gun away and, turning to Elvin, gave him an oily grin. "Come on, let's have it."

Elvin dug a trembling hand into his trouser pocket and, after much fumbling, produced the key.

"Right. Now open the bag, there's a good boy, and we can all relax."

The bus rocked from side to side as Glan Hopkins, his mouth dry with fear, negotiated the narrow lanes. Elvin, whimpering now, tried hard to fit the key into the lock.

"Give the bloody thing to me." Jewell snatched the key from the youth's hand and tried to open the bag himself. He gave up after a couple of attempts. "This is the wrong key, damn it. Come on, own up. Who's got the right key?" He put the gun to Lloyd-Price's head again.

Dai Fargo was delighted with the way his old bus was behaving. He had no idea how far he was behind Hopkins's bus, but there couldn't be too much in it if he could keep up this speed.

Burns craned forward, urging Dai on and searching the winding road ahead for the other vehicle. They began to sing. "Onward, Christian soldiers", they carolled, high with the excitement of the chase.

A long way ahead of the other Zulus, Berwyn Llewellyn pedalled in a kind of ecstasy of anger. His blood lust was aroused and from time to time the country lanes echoed to a fierce Zulu war cry learned at his mother's knee. He came from a warrior tribe on his father's side, too. Old Tom Llewellyn had brought back his bride from Africa, where he had served with the Royal Welsh Fusiliers in the Boer War. He had had to put up with fierce opposition from the Army and had bought himself out so that he could marry the proud black girl he loved.

Like his father, Berwyn had the same stubborn determination when he wanted something badly and right now he wanted the man who had stolen his money. He stood high on the pedals of his bike as he rode down the steep hill which led into the little village of Dan-y-graig and, waving his spear, let out a hideous yell.

An old man, nodding off on a wooden settle outside The Three Feathers, looked up in amazement at the sight and sound of a Zulu riding a push-bike in full war regalia. A veteran of the Zulu Wars, he knew the real thing when he saw it.

Dropping his pint, he charged into the pub, and to the astonishment of the landlord, who was the sole occupant of the saloon bar, wrested one of a pair of ornamental swords from its position over the mantelpiece.

"The black devils are back," he cried. "Defend yourself, boyo!"

"Come on, Ianto, pull yourself together," said the landlord. "There's nobody coming for you."

"Isn't there be buggered?" he cried. "Look out of the window."

At that moment half a dozen Zulus went pedalling past.

The publican reeled to the door of his hostelry, unable to believe his eyes.

In the wake of the cycling savages, a smartly-dressed woman with a veil blowing across her face came riding down the hill on a motor bike, her skirts above her thighs, while in the side-car of the bike sat a policeman waving a shotgun.

The publican went back into his bar without a word. He poured himself a tumblerful of whisky and knocked it down in one gulp. Tucking the bottle under his arm he took down the companion sword from over the mantelpiece and joined old Ianto who lay full-length behind the overturned settle on which he had been sitting.

He put the bottle on the ground between them. "We'll get 'em when they come back," he said. "Whoever they are."

Sergeant Powell adjusted his helmet more securely and took a sly glance at the gap between suspender and thigh which the mysterious lady motorcyclist was displaying. There had been no time for conversation and he was wondering who this creature could be. He couldn't remember seeing her in Panteg, and yet there was something familiar about her.

"Turn left here towards Pentwrch, and we'll cut across the mountain. We should be able to see where the others are."

The veiled lady nodded at the policeman's shouted orders.

Powell looked over his shoulder. The Zulus had been left well behind, although he could still see Berwyn Llewellyn about half a mile back as they began the climb to Pentwrch, a little village in the valley to the west of Panteg. The bag his wife had given him still lay in his lap, and temporarily taking his eyes off the road, he opened it. "Good God — croissants!" He was both stunned and delighted by the sight of the French pastries. Where in the world had his wife bought them? Without wasting any more time on conjecture he sank his teeth into one. Delicious — just like the ones he had shared with Marie in Amiens. He closed his eyes in ecstasy, the chase forgotten as the delicate pastry melted in his mouth.

At that moment Jammy took a bend too recklessly and bike and side-car parted company again. The sergeant found himself suddenly confronted with a face full of hedge as the side-car plunged off the road, burying itself in a thicket. He groaned as the sharp twigs lacerated his skin. The rest of the croissants had crumbled into small pieces on impact and he was gripped with a great sense of injustice.

"Are you all right in there, Sergeant?" said an anxious voice about three feet from his right ear.

"Get me out, Madam, please."

"Hold on, love, I'll try and pull you out," said Jammy, heaving at the back of the now useless side-car. He was pretty strong for his size, having found in his youth that being effeminate meant being bullied, and consequently having taken up weight training for his own protection.

The groaning Powell suddenly came free from the hedge in what was left of Jewell's landlady's husband's ancient side-car. He took Jammy's arm, surprised at the strength of it as he was pulled from the wreckage. "Thank you, dear," he said gratefully.

"Think nothing of it," said Jammy, affecting a higher-pitched voice. He had not realised that in the struggle to free the policeman, the veil had come away from his hat.

"Good God! Jammy Wicks! What are you doing dressed like that? "Powell couldn't believe his eyes.

Jammy curtsied, putting his finger under his chin in an exaggerated little-girl gesture. "Why, don't you like it?"

"I should arrest you for this," blustered the sergeant.

"You wouldn't really, would you? Because I know where that bloke who pinched the money is going tonight if we don't catch up with him now."

"What do you mean?" Powell fumbled in the wreckage for his shotgun. He found it covered in croissant crumbs.

"It's a long story, Sergeant, but I know for certain where you can pick him up if he gets away."

"All right. All right. But first let's try to get after him. Is the bike working?"

"I think so." Jammy went back to where the bike lay in the road. He righted it, and gave the starter an experimental kick. The engine spluttered and died. He kicked again and this time the machine stayed alive. "Jump on the pillion and hold tight to my waist."

Reluctantly Powell did as he was told, shouldering the shotgun and catching Jammy's waist gingerly.

"Ooh, that's nice," said Jammy with a grin.

"Take the next turn right across the mountain before we get to Pentwrch and get on, you bloody cissy," growled Powell.

"Sticks and stones," cried Jammy gaily over his shoulder as he let in the clutch.

Glan Hopkins winced every time he heard the sharp hedgerows cut into the side of his borrowed bus. In his mirror he could see Jewell and Lloyd-Price arguing fiercely.

Jewell lowered the gun from Lloyd-Price's head. "Somebody must have the key, man. How the hell did you expect to pay out if you couldn't open the bag?"

Lloyd-Price, his voice hoarse with pleading for his life, pointed a shaking finger at Elvin who cringed in abject terror in his corner seat. "He's supposed to carry the key in case anything happens to me." He stopped. "Glynis," he cried in anguish. "Glynis did this to me. She must have switched the keys. No wonder she didn't want me to unlock the bag in the office."

"Bugger Glynis," said Sid coarsely. "Now what do we do?"

Hopkins swung the wheel to miss a straying sheep, throwing Jewell and Lloyd-Price off balance. They fell to the ground, the clerk crying out in pain as the bag, still wound around the pole, cut deeply into his wrist.

Elvin, grasping the sudden opportunity, leapt over both men like a startled gazelle and made for the door.

"Come back here," shouted Jewell, scrabbling for the gun on the floor.

"Oh Mam, Mam," sobbed Elvin, grappling with the door handle. He managed to open it and throw himself out before Sid could squeeze off a shot at him. The shock of the fall knocked all the breath out of him, and he lay sobbing and panting in the ditch. As he got to his feet, Dai Fargo's bus rumbled around the corner in hot pursuit. Dai pulled up sharply.

Burns jumped from the bus and dragged the unwilling boy on board. "What's going on in the other bus?" asked Burns, as Dai set off again.

"He's got Mr. Lloyd-Price in there and he's got a gun and Glynis changed the keys over and . . ."

"Slowly, boy, slowly." Burns patted the sobbing clerk on the back and made him tell his story all the while aware that they were gradually getting closer to the other bus.

Jewell got to his feet, cursing. He was in two minds as to what he should do. There was no point in terrorising the man with the bag — he clearly hadn't got the key. But somehow he'd got to get the bag away from him. He looked over his shoulder and saw for the first time that Dai Fargo was within sight.

Lloyd-Price was not going to be any trouble for the moment, he was too busy being sick. Sid looked out of the window and realised that if they kept going on this road they would soon be in Panteg and once there, they'd never get out of the valley. There was a turning coming up ahead. He made a sudden decision. "Turn left towards Pentwrch at the next crossing," he shouted, banging on the window with the gun.

Hopkins pulled the bus around in a tight turn, making Jewell hang on to the pole to stop himself falling over the retching figure of Lloyd-Price. The tyres squealed in protest. The lane was narrower now but there was a straight stretch of clear road ahead. Behind them, Dai Fargo urged his ailing bus around the bend and came clattering after them, slowly losing distance.

Hopkins had almost got to the end of the straight section of road when Jammy Wicks and Powell came belting around the bend towards them.

Glan tugged frantically at the wheel to avoid the strange pair astride the bike which seemed to be coming straight at his bonnet. He scraped a telegraph pole, making a tremendous dent in the side of the bus as he did so.

Jammy Wicks shut his eyes and, holding a steady course, prepared for the crash. Powell put his head down and gripped Jammy tightly around the waist.

They missed each other by a whisker, the bus removing part of the hedge. When Jammy opened his eyes again he could hardly believe his luck. Neither could Powell. They had come through unscathed, but were now heading the wrong way.

Dai Fargo stopped short to avoid colliding with the bike as Jammy turned it around in the road.

Powell climbed stiffly off the pillion and heaved himself on to the bus, shouting to Jammy to leave the bike and follow him. "You've got a lot of explaining to do," Powell shook his finger in Burns's face.

'We've got no time to waste — Jewell's got a gun. I'll have to explain later." Burns watched over his sergeant's shoulder as the strange figure of Jammy Wicks, now minus hat and veil, clambered on board. "Good God, what's he doing dressed up like that?"

"All in good time, Burns. Let's get after that man in front." He unslung his shotgun as he spoke, bracing himself against the seat as Dai slammed his foot on the accelerator. From his pocket he took two cartridges which he carefully loaded into the twin barrels.

"Oh God," said Elvin.

In front, Jewell was frantically trying to make up his mind what to do. The collision with the telegraph pole and the encounter with the hedge had slowed down the bus and Dai was coming into view again. He wasn't familiar with the district but assumed that Hopkins was.

"Shake him off," Jewell yelled, indicating the other bus over his shoulder and brandishing the automatic.

Glan Hopkins, who had no idea where he was after he had forsaken the Swansea to Panteg road, swerved off the lane down a track, the trees either side whipping the paintwork mercilessly. He had ceased to worry about the damage being done to the bus, his only concern now was to preserve his own life. Meanwhile, in the back of the rocking vehicle Miss Rice-Morgan dreamed of switchbacks and roundabouts at the fairs of her childhood.

"He's taken the road to the quarry," shouted Dai in amazement. "There's no way out of there and it's bloody dangerous."

"Go on, man, follow him." Powell grinned in triumph, his shotgun at the ready. "We've got him trapped."

Burns looked nervously at his superior. "Don't you think we should telephone the Swansea Constabulary now? There'll be hell to pay when they find out what's been going on."

"There's no telephone out here, lad — and Jewell's mine, all mine." He sounded like an old-time villain.

Burns thought of his ruined bike and his accident with the cucumber frame. "I'd like tae have him, too," he said grimly, his Scottish blood flowing hot again.

"I'd like to have my Mam," whispered Elvin.

"Never mind, love," said Jammy Wicks, patting his hand and moving close.

"Geroff." Elvin pushed him away.

"Please yourself, dear." Jammy patted his hair into place and hummed a little tune.

Inspector Northwood of the Swansea Police stood with his legs apart in his office, jingling the loose change in his pocket. He was a lanky man with mournful features who had the reputation of being a droll. He addressed the sergeant who had just entered his office with a piece of paper.

"Another message? Just what is going on up around Cwmgorse, sergeant? It appears that half the women from Panteg are being assaulted by Zulus, or, knowing some of the ladies in question, it could be the other way around." He nodded at the message in the sergeant's hand. "What's that all about? Has a band of marauding Eskimos taken over the Kardoma café? If so I'll have to make other arrangements for lunch."

"It's from a Miss Thomas, sir. Headmistress at Panteg school. She telephoned in from a sweet shop in Cwmbwrla. Had to walk miles, apparently. It seems that the wages for the Colliery have been stolen by a fellow pretending to be a *South Wales Evening Post* cameraman. Had a camera with him."

"Good thinking on his part."

"Anyway, he made the driver of a S.W.T. bus drive off with him and the two clerks on board. Got a gun on him."

"Has he indeed?" The Inspector reached out and took the message from the sergeant. "Get me Panteg police station, quick." His tone was brisk and the banter gone.

"That's another thing, sir. There's nobody there except an old reserve copper who says he's been asked to mind the shop while Powell and Burns went after a suspect. And from what I gather from another report that Constable Perryman is just taking down, they've gone after the other bus. At least Burns went in Fargo's bus after the S.W.T. bus, and Powell followed later on a motor bike and side-car ridden by a woman. And a big black bloke — a real blackie — has also gone chasing after them on his bike with a spear."

The Inspector sat down abruptly on a corner of his desk. "This has all the ingredients of an interesting case, Sergeant. No mention yet of Snow White and the Seven Dwarfs being involved?"

"Not yet, sir." The sergeant was used to his superior's jokes even if he didn't understand them.

"Better get some men up there, hadn't we? And get my car ready. I'll have to chase up those two errant coppers." As the sergeant began to leave the room he called him back. "It might be an idea to arrange some sort of transport for all those women with their shopping bags on Cwmgorse Common. Get them taken back to Panteg before they march on Swansea."

The track leading to the disused quarry began to open out as Glan Hopkins got nearer to the workings. As it widened, one thing became clear to Sid Jewell. Fargo's bus would be able to overtake and perhaps force Hopkins to stop. He looked down at Lloyd-Price who lay moaning, covered with vomit, his arm held high in the air by the chain which was still wound around the pole. If only he could get the bloody bag off the clerk's wrist, he could jump out and take a chance running away. Fargo's bus was nearer now, and he could see the police sergeant leaning out of the window with a shotgun. He estimated the distance left before the track forked. The hillside was pretty bare ahead, one fork going directly to the quarry where there would be no way out, and the other just a track leading upwards over the top of the quarry.

"Take the right fork ahead," he screamed at Hopkins.

'He must have gone mad," yelled Dai when he saw the other bus taking the track to the right. "That goes over the top of the quarry and finishes back on this road."

"Keep on this road and we'll catch him coming down." There was a light of triumph in Powell's eyes as he gripped his shotgun tighter.

Hopkins suddenly became aware of the danger he was about to run into. He began to slow down.

"Keep going, keep going!" Jewell banged on the glass with the gun and Glan, his bladder releasing more little spurts of water, needed no further bidding.

Jewell looked behind at Dai's bus and saw him keep to the main track. He wondered why. There was little time left to him now. If only he could open the bag! Then an idea came to him from a gangster film he had seen — a Warner Brothers film it was. They had blasted open the lock of a door with gunfire. That was it! He levelled the gun at the point where the chain joined the bag and squeezed the trigger. The noise was hideous in the confined space of the bus and Lloyd-Price, who had been slowly coming to his senses, promptly left them again. Hopkins gibbered with terror at the sound, the wheel spinning under his grip as the bus fought the steep track.

Sid examined the chain. It was dented but the bag remained firmly attached to it. One more shot might do it, though. He steadied the gun with both hands and, breathing in, took aim. The bullet ricocheted from the lock through the glass behind Hopkins's head, carving a neat furrow across the top of his sweating scalp. He fainted away immediately and the bus, without his hands on the wheel, but with his foot jammed on the accelerator, reached the top of the quarry and made for the edge.

Sid, elated to find the bag free from the chain, grabbed it to his chest as the bus began its plunge over the side of the quarry. He leapt clear just before it plummeted down.

Below, Dai and the rest watched with horror as the brand new vehicle came tumbling down towards them, carrying tons of rubble with it. A large boulder hit the front of the Fargo bus and the engine expired in a cloud of steam. Dazed, Dai managed to force open the cab door and join the others, who had made for the exit the moment the boulder hit.

It was impossible immediately to assess what had happened to the other bus because of the dust which now filled the quarry.

Then, as the air slowly cleared, they could make out the shape of it. Miraculously, it had landed on its wheels after somersaulting several times, but the top was crushed and the windows were shattered. Powell and Burns looked at each other with wild surmise. They hadn't seen Jewell leap from the bus at the last moment because they were too far below at the bottom of the quarry. They expected to find corpses, Jewell's included, as they ran towards the wreck. First they pulled out the unconscious, but not seriously hurt, Lloyd-Price. The sturdy interior had protected him on the way down. Glan Hopkins was eased from his wrecked cab by Jammy Wicks and Dai. He was alive and breathing, though his ribs appeared to be crushed and one of his legs looked as if it might be broken.

"Look in there for the other one. Jewell's got to be in there," said Powell. He was kneeling at the side of Lloyd-Price and could see that the chain attached to his wrist was broken.

"He's not in here," shouted Burns from the wreck. His bandage was filthy with dust and he slapped at his uniform in disgust. What a day it had been. The glass crunched under his feet and he watched the floor carefully as he walked gingerly up the aisle. His eye caught a glint of steel under a seat. The gun. Thank God for that, he thought, as he picked it up. He sniffed the muzzle and smelled cordite. The gun had been fired recently. He wrapped it in his handkerchief and put it in his side pocket. He looked around the interior of what should have been the pride of the South Wales Transport's new fleet. Seats lay broken and glass was everywhere. It was a miracle that Lloyd-Price and Hopkins had survived. What had happened to Jewell, though? He might have been thrown out as the bus came somersaulting down the quarryside. Or he might have . . .

"Yoo hoo," said a little voice.

Burns started in surprise. From the back of what was left of the bus, a tiny figure in red picked its way through the debris towards him.

"It was a very nice ride until that last bit," said Miss Rice-

Morgan. "We'll have to do something about these country roads."

The policeman helped her from the bus, unable to speak with the shock of her unexpected appearance. She nodded politely to Dai and the others, boarded the Fargo bus, and promptly went to sleep in a back seat.

Powell was the first to recover. "There's a lucky lady for you. Good job she was in the back seat, the cushions must have protected her from the fall. Now, where's Jewell? The bag's not here and either he and it are buried under the rubble or he's got away with the money."

"We can't possibly shift all this lot with our bare hands," said Dai.

Burns nodded in agreement. "And we've got to get these two to hospital as soon as we can," he added.

Elvin sat awkwardly on the ground alongside the stricken figure of Lloyd-Price. He was only just beginning to appreciate his good fortune in jumping from the bus before Sid Jewell had forced Hopkins to take the road leading to the quarry. On reflection there was little he could be proud of in his behaviour. Jewell had taken the gun from him with consummate ease, and he had gladly given up the key, even though it had proved to be the wrong one. He wondered what the Colliery Head Office would have to say.

"He took the bag. Shot the chain off it."

Elvin turned and saw that the words had been spoken by Lloyd-Price.

"Sergeant," he shouted. "Mr. Lloyd-Price is awake."

Lloyd-Price tried to raise himself on his elbows, but cried out with pain at the effort and fell back again. He spoke in short bursts. "He — he fired at the lock. Then I passed out. Wouldn't let go of the bag, see. Money belongs to the firm."

"But you told me to give him the key. And then you said it was Glynis's fault because she . . .' Elvin stopped dead in his tracks. Lloyd-Price was actually winking at him and shaking his head painfully to halt any further revelations.

"It looks to me as if the wicked sod has got clean away with it," said Powell savagely. "Burns, get down on to the main road and get through to Swansea Police. We've got to get these people to hospital." Then he remembered what Jammy Wicks had said about knowing where Jewell would be later on that night. He looked around for him.

Jammy had Glan Hopkins's head resting in his lap and was crooning to the little bald-headed man, who was slowly showing signs of returning to life. "There, there, Jammy's got you."

Hopkins became aware of firm thighs and a reassuring voice and gave a little sigh before lapsing into unconsciousness again.

"Hey, Jammy, what's all this about knowing where this Jewell bloke has got to with the money?"

"Hush up," said Jammy, putting a finger to his lips. "He's just gone back to sleep again."

Sid Jewell lay panting for breath just above the lip of the quarry. The bag lay safely under him and the feel of it sent a warm glow coursing through his body. He could hear the voices of Powell and Burns coming up from down below and he wondered whether they had yet realised that he had jumped from the bus. He looked around him. The hillside was pretty bare except for the odd clump of gorse and offered little in the way of a hiding place. Keeping on all fours, Jewell began to inch his way towards the nearest gorse bush where he could examine the situation and plan his next move. He had to get to Swansea Docks by nightfall and then — South America here we come! But first he had to open the bag and see the money that he had risked his life for.

Slowly and with much subdued grunting he settled himself out of sight among the prickly gorse and placed the bag in his lap. The lock had sprung with the impact of the bullet and Jewell' s eyes shone with greed and excitement as he looked at the piles of notes and the bags of silver. He put his hands into the bag and allowed himself the luxury of riffling the elastic-banded stacks. He was unaware that he was being watched by a shadowy figure who had come upon him unexpectedly, drawn by the commotion in the quarry, but who had now sought refuge in an adjacent clump of gorse the better to observe him.

The mountainside now held two full gorse bushes — accommodation was getting scarce.

Inspector Northwood's car almost ran over P.C. Burns as it came level with the turning which led to the quarry. "What have we here? Half the Panteg constabulary bandaged and out of breath," he remarked to his driver.

Burns saluted smartly when he saw who the occupants of the car were. "Could you come down to the quarry, sir? There's been a nasty accident."

'Get in, constable, and tell me your story on the way. It had better be a good one."

When they arrived at the quarry the Inspector, now up to date with events, unwound his long frame from the car and surveyed the scene before him. Lloyd-Price lay with his head on the rolled-up jacket which had been placed there at the command of Sergeant Powell. Beside him sat the reluctantly shirt-sleeved Elvin. Dai Fargo was ruefully examining the damage done to his bus by the falling boulder, and Powell was standing over the prostrate Hopkins whose head still lay in Jammy Wicks's lap.

"Ah — Jammy Nightingale," said the Inspector.

"Hello, Charlie," called Jammy cheerily.

"You know him then, Inspector?" Powell was surprised.

"Yes, Jammy and I are old friends. He's been doing us a favour recently — helping us to catch a gang of villains working a racket on the docks. They've been smuggling undesirables out of the country in a banana boat — for a price, of course — and Jammy here with his peculiar talents, shall we say, has been extremely useful in penetrating their operation."

"Then what he's been telling me is the truth? That Jewell will definitely be at the banana boat tonight, if he's got out of this lot alive, that is?" Powell pointed at the wrecked bus and the tons of rubble which it had brought down with it.

"That's right, Sergeant. But first things first. We'd better see to these poor people." He turned to his driver. "Go back to town and get an ambulance and issue a description of Jewell to all units. Not to be approached, just observed."

The car sped away.

"Aren't you going to throw a cordon around the area? The man's armed," said the bewildered Powell.

"No, he's nae armed, Sergeant. I forgot to tell ye I found the gun on the floor of the bus." Burns produced the Smith and Wesson from his dusty uniform pocket.

"So there you are, Powell. We could make a big fuss, stop cars, search empty premises, thrash around the bushes and frighten Jewell into hiding. If he's escaped he will certainly make for the Swansea Docks and that banana boat. It makes sense. Then we catch him and we also catch our friends who have been doing the smuggling. We've never been able to pin them down with solid evidence before. Tonight's the night, as they say." Northwood produced a snowy white handkerchief from his pocket and blew his nose.

"Well, what about Jammy Wicks being dressed as a woman? There's a law against that." The sergeant was dying to arrest somebody.

"Strangely enough, Sergeant, that was my idea. Jammy is being used as a decoy tonight and the plan requires that he dress as a woman. To test his disguise I asked him to come along and see me this morning on the bus. If he could pass muster in broad daylight he would be bound to be all right tonight."

"And when I heard that the South Wales Tranport were running a special for the ladies of Panteg I decided that would be the ideal time to try out my new outfit." Jammy spoke up from where he sat cradling Glan Hopkins's head in his lap.

"Good thinking, Jammy. There's only one mistake you

made." The Inspector slapped his stick against his leg.
"What was that?"
"You should never wear diamanté earrings in the daytime. It's rather vulgar."
Powell snorted at this exchange and Burns looked puzzled.
The Inspector turned to them, his eyes like steel. "There's going to be an inquiry into your conduct in this business — both of you. You didn't inform us about the plan to rob the bus, and you left your own station unattended. And, in addition, you've gone around commandeering vehicles."
"That's a point." Dai Fargo strolled over to the group of policemen. He was wiping his hands on a piece of oily rag. "That old bus of mine is finished. Bloody boulder's ruined the engine and I think the front suspension has gone. Who's going to pay me compensation?"
"Don't worry, Mr. Fargo, I'm sure we'll be able to sort something out." The Inspector was politely evasive. "Now, while we're waiting for the ambulance, let's have a few statements. It's all jolly exciting, isn't it?"

Sid Jewell sat in his gorse bush trying to make up his mind what to do. So far there was no sound of police whistles or barking dogs as there always was in the American gangster films when a fugitive was on the run. The only discomfort he felt was the prickles in his backside, yet he couldn't stay there for ever. He had to make a move some time. The bag in his lap began to give him pins and needles in his legs. It was going to be a heavy load to carry around all day. He wondered whether he should make a reconnaissance of the mountainside and find out how he could get into Swansea. There would be no bus from Panteg today from the sounds he had heard from the quarry. Without the bag he could move more quickly. Nobody knew him locally except for his ex-accomplices and the Capone family, so he had a chance of getting away with it. But the bag would be a dead giveaway. People would be looking out for somebody with a wages bag. He would have to hide it until he made arrangements to get into Swansea where he could hide up in an empty warehouse in the docks.

He looked around him in desperation, thrusting his hands into the prickly gorse for a likely hiding-place. Again he was lucky. To his right he felt an open space beneath his hand. Forcing back the gorse, heedless of the scratches he was receiving, he found a small fissure in the side of the mountain. It was too small to be called a cave, but it was dry and as far as Jewell could judge, was about three feet wide and as many deep. His heart thumped as he tried to make up his mind. He could take the bag with him while he looked for a way off the mountain, but he'd be taking a big risk — or he could leave the bag and the money and have a good chance of going unchallenged. Then, when he had arranged a method of getting to Swansea, he'd come back and get it. Perhaps they think I was killed in the fall; that I didn't make it; that I'm buried under all that rubble that crashed down into the quarry.

He was convincing himself slowly. Suppose I took some of the money on me? Then I could buy a bike off a local. Not a bad idea, he decided. He stuffed the money in his pockets, packing away on his person about four hundred pounds. He would have taken more but he didn't want to look conspicuously bulky. With reluctance and more than a little agonising he put the bag containing the rest of the money into the crevice and the gorse sprang back over it. After satisfying himself that there was little chance of the casual passer-by stumbling across his cache, he rose cautiously to his feet. It was now or never.

He could still hear the sound of voices from down in the quarry but there was no sign of any activity on the mountainside. About a mile away he could make out a little hill farm. They might have a bike there that he could persuade the farmer to sell him. He got down into a crouch and set off at a half run, expecting police whistles and, to his surprise, hearing none. They must think I'm dead, he exulted, and, straightening up, walked arrogantly away.

Behind him the figure in the other gorse bush waited until he had reached a safe distance then rose stealthily and went to inspect Sid's hiding-place.

The farmer's wife viewed Sid with suspicion. She kept him on the doorstep of the dilapidated farmhouse while she went to consult her husband.

"Feller at the door wants to know if we've got a bike to sell." She spoke in Welsh because she and her husband both came from Cardiganshire.

"There's lucky he is, then," said Idris, her husband. "He might want to buy that motor bike I found on the Pentwrch road."

"What bike?"

Her husband rarely confided in her. "The one I've just brought back. I found it in the ditch when I was chasing a cow that got out of the top field. A bit battered but he might want to buy it if he's desperate."

"Why should he be desperate?"

"Because there's been a robbery hereabouts and he might pay anything to have something to get away on."

"How did you know . . . ?"

"That there was a robbery? A big darkie on a push-bike told me about half an hour ago when I was looking for the cow."

"Darkies on push bikes, robberies — you're going 'twp', Idris."

"Wait and see, Nerys. We'll get a lot of money for that bike." The farmer rubbed his hands together in anticipation of a quick lucrative deal, his Cardiganshire instinct for a bargain strongly aroused. He went to the door where Sid was trying to repel the amorous advances of the large Alsatian dog which had him pinned against the front porch. "Want to buy a bike, is it, Mister?" enquired Idris, hissing his "s's". "It will cost you."

Sid, recognising when he was beaten, nodded wearily. Twenty minutes later and fifty pounds lighter, he took possession of the same bike which he had hired from his landlady for two quid, only now it was minus the side-car.

"We'll go to Aberystwyth for the weekend, Nerys," said Idris, counting out the money on the kitchen table.

"When, Idris?" Her face brightened.

"Next year, perhaps."

Berwyn Llewellyn had lost touch with the buses after they had turned off for the quarry. He cycled up and down the Pentwrch road, meeting only a farmer from whom he had gathered no information but to whom he had told all that he knew. He decided to cycle to the Colliery to see if there was any money being paid out. He was met at the gates by a mine official who told him that owing to unforseen circumstances there would be no pay today. Quite a crowd of miners had gathered for their money and the news was greeted with angry shouts.

Berwyn, barely conscious of the fact that he was still in his Zulu outfit, grew tired of the jokes levelled at him by his workmates. He mounted his bike and pedalled off on a last desperate search for Sid Jewell and the missing wages, deciding to retrace the route back to Cwmgorse Common.

As he freewheeled down into Dan-y-graig he found himself assaulted by two drunken men wielding ancient swords, who dashed at him from behind an overturned settle.

"Piss off, you silly sods," he yelled, easily fending off their wild blows with his spear.

"It's a Welsh Zulu, Ianto," said the landlord of The Three Feathers through a split lip, as he backed away.

"That's the worse kind," cried Ianto as he struggled two feet off the ground in the grip of the gigantic negro.

"Don't be so daft. Now come on, stop fighting." He returned the old man to terra firma.

"No hard feelings, Sambo." The publican held up the whisky bottle. "Have a drink."

"It's empty, mun," pointed out Berwyn.

"So it is." The other man examined the bottle carefully. "Come on inside, there's plenty more in there."

The three men entered the pub and shut the door. A "Closed" notice appeared in the window and some serious drinking began.

Sid wheeled the motor bike cautiously into the lane outside the farmhouse. It would be asking for trouble to ride it back to where he had left the bag. He looked at his watch. It was only half past two and there was a long time to go before he could get aboard the boat. The farmer might raise the alarm, but there were no telephone wires attached to the house, and if he judged the man correctly he wouldn't be too anxious to talk about selling a bike which didn't belong to him. The best thing to do would be to lie up somewhere until late afternoon, go back for the bag and then head for the docks. Where to lie up, though? All around his body he could feel the weight of the notes he had stuffed in his pockets. He could afford a suite at the Ritz, but he'd have to make do with the hedgerow or at best an empty barn. Sighing at the irony of the situation, he kicked the bike into reluctant life and puttered up the lane in search of somewhere to hide.

He came across a tumbledown, abandoned cottage about half a mile away from the farm. The roof had fallen in and there was a rustle of wild creatures as he walked up the overgrown path, wheeling the bike. Ideal, he thought, sizing up the surrounding countryside; remote and yet not too far from where he had hidden the money. He parked the bike out of sight behind the cottage and took up residence in the front room. The floorboards were rotten and the ceiling had collapsed but it would do for a few hours. Some of the floorboards gave way under him as he settled down with his back against the peeling wall. A text in a broken glass frame hung drunkenly from a nail on the opposite wall. Sid turned his head sideways to read the faded brown words.

"Honesty is the best policy," it said.
"Bollocks," said Sid, and grinned evilly.

Inspector Northwood had a busy afternoon. After seeing Lloyd-Price and Hopkins into the ambulance along with Miss Rice-Morgan, who kept wondering what the fuss was all about, he despatched Dai Fargo, Jammy Wicks, Powell and Burns back to Panteg in a police vehicle. He then put Elvin in his own car and took him back to the Colliery Head Office in Swansea, where he informed the pale-faced and shaken General Manager what had happened.

"This young chap has had rather a rough time, so I advise you to send him home. I'd like him to be rested for tomorrow morning when I want a full statement from him about the whole affair. What I've got from him so far is a bit incoherent. Anyway, let him go. By the way, I should get some wages up to the Colliery as soon as you can, I hear your miners are getting a bit restless. Send the money up by private car with an escort — much safer than public transport, as you've just discovered."

His next step was to visit his Chief Constable.

"Hello, Charlie," said his superior. "What the hell's going on?"

"It's a long story, sir, but I'll try to cut it short. As you know, there's been a wages snatch which involved the thief making off with a brand new South Wales Transport bus, which was then followed by the Fargo bus from Panteg with Constable Burns on board, which in turn was chased by Sergeant Powell in a motor bike and side-car ridden by Jammy Wicks in female clothes."

"Jammy who?"

"I'll explain him later. The S.W.T. bus was forced to take evasive action by taking a track which led over the top of a disused quarry, out near Pentwrch. The bus charged over the edge for some reason we have not yet ascertained, and a wages clerk and the driver received injuries which, fortunately, as near as I could make out are not too serious. Bad enough, but not all that bad. And — oh, I forgot — Miss Rice-Morgan was also in the bus that crashed over the quarry but she was completely unhurt."

"Yes, I see. But what about all these stories I've been hearing about Zulus, and you not finding the bloke who took the money? Where is he? Who is he?" The Chief Constable was going red in the face. "Why isn't there a cordon around the quarry, for a start?"

The Inspector took out a cigarette case from the left top pocket of his uniform, opened it and offered it to his superior. "Passing Cloud, sir?"

The Chief Constable shook his head irritably.

Northwood lit a cigarette and took a deep pull at it before continuing. "For some weeks now, sir, we've been keeping a close eye on a racket that has been going on down at the docks. The first mate of a banana boat, the *Heracles*, has been smuggling people out of the country in his ship. We don't think the captain's involved, but the mate has a woman accomplice who is part of the bait. The men pay extra because they think they're going to share their cabin with her. Of course, when they've paid their cash over — always cash, naturally — and they go aboard, there's no woman and they find themselves sometimes three to a cabin."

"Who are 'they'?"

"Mostly undesirables, sir. Criminals evading justice. They rendezvous at The Grapes — a pub at the bottom of the Strand. Obviously there's a tie-up with the underworld network, because we've observed villains from London in the pub."

'Why haven't you arrested them before now, then?"

"We've not been able to catch them in the act, because to be honest we didn't know exactly how the racket was operated. We missed the last boatload by a couple of hours. But tonight we've got the whole operation covered."

"How did you managed to infiltrate their modus operandi then, Charlie? Don't keep me in bloody suspense."

"Jammy Wicks. That's the man who told us what was going

on. He's, you know, what they call a nancy boy, but harmless and very public-spirited. He'd been knocking about with this first mate who happens to be a bit that way too, and one night when they were both pretty drunk he told Jammy what he was doing. As I say, Jammy is very public-spirited and he rang me and told me what was happening."

"Why you?"

"He's my first cousin on my mother's side. I've known him since he was a little — well — girl."

The Chief Constable grunted.

"Anyway, it was too late for us to do anything that first time. As I said, we missed the boat by a couple of hours. This time Jammy has pretended to go along with his mate — the first mate — and has reported to us all the way down the line. Who is going to be on the boat, and what time they're being smuggled aboard."

"All right, fine. But what's this all got to do with the wages robbery and your apparent reluctance to catch the feller who did it?"

"Because he is one of the men who is being smuggled aboard tonight. He met up with Jammy and the first mate two nights ago and they made all the arrangements then. Jewell his name is. Sid Jewell."

Chief Constable Arthur Jewell went white. "That no-good bastard! It's time he was put behind bars."

Inspector Northwood examined the ash on the end of his cigarette. "Any relation?" he asked, without looking up.

"No. Yes, dammit. Second cousin on my father's side. Never been any damned use to anybody since he was born."

"So, you see, sir, it's pretty obvious that if he's not under the rubble in the quarry he'll be ripe for the picking at the gangplank."

"How are you going to go about the arrest? By the way, he's not known by any other name, is he?"

"Sorry, sir, but of course his real name will have to come out in court."

"Pity, pity. Give me a cigarette." He took the proffered Passing Cloud and dragged smoke into his lungs. "Go on, then."

"Well, tonight we're going to pick up the first mate and his lady accomplice, and substitute one of our blokes and Jammy Wicks, who will be dressed as a woman for the purpose. We wait on board and nab the naughty passengers."

"Yes, but why does the Wicks cissy boy have to dress up as a woman? Couldn't one of our chaps do it?"

"Not as well, sir. He's also rather a tough customer, our Jammy, and he'll do a good imitation of the lady crook he's replacing. Besides, it's a little bonus for him for being a good citizen, don't you think so, sir?"

"If you say so, Charlie. But just a minute. If you pick up the first mate and the woman before they've taken the money from the passengers you've got nothing to charge them with." The Chief Constable sat back in triumph.

"As I said, sir, none of the passengers must know that anyone except the woman is going to share the cabin, so they all go aboard at different times. We'll let them take the first passenger up the gangplank, which will give us the evidence we need. Then we nab them and make the substitution. Jewell's rendezvous is at nine o'clock — he's the second one. The first bloke is due to meet them at eight o'clock." Northwood stubbed out his cigarette and stood up. "Anything else, sir?"

"What about those two clowns Powell and Burns? They seem to have exceeded their duty from what I gather."

"I shall be including everything in my report, sir."

"Let me have it as soon as possible, then." As Northwood reached the door, the Chief Constable called him back. "You're sure there's no way that we can keep my second cousin's name a secret? Could be a bit embarrassing for me. Jewell's an unusual name, you know."

"Sorry, sir." Northwood was polite but firm. He started towards the door again.

"At least my cousin's not a nancy boy," said the Chief Constable acrimoniously

The police car dropped Jammy Wicks off at his back door so that he could enter without being seen. "Tell Inspector Northwood if he wants me at the docks he'll have to send a car for me."

"Right," grunted the driver.

"Ta ta, folks," Jammy waved to the others in the car and ran nimbly for his house.

Powell and Burns, with whom he had been sharing the back seat, looked at each other.

"Funny way of going about police business, if you ask me," said the sergeant, still smarting from the going-over the Inspector had given him in the quarry.

"He gets results, though. Crime in Swansea is on the decrease since he took over." Burns admired Northwood and his methods.

"Well, I hope he can do something about getting another bus for me," said Dai Fargo over his shoulder from the front seat. "I know it was past its prime, but there were a good few miles left in her. After all is said and done, you blokes commandeered my vehicle for police purposes."

"Yes, well, we'll see. We get out here." The two policemen were as evasive as Northwood on the subject of compensation, a point Dai made to his mother and Elspeth when he reached home, after they had got over the emotion of his return.

"We didn't know what had happened to you. Rumours have been flying around Panteg all afternoon. Couldn't make head or tail of some of them. Old black men with spears, and buses chasing each other. Where is the bus, anyway?" His mother rattled on, nineteen to the dozen.

Elspeth just clung to him.

"Hold on, Mam. I'll tell you, but first get the kettle on for a cup of tea. I'm parched with all that dust from the quarry."

As his mother turned away, Elspeth took the opportunity to give Dai a big, smacking kiss that took his breath away. He was about to grab her when the door burst open and James Henry burst in shouting "Uncle Dai! Uncle Dai!"

He stopped short when he saw his uncle and his school mistress in each other arms.

"Now, hold it, James Henry," said Dai. "I'm not trying to kill Elspeth. I'm just going to give her a big kiss. There, see? You'd better get used to it, my lad."

James Henry grinned sheepishly. "Right ho, Uncle Dai. What happened today? Did you catch the robbers?"

"Not exactly. Anyway it was like this . . ." And Dai told the tale he was to tell more and more elaborately as the years went by.

"What happened to Bryn?" asked his mother.

"God knows. Apparently he did a bunk when Sergeant Powell started to ask him questions. Could be anywhere."

Bryn Willaims was at that moment making his way back to Panteg on foot, avoiding the main roads and whimpering with every step. He was too much of a coward to run far. Australia would have been a great place to go to if he had had his share of the wages, but without any money he could see no future in leaving home. He reasoned that if he could get back to Panteg there might be a chance of being let off with a caution. After all, he hadn't done anything wrong, really. The biggest mistake he had made was bolting when Powell confronted him. He should have stayed and brazened it out. Thus his mind worked, going over the subject again and again as he trudged towards Panteg.

Elvin was beginning to feel better. Mr. Thomas Picton, the General Manager, sat him down in his office and gave him a cup of tea in his best china. In the version of the story which he told to Picton, he omitted to mention that Glynis had switched the keys, remembering Lloyd-Price's warning wink at the quarry when he had started to tell Powell. It made his own part in the affair look a little more heroic if he made out that he himself had deliberately given Jewell the wrong key. When Burns had questioned him on the bus he had been too hysterical to make much sense to the constable. With a bit of luck he and Lloyd-Price could come out of the whole affair with flying colours.

On his way out he went down to the pay office. Glynis looked up at him from her desk, her face tear-stained. She threw herself into his arms and sobbed. "I didn't mean to do it."

Elvin patted her awkwardly on the back. "I won't say anything about the key if you don't. And I don't think Mr. Lloyd-Price will either."

Glynis squeezed him tightly with gratitude and Elvin found himself liking it immensely. She felt him stir and looked down at him with big eyes. "You won't regret it, Elvin," she said, moving her hips against him.

Elvin shivered with pleasure. Mr. Lloyd-Price had better watch out, he thought, as she glued her lips to his.

Berwyn Llewellyn, after sinking a bottle of whisky and six pints of draught beer, was more Zulu than Welsh. The fighting instincts of his mother's warrior nation came rushing to the fore and once again he let out a blood-curdling yell. His two companions slept on, oblivious to everything, their heads lying in pools of spilled beer on the bar-room table. Berwyn had drunk them into a stupor hours ago. Some of the locals had come and banged on the door, surprised to find the pub closed during opening hours, but they had gone away after a while.

The huge black man rose unsteadily to his feet and reached for his spear. Revenge for his lost wages was uppermost in his mind. He would find the man who had stolen the money and spear him through the heart. He would wash his spear in blood and then tribal honour would be satisfied. But first he would have a drop more whisky. He grabbed a bottle from the bar and staggered towards the door. After falling from his bike twice and nearly breaking the bottle he threw the machine in the hedge and started off across the fields towards the mountain ahead, using the steady lope with which his ancestors had tracked their enemies for centuries.

Sid Jewell awoke with a start, and stared around him with no idea of where he was. Then he remembered and looked at his watch. Five-thirty. He had to be at the docks at nine. The thought of a boat trip to South America in the company of a pretty woman filled him with pleasurable anticipation. She had looked good in the gloom of The Grapes, but he hadn't been allowed to touch her when he had made the arrangements for the trip. First things first. He had to pick up the money from its hiding-place. There was a saddle-bag on the motor bike into which he could put the cash. Time to get it, no sense in risking leaving it there on the mountainside any longer. Someone might have found it by accident! Perhaps the police were already climbing the mountainside!

He broke into a sweat and went round the back of the ruined cottage for the bike. He wheeled it into the lane before starting up, having made sure that no-one was around. The afternoon was drawing to a close and the rain clouds which had earlier dissipated were gathering again, darkening the sky.

When he reached a break in the hedge past the farm, he carefully hid the bike and began the trek back to where he had buried the money bag. He proceeded cautiously at first, looking all around for signs of being watched, his senses heightened by the nearness of the quarry. The sky was blacker now and a downpour appeared imminent.

Inspector Northwood put his receiver back on its hook with an air of satisfaction. He looked up at the sergeant standing before his desk. "No need to send that heavy lifting equipment up to the quarry, Sergeant. Our man's alive."

"Who was that on the telephone then, sir?"

"A farmer's wife, calling from her nearest neighbour's house, two miles from her home. It appears that a man answering Jewell's description came to their farm wanting to buy a bike. He had plenty of money on him in notes and her old man sold him a motor bike he had just found for fifty quid. Her husband's a Cardi — you know what they're like for money."

The sergeant, who happened to come from Cardiganshire himself, remained stony-faced.

The Inspector realised his mistake. "Sorry, Sergeant Rogers. Anyway she's spilled the beans because her husband won't take her to Aberystwyth with the money. It would appear that being avaricious doesn't pay in the long run. We'll be taking that money off her old man as evidence."

"Yes, sir. Any other instructions?"

"Inform everybody that Jewell is definitely in circulation and that he's not to be approached on any account. And send somebody up to that farm to get the money — I've put the address down on this piece of paper." He handed it over to the sergeant. "Sam Rogers, Hillside Farm, Pentwrch. Same name as you. Any relation?"

The sergeant coloured deeply. "Sort of third cousin, sir — on my father's side."

"Fancy," said the Inspector with a smile. "You and the Chief Constable have something in common — cousins in crime."

The sergeant saluted and left the office, confused.

"At least *my* cousin is on the side of the law," said Northwood to the empty room. "Has to be on the side. I wouldn't trust him around the back." He turned in his chair and looked out of the window. The sky was very black and big drops of rain began to splatter against the panes. It was going to be a nasty night.

The rain hit Jewell halfway across the mountain, driving into his face. He cursed as he struggled to pull his coat tight against his body. Thunder crashed and lightning cracked above him. The sooner he recovered the bag and got under cover down in the docks the happier he'd be.

He found the gorse bush where he'd planted the money and reached down anxiously into the crevice under the gorse. The rain coursed down his nose. Thrusting his hand deep he felt around for the bag. It was there! His heart stopped playing the xylophone against his ribs and he pulled the heavy object up through the cruel thorns with a cry of triumph.

It seemed heavier than he remembered it. He hefted it a few times, not wishing to open it and get all the lovely money wet. A little seed of suspicion planted itself in his brain and, turning his back to the rain, he opened the bag about an inch, then, unable to believe his eyes he opened it wide. Stones, by God! He turned the bag upside down and the grey stones tumbled out on to the soaking wet grass of the mountainside.

He stood motionless, uncaring that the rain was now beating his overcoat and its contents into a saturated pulp. Then, throwing back his head, the great scimitar nose pointing accusingly at the black sky, he let out a howl of anguish which came from the depths of his rotten being. He threw the bag from him in his fury as the full import of what had happened hit him. He fell to the ground, smashing his fists against the stones which had so cruelly replaced the money. No South America! His teeth savaged the grass. No life of luxury! Again his molars bit into the mountain. He pounded and kicked the unfeeling fold of Cambrian rock until he was forced to give up, his energy spent. Slowly he regained his sanity as he lay face down, the rain still remorselessly pelting the back of his steaming overcoat.

As he turned his head to get a lungful of fresh air, he saw a sodden pound note on the grass. At first he thought it might have come from the bag and then he realised that it had slipped from one of his pockets. He rose damply to his feet, his overcoat squelching as he patted himself all over. There should be enough on his person to get out of the country. Three hundred quid, they wanted. He must have that much on him. As he ran towards his bike he wondered who had done this to him. Who had seen him bury the bag? Was it a police trap? He'd have plenty of time to think about it all on the boat to South

America. He started the bike with difficulty. Before he rode off he took one last despairing look at the mountain. A jagged streak of lightning broke in the sky and seemed to aim directly at the place he had buried the bag. Thunder rolled. That's close, he thought. When you hear thunder and see lightning at the same time, it's right overhead. He was not a religious man, but deep down in his soul he believed in Divine retribution.

He shivered and let in the clutch. "Bastards!" he cried as he fought to keep the bike upright on the now very muddy lane. "Bastards!" he shouted to the whole world, and his tears mingled with the rain all the way into Swansea.

thirteen

At the same time that Sid Jewell reached the dockside in Swansea, Flasher, taking his early evening prowl over the mountain, came across the empty wages bag so recently discarded by the fleeing crook. The rain had eased somewhat and the bag intrigued him. It would come in handy for something, he thought to himself. There was a certain dignity about it. Perhaps he could carry sandwiches and a drink in it to ease the monotony of his late night flashing. He stood tall on the slope of the mountain, revelling in the feel of the handle, the weight of the bag against his leg. There was a change in his bearing as he moved off in the rain.

Berwyn Llewellyn saw him from the lane which ran past the farm. The amount of whisky he had drunk had dulled his senses. The fury and the desire for vengeance were there, but the picture in his mind of Sid Jewell was now blurred. Any man holding a wages bag was fair game to his befuddled brain. He began to stalk Flasher in the gradually increasing gloom, bottle in one hand and spear in the other.

Miss Thomas, alone in her bedroom, had had a most degrading day. After walking for miles to inform the Swansea police that she and the other ladies from Panteg had been stranded on Cwmgorse Common, she had had to suffer the indignity of being driven to the school in the back of a pop lorry along with a batch of women who had sung obscene songs all the way home. She had also had a bruising experience with the school inspector, who wanted to know why she had taken so much time off recently.

When she finally reached home she allowed herself the luxury of a good cry and then, going against the habit of a lifetime, she decided to break open the bottle of South African sherry she was keeping for special occasions. It was easy to down three or four glasses and she was feeling no pain by the time that the clock on her mantelpiece chimed seven. Outside her bedroom window it was darker than usual. The rain had steadily increased in intensity, and occasional claps of thunder rattled the panes.

The sherry released her inhibitions. She thought of the time when poor dead Richard Neapes had taken her virginity. How she had revelled in the experience! Her one and only experience. There had been a faint glimmer of hope that Glan Hopkins might have been someone with whom she could have formed a closer relationship. But now there was no chance of that. From what she had heard he was in hospital after a crash in the quarry, and he'd probably be blaming her for hiring the bus in the first place. Men! She poured herself another tumblerful of sherry and walked unsteadily with it to the window, pressing her forehead against the frame when she got there.

In her garden, Flasher stood looking up at the bedroom window. He still held the bag in one hand and was debating whether to do a quick flash before heading for home. There seemed little point in it, really, in view of the pouring rain, but Flasher was not one of your fair weather flashers, he was a pro.

The headmistress sensed movement in the garden and tried to focus through the streaming panes. She went to the bedroom switch and put on the main light. Flasher showed up quite clearly now and she recognised him for what he was. In a sudden fit of recklessness she flung open her window, illuminating the man below.

"Come on," she cried drunkenly. "Don't wave that thing about out there, bring it in here if you're anything like a man."

The challenge froze the Flasher in the classic pose of his

kind — the mac held wide open with both hands. Then, before Miss Thomas's eyes, a terrific flash of lightning lit up the sky and Flasher let out a strangled cry. From his chest the point of a spear sprouted suddenly and he slowly toppled over.

The headmistress watched in silence for a couple of seconds and then she started to scream.

Northwood crouched behind the stanchion of a lifeboat, the rain soaking his uniform mackintosh. His men were in position to nab Jewell as soon as he had climbed the gangplank and handed over the money to Jammy Wicks, who was waiting in the cabin. The first would-be passenger had been picked up according to plan along with the first mate and his lady partner. The Inspector knew that Jewell was in the area. He had been observed on his journey into Swansea and allowed to move freely. Northwood looked anxiously at his watch. Five minutes to go. He hoped nothing would go wrong at this stage. The Chief Constable would be unrelenting in his condemnation of his tactics if they didn't work. The gamble had to come off, or he might find himself back on the beat.

Sid Jewell held his wristwatch up to his eye level. Time to be going. He hesitated to leave the shelter of the deserted warehouse. In his pockets the money pressed damply against his body. He had counted the notes carefully and found that he had three hundred and fifty pounds. After paying his fare he'd be left with fifty pounds to start a new life in South America. At least it was warmer there, and the cabin with his pretty shipmate called to him. He plodded wetly from his lair after making sure that there was nobody around. The boards clattered under his feet as he mounted the gangplank of the *Heracles*.

Northwood and his men tensed themselves as Jewell came into view. He stood uncertainly on the deck, his coat collar turned up against the back of his neck.

"Anybody there?" he called hoarsely.

"This way, please." A man who looked familiar from a

distance beckoned him forward.

Sid walked thankfully towards him across the slippery deck. "Where's the woman? I want to see the woman before I hand over the money."

"In here, she's waiting for you." The cabin door opened and Sid saw a seductive figure lying invitingly on a bunk bed.

"O.K. Here's the money." Sid handed over £300 in wet notes and moved in through the door, his arms stretched wide. "Hello, beauty," he said, smiling broadly in anticipation.

"Hello yourself, shipmate." Jammy Wicks sat up and wiggled his shoulders provocatively.

"Hey, just a minute!" Jewell backed towards the door. "You're not a woman, you're a feller."

"That's right, Sid," said Northwood from behind him. "It's a lovely make-up though, isn't it?"

Jewell made no move to resist arrest. The fight had gone out of him.

"Now, where's the rest of the money, Jewell?" asked Inspector Northwood, rubbing his hands together. His "softly softly" ploy had worked. He had "killed two birds with one stone". "All's well that ends well." His mind filled with happy little clichés.

"That's all I've got, honest. Some bastard stole the money from where I'd hidden it and filled the bag full of bloody stones." Sid was righteously indignant.

"Now, come off it, Sid, we know you're lying." A tiny alarm bell rang in Northwood's head and another cliché popped up. "Don't count your chickens before they're hatched." "There's many a slip" followed rapidly. He was still questioning Sid in the captain's cabin when the third passenger was brought in. "Pitchford," said Northwood. "How nice to see you."

The South Wales Transport executive shook with fear. He had arranged this trip some weeks ago. He had fiddled a large amount of money from the firm and Glan Hopkins's cash had been his last pick-up. Since the hullabaloo had started at Head Office after the news of the wrecking of the brand new bus, he had sought refuge in the back room of The Grapes.

"Let's get this little lot under lock and key," said the Inspector, addressing Sergeant Rogers. "Keep those damp notes there on the table separate from the others. That's the money from the wages snatch."

"Is that all there is, sir?" The sergeant was enjoying himself. He knew that Northwood had staked his reputation on picking up Jewell with all the money intact. It had been hard work, too, getting his cousin to hand over the fifty pounds he had received for the motor bike, and he hadn't forgiven the Inspector for his remarks about Cardis.

"Don't worry, Sergeant. We'll find it." Northwood waved his hand in the direction of the distant mountains. "There's gold in them thar hills." He spoke lightly, but his mouth felt full of ashes.

Bryn Williams was the first to bring the news of the death of Flasher Roberts to Panteg. He had been slinking into the village the back way, his head down against the driving rain, when he came level with Miss Thomas's back garden gate which opened on to the mountainside. His eyes caught the movement of Berwyn's huge form rising up from the grass. He looked towards the headmistress's house and saw Flasher outlined in the light from her bedroom window. Then came the lightning flash and he stood transfixed at what was happening.

He saw Berwyn Llewellyn creep up behind the other man and throw the spear into his back. The screams of Miss Thomas followed him as he made for the police station. Even in his panic he thought that he might be doing himself a favour with the police by recounting what he had seen. It could be helpful when his own case came up.

Powell was sceptical at first when Williams blurted out his story, but Burns could see that the man was telling the truth.

"Christ Almighty! Sergeant, let's get up there." He pulled on his overcoat as he spoke.

"Well, all right." Powell took a pair of handcuffs from a

drawer and put them on Bryn. "You're under arrest anyway, Williams. I'm not taking any chances on your running away again." He locked the door on the bus conductor and put on his overcoat.

"Vindictive bastards!" shouted Bryn as the policemen left. Then he settled down to a good weep.

"Hey, David, your photo's all over the front page of the *Western Mail.*" Mrs. Fargo burst into Dai's bedroom with a cup of tea and the morning paper.

Her son sat up, bleary-eyed. The previous night had been something of a nightmare. His sister had come around to the house crying about Bryn being arrested. Then there was the terrible news about Flasher's murder and Miss Thomas being taken away to Cefn Coed where the mentally disturbed were housed. It seemed she would be there for some time. He reached out and took the newspaper from his mother's hand.

"Panteg hero," ran the caption under a photograph of Dai taken years ago.

"Where did they get that picture from?"

"Well, when you were up at the police station answering all those questions, a nice man came to the door and asked me for a photo of you. So I gave them the one of you I had on the mantelpiece."

"Good God, Mam, that was taken when I was seventeen." Dai was annoyed.

"Yes, but it's the best one you've ever had taken. You look so much like your old Dad in that picture." Mrs. Fargo blew her nose in the handkerchief she kept in her apron pocket.

"All right, Mam," Dai patted his mother's arm.

She left the room, dabbing her eyes, and he settled back against the pillows to read the paper. He felt strange not being up and about, preparing the old bus for his first Swansea trip of the day. Still, he'd have to get used to it.

There was a garbled description of what had happened,

including the arrest of Sid Jewell at the docks, and a statement from Inspector Northwood which touched only briefly on the fact that all the money had not yet been recovered. The two pay clerks came in for a fair share of praise for the way they had defended the wages until forced at gunpoint to yield. Tommy Rees was reported to be still unconscious and under guard in a ward in Swansea Hospital. There was also a photo of Glan Hopkins and Lloyd-Price, bandaged and unrecognisable, in their beds in the same hospital.

Side by side with the headlines of the robbery was the story of how Flasher Roberts had met his untimely end. The full details were not revealed, but Sergeant Powell was reported as saying that a Clydach man had freely confessed to the murder and was assisting the police in their enquiries.

The editorial said how much the public owed to the bravery of Elvin and Lloyd-Price and paid a tribute to the sacrifice Dai Fargo had made in the pursuit of justice: "Should this man be allowed to suffer because he has given up his livelihood to bring a villain to book? His bus, his sole means of support, lies useless in the quarry alongside the wreck of a South Wales Transport bus. It has been rumoured that the big firm had been about to swallow the one-man operation that David Fargo has provided faithfully over the years. In these lean days any man who deliberately sacrifices his life's work and his future needs all the assistance we can give him. The *Western Mail* proposes to open a Dai Fargo Fund to provide this brave man with a new vehicle with which he can pursue his most useful and much needed service. All donations to be sent to 'Fargo Fund', Western Mail Office, Wind Street, Swansea."

Dai put down the paper, his eyes blurred with tears. It could happen, he thought. I could have a new bus, and a new wife and a sound future. He lay back against the pillows and began to plan.

Inspector Northwood sat in the Panteg police station, his legs elegantly crossed. In his hands he held a cup of coffee which shook just slightly as he spoke.

"It was quite a day yesterday, wasn't it, chaps?"

Sergeant Powell and Constable Burns nodded in agreement. They both had a hint of smugness around their mouths. Northwood had overplayed his hand in the Jewell affair. The bulk of the money was still undiscovered even after an exhaustive search of the mountainside by a whole army of policemen and miners. Not even a threepenny piece had been found.

"The murder of Flasher was one for the book, wasn't it? Killed by a spear in a flash of lightning whilst flashing. Poetic justice in a way." The Inspector tried to keep his voice bright. "The blackie gave himself up, then?"

"As a matter of fact he met us half way between the police station and Miss Thomas's. He was carrying poor old Flasher in his arms. Crying buckets, he was. Thought it was Jewell, you see. Deep emotions they have, those black blokes. You can never really fathom them out." Sergeant Powell spoke easily, relaxed on his home ground and knowing that he had the measure of his superior. "Have a croissant, Inspector?" He pushed a plate of warm French pastries towards the other policeman.

"Nice," said Northwood, munching. "Where did you get them?"

"The wife found this little café near where Fargo's bus broke down. Went along there this morning myself to make some routine enquiries and I brought some back." Powell twirled his moustache and relived his reunion with Marie. Being a baker, her husband worked nights, and the policeman's reception had been warm.

"Ah, Marie's," said the Inspector, winking. "Hot stuff — the croissants, I mean."

"Ah — yes," Powell lost some of his earlier bounce.

"Now, about this damned money. Who do you blokes suspect did the switch with the stones? Somebody must have been watching Jewell all the time, and in the period between his hiding the bag and coming back at half past five the change-over was made. Jewell has shown us where he hid the bag, and believe me, someone must have been looking very closely to find that little crevice under the gorse bush. Any suspects at all?" Northwood was pleading now.

"As far as Burns and I are concerned, the only two people who might have been able to do the job and knew the mountain well enough have been ruled out. Flasher's dead and Bryn Williams is in custody without a penny to his name." Powell was clearly convinced. "Short of making a house-to-house search of Panteg there's nothing we can do until the thief shows his hand by spending some of the money. Everybody in the country must have the serial numbers of the notes by now. We'll just have to sit back and wait."

"The Chief Constable will have my guts for garters over this." The Inspector's face was even gloomier than usual.

"I suppose he will," said Powell with a little smile, linking his fingers behind his iron grey head.

"How are you feeling now, Mr. Lloyd-Price?" Elvin stood by the chief clerk's bedside.

"Getting better, boy, thank you. Arm seems to be mending." He held up his plaster cast. "And the pelvis wasn't broken after all." He motioned the young man to lean closer. "You've not mentioned anything to the police about the key, have you? Might make things look a bit different. Know what I mean? Got to protect Glynis."

"That's right, Mr. Lloyd-Price," whispered Elvin. "And I've got a surprise for you." He went to the door and called to someone. He came back to Lloyd-Price's bedside, leading a girl by the hand. "I'd like you to meet my fiancée, Mr. Lloyd-Price."

"Hello," said Glynis, fluttering her lashes.

"Good God — no!" cried Lloyd-Price, bringing a nurse

hurrying to the bed.

"You'll have to leave," she told the couple. "He appears to have had a relapse."

In another ward Glan Hopkins lay surrounded by flowers, being fed custard by a visitor. He was really happy for the first time in his existence. At last he had found somebody with whom he could share his life, someone who didn't care about his baldness or his lack of stature, who loved him just for being himself.

"Comfy, dear?" Jammy patted the pillows behind Glan's head and prepared to feed him another spoonful of custard.

"Who would ever think that last week there was a murder down there and all that excitement about the robbers?" Dai raised himself on his elbows and indicated with his head the tranquil scene below.

"Who indeed?" Elspeth sat up and looked down at Panteg.

It was a lovely Sunday afternoon and the grass of the mountainside was warm beneath them. The pithead wheel was still and the grey slate roofs of the terraced houses gleamed in the sun. People moved at a Sunday pace in the little streets.

Dai lay back again, taking Elspeth in his arms. "And who would think that you would be appointed temporary headmistress? Good job you withdrew your resignation." He stroked her hair, removing bits of grass from it.

"Fancy all those people sending money to the *Western Mail* for a new bus for you, too. You'd never think that only a week ago everybody was saying what an awful bus service you were running. And now you're a hero." She removed Dai's roving hand from under her skirt. "Hero or not, keep your hands to yourself."

"Ah, come on, we're going to be married soon," Dai persisted.

"That's another thing," said Elspeth, pushing him away and sitting up. "The Vicar says that we can can't be married until you're baptised in the Church of England. You'll have to be christened." She looked at Dai speculatively.

"Not at my age, I won't. White wedding or no bloody white wedding." Dai spoke very firmly. "I'm fed up with churches and chapels." He plucked a piece of grass and stuck it in his mouth. "That Iorwerth Jenkins has been all over me since my name's been in the papers. Hypocritical old fart." He turned to Elspeth and held her by the shoulders. "Look, I can't hold out much longer. What if we go to Swansea some day next week and arrange to get married in the registry office?"

Elspeth stared away down into Panteg. She'd set her heart on a white wedding in church, but she knew that Dai's mother wanted a Chapel wedding. They were not getting any younger and she had had enough arguments and traumas lately. And besides, she wanted this big, gentle man to bed her as soon as possible. It had been a long engagement. She turned her face back to Dai's. "All right then."

"Oh Duw, there's lovely," said Dai happily. He spat the grass stalk from his mouth and, putting his lips to hers, drew her down into the grass, his hands moving to the buttons on her blouse.

"No, no, Dai. Stop."

"Good God, woman, we've done it once before."

"Yes, but only after you'd poured half a bottle of Green Goddess down me." Elspeth sat up again, brushing the grass from her skirt and buttoning up her blouse.

Dai struck his forehead with his hand. "Where the hell can I get a bottle of Green Goddess from on a Sunday afternoon in Panteg?"

Elspeth looked at him, her eyes dancing. "As a matter of fact, I know where there is one." She stood up and grinned down at Dai.

His eyes opened wide in wonder. "Where?"

"On the mantelpiece in my bedroom along with two glasses. I bought it yesterday. Dad's courting Mrs. Wicks. They've gone to Porthcawl on a mystery trip. They won't be back till late."

"Are you serious?" Dai's face was a picture.

"Find out for yourself, David Fargo. But you'll have to catch me first." Elspeth started off down the slope.

"You devil, you crafty little devil!" Dai got to his feet and ran after her. They chased each other down the mountainside like kids at play.

"That's a nasty cough your mother's got." Al Capone, trying to suppress a smile, looked up from his newspaper and listened to the sound of his mother-in-law's chest-rattling spasms filtering down from her bedroom. He spoke in Italian.

His wife, knitting in the armchair opposite, cocked her head to one side and nodded. "She's taking her own medicine for it. She won't go to the doctor. You know what she's like."

"Yes, I certainly do know what she's like. She's a witch, that's what she is." Al shook his paper angrily. "Serves her right for wandering about the mountain in all that rain last week, gathering her damned herbs. She came back with a whole shopping basket of them one night. Always boiling the things on the kitchen stove, stinking the place out."

"Yes, dear." His wife, serene as ever, went on knitting.

At the dining-table James Henry and Teresa quarrelled over a game of ludo.

In her little bedroom, Magdalena Bellini lay fighting for breath. Her efforts on the mountain the previous week had brought their reward but she was now paying the price. God had sent the man with the bag to her, she knew. She had watched him from the cover of her gorse bush, curious to see what he was doing. When she saw him stuffing the notes in his pockets she knew that he must have done a robbery. Where she came from in Sicily such things happened frequently. She waited until he went off to the farm and then moved into the other clump of gorse to see where he had hidden the bag. It took her no time at all to pull it from the little crevice under the bushes.

The amount of money took her breath away. She could go back home to her beloved Sicily with this — it was a gift from

God to enable her to be independent of her hated son-in-law. She set to work at once. First she took the bag into the gorse bush where she had originally been hiding and emptied it. The bags of silver she hid among the roots of the tough bushes. Taking off the kerchief from around her head she put as many packets of notes as she could carry in it, then, collecting stones from a collapsed dry stone wall which had once formed the boundary to a farm property before the quarrymen came, she carefully made a cairn over the remaining notes. It was a back-breaking task for an old lady, especially in the rain which had begun to fall, but she was a tough peasant woman used to hard work.

She then filled the bag with stones and put it back where she had found it. The walk back to Panteg with the first haul of notes took her an hour, and she realised that she would have to use something bigger than her kerchief to bring the rest back. That was when she had taken the big shopping basket. In it she managed to cram all the remaining money, covering the top of the basket with herbs in case anyone stopped her. She put the stones back on the wall and was gone about five minutes before Sid Jewell returned for the bag. The rain beat down on her all the way, but she hardly noticed it.

When she returned she went straight up to her bedroom, unobserved by her daughter and son-in-law who were both serving in the café. Under her bed she kept the trunk in which she had carried all her belongings from Sicily. She dragged it out and packed the money at the bottom, piling her wedding dress and her underwear and all the rest of the contents on top of it. Then she knelt and said a prayer to thank the Madonna for sending her the means to return to the sunshine of her native land.

Now, between fits of coughing, she schemed about how she would get back. She would use the silver to buy a train ticket to London and on to France. There were plenty of half-crowns and florins in the trunk and they were not traceable like the notes. Then, when she got to Paris, she'd change some of the money and get a train down into Italy. In no time she would be home.

No more son-in-law. She made an obscene gesture from the bed at his wedding photograph on her chest of drawers. That started her coughing again.

Libraries Information and Culture

ALSAGER LIBRARY
Sandbach Road North
Alsager, ST7 2QH

Tel: 01270 873552

Alsager.infopoint@cheshire.gov.uk

Mon: 9.00 – 5.00 Tues: 9.00 – 7.00 Wed: Closed
Thurs: 9.00 – 5.00 Fri: 9.00 – 7.00 Sat: 9.30 – 1.00

With Compliments